FANTOME

ISBN 978-0-9834469-9-6   (Trade Paperback)
ISBN 978-0-9834469-4-1   (epub)
ISBN 978-0-9834469-5-8   (Kindle)

Connect with the author:
facebook.com/mcsiemsen * www.michaelsiemsen.com
mail@michaelsiemsen.com * twitter: @michaelsiemsen

Also by Michael Siemsen:
The Many Lives of Samuel Beauchamp (a demon's story)
The Dig (Matt Turner Series Book 1)
The Opal (Matt Turner Series Book 2)
Return (Matt Turner Series Book 3)
Exigency

This book is dedicated to Ana.

Table of Contents

A Warm Place to Call Home

(a demon's story)

Michael Siemsen

1. I am a Demon

Who's ever heard of a demon named Frederick? I'm the only one that I know of. But, to be honest, that statement should carry little weight, as I've never met another demon. I've heard of others, and they have striking monikers like Rashk, Xaphan, or Neqa'el. Am I envious? Yes. I quite like those names. But here's the thing—I don't believe in those characters. I think they're all bullshit. There's no such thing as a demon, and certainly not the sort cited in the Holy Bible or discussed throughout the world's mythology. The concept of these fallen angels doing the bidding of Lucifer is laughable. It's all superstitious hokum, and anyone who subscribes to such nonsense is a moron. That said, I am a demon. And I'm self-employed.

What makes me a demon, you ask? Good question. Well done. I like you already. Overall, I am not so different from you. I eat, drink, read, fornicate, text, watch TV (I'm quite fond of sitcoms and forensic investigator crime dramas), and pore over YouTube videos like they're the pinnacle of creative expression. Oh yeah, I also take over the bodies of human beings.

As far as I know, I am immortal, though I haven't been around for thousands of years, watching empires rise and fall. No, I only came to be in the early 80's. Reagan had just become the President, Brezhnev in Russia, Thatcher in England. IBM launched the first PC running Microsoft DOS, the Post-It note was invented, and China cloned a fish. If memory serves (and my memory is perfect, when aided by

Wikipedia), the average cost of a new house in the U.S. was $78,000, and a gallon of gas was $1.25. Unlike the prolonged extra-uterine gestation of human babies, I was conscious and aware the instant I appeared, if a bit confused.

I have few complaints. Usually no aches or pains, no deep emotional struggles or feelings of loneliness, no yearning for "something more" or a desire to "belong." I live the perfect life and I do not take that fact for granted. You see, the problem with human existence is *problems*. When you have them, you must *deal* with them, because if you don't you will suffer the consequences—potentially for the rest of your lives. Ugh, horrible. That's no way to live. Me, if I have a problem I can either ignore it, deal with it in a somewhat more brazen fashion than you might choose, or simply leave. Move to a new body. Bam. No more problem.

You may have difficulty sympathizing with my story, let alone empathizing. Empathy is a trait which I do not myself possess, and thus being engaged by a protagonist such as I could be a challenge. If I lack empathy, how could I expect you to identify with me? Another valid question, and one with a simple answer: I honestly don't care if you do. How could I? I'm incapable. Instead, perhaps feel sorry for my inability … yes, do that. Pity me my incapacity while you contemplate my status as protagonist or antagonist.

I'm a fascinating character. Captivating volumes could be written about my entire existence if I do say so, and I do say so. But this story will be limited to a relatively brief period: a recent and pivotal slice of my life beginning with my introduction to a man named Joseph Cling, and ending with the death of said man, Joseph Cling. I suppose that gives away the ending, but bear with me and there should be a tremendous payoff. Or, I could be lying (I am, by my very nature, a liar), just stringing you along. But tell me you're not at least a little curious where this is going, and we're only 638 words in.

There are a few important details about me that you must know before I go on: logistics, history, and whatnot.

My beginning came as a surprise to me. That is to say, I was not expecting to come to be, and then I was!

I sat perched upon the bronze head of a soldier in front of the historic Leesburg, Virginia courthouse. To my right and left, pigeons flapped away and shot me disgruntled looks. I knew they were pigeons, that they were disgruntled, and I knew that I *hated* fucking pigeons. I knew the statue on which I perched was made of bronze, and how the depicted soldier stood in tribute to Confederate soldiers who had died during America's Civil War. I knew I was called Frederick, though I didn't quite realize what I was. The critical things that I didn't know were a) how I knew *anything*, and b) how I had come to be.

I sat there for a few minutes, fairly certain I could leave if I so wished, but chose to remain for a time. I watched the trees sway in the wind, the white buds sail through the air then tumble across the grass, the squirrels hopping about in a seemingly constant state of panic, and I watched the people. Oh, the *people*.

There are these waves that emanate from you, like a hot road in the desert. They're terribly beguiling. It's a beckoning energy.

It says, "Hey, Frederick, come inside and have a look-see around!"

It says "Be in here now!"

It says "What the hell are you doing out there naked, dry, and loose?"

Sea turtle hatchlings spend days digging themselves up through sand until they near the surface, wait for nighttime, and emerge. Then, inexplicably, they decide they must go into the ocean and swim frantically for a couple of days. Like countless species, they just know what they're supposed to do. I knew I needed to be *inside* somebody.

I sensed a distinct outflow of waves from the center of a group, there! But I held back despite the primal urge to go, looking over the rest of the passers-by. No other candidate's display could come close to the captivating, luminous plumage beckoning me forward. And so I was off.

Now, it's not exactly flying, what I do outside a body. It's more of a loose hovering, as if gravity has a light hold of me, but some sort of magnetic field doesn't want me touching the ground. I jumped from the statue, scraped the pavement and floated along the curvy path toward a group of children, teachers, and a uniformed guide.

Weaving between the whispering and giggling kiddies, I found the source of the waves: a girl—bright, shiny, curious and happy, with blond coils of hair and a ruffled white blouse. She was holding hands with an assigned "buddy"—in her case, a boy her age. As I neared, it was almost as though she began to suck me in. Beyond my own control, I accelerated, passed through her neck and back, and BOOM! I was in there! It felt amazing! Like bathing in warm, static-filled Jell-O.

But I had stopped her walking, and those behind her suddenly bumped into each other—including me—like a low-speed, in-traffic fender bender. Her buddy yanked his hand away at once, as if burned, and gawked.

"Keep walking, Morgan," The teacher said, and so I complied, realizing that was my name.

It was easier than you might imagine, walking for the first time. Probably the same as what you do. You stand somewhere, you want to walk, and so you just go. Your legs and feet begin to move without you having to think too much about it. For me, it is just like this. I am not some tiny alien in your brain, pressing buttons and pulling levers in rhythm. Well, perhaps metaphorically I am, but logistically, there are no logistics.

A boy with messy hair turned around in front of me with an overstated expression of annoyance. He said in a singsong, "Hellooo … Morgan? Time to wake u-u-up …"

I looked him in the eye and said, "I *am* awake. Just go, you little dork."

His new expression was delicious, and he cut through the kids in front of him as he scurried away. Only later did I realize that my words were not what had alarmed Little Dork. It was young Morgan's sudden change of voice and manner.

My "buddy" refused to rejoin hands with me, continuing to stare as he walked a safe distance away from my side. The look was more suspicious than frightened, but I simply shrugged and skipped gleefully along with the group.

After a week passed it had dawned on me what I was and, more importantly, that I needed to do a little more research before climbing into one of you people. For one, certain religions will make life a living hell for a demon. Exorcisms are obnoxious. I mean, who the hell are these grown men believing in a fucking invisible entity occupying human bodies? To me the concept of a demon should be no different than any other monster myth out there—Yeti, Chupacabra, Robert Pattinson. Disregard for a moment the fact that I happen to exist. No one should believe in me. It's stupid. There's as much evidence to support my existence as any other silly legend. And yet, someone decided there should be trained "professionals" dedicated to the holy mission of pissing me off.

Second, you have to know a bit about the person you're taking over. How they talk, mannerisms, posture, details like that. Little Morgan was a big rookie mistake on my part, and a huge waste.

See, when walking in her body, I had more of a skulk than a walk. I imagine that it looked like this cute little girl was lurking to the water fountain, creeping onto the school bus, and prowling to the dinner table. And I wasn't using her voice. The other kids moaned "stop talking like that!" Morgan's Mom and Dad were initially amused, then it turned to "Okay, honey, enough with the voice." But I didn't know how she'd sounded before, so they thought I was sassing them when trying out different pitches and tonalities. Eventually, I got annoyed with Morgan's father and told him if he didn't like my voice, maybe he should go read the dirty magazines under his mattress and make the blankets go up and down again. It didn't go well.

First, it was the therapist, followed by a psychiatrist, and then the priest. These meetings were interesting enough. I got to meet new people and see new places. I came to realize that I loved being human! The littlest things were sources of pleasure. The feel of textures on my little fingers, the taste and feel of gummy bears, and the smells! Everything smelled wonderful. Even dog shit. You probably don't appreciate it, but shit lights up the senses, inside and out. There are few things like it. So as much as I complain, I honestly enjoyed living in Morgan during my brief stay. No one around me had the same appreciation, but that was just because they thought something was wrong with the girl they knew. There was nothing wrong with her, she'd just been replaced.

"Morgan, dear," Mom said gently. "Would you tell Father Humphrey what you think of bedtime stories?"

I turned toward the priest who was smiling at me with his bushy eyebrows raised. He peered over the tiny rectangles of his eyeglasses. Behind him loomed a wall of books. To me they were all Bibles of a thousand sizes and colors.

"I like them," I said in my version of a sweet little girl voice.

Mom frowned and glared at me. She stuck out her jaw and went on, "No, honey, tell him what you said last week when I wanted to read you Little Red Riding Hood."

I smiled, "Oh right. I said I already read all the books in my room."

"And then what did you say?"

"I said … you don't have to try to knock me out …" She encouraged me on with a deep nod. "… just 'cause it was you and Daddy's *special* night."

Her chest heaved up and down and I could hear the air whistling in and out of her ugly nose. To me, her nose looked like a dog's backside was sticking out of her face, squatting to take a dump. She fought to keep the "nice Mommy" voice, but she wasn't fooling me or the priest.

She spoke through her teeth. "*Almost*, dear. What were the real words you used? The bad words. It's okay to say them again, just this once."

I shrugged, "Fine. I said '… just 'cause Daddy wants you to suck on his ding-a-ling.'"

She turned triumphantly to Father Humphrey. His eyes were like saucers.

He stammered, "And-and-and where did you learn of such private … such *grown-up* things, young lady?"

"I guess from hiding in the closet and watching her suck Daddy's ding-a-ling." I shrugged. "See, I thought I was letting her off the hook with the story, and really wasn't interested in Red Riding Hood that night. I think it's about sex stuff, anyway, and I'd rather do my own sex stuff to my body than hear a boring story about it."

They shared a look. Mom made a "See?" face. Then they needed to talk alone. I eavesdropped against the door. The priest expressed his suspicion that I was being molested. He began interrogating her about every single male with whom I'd come into contact for the past year. I was brought back in and asked squarely if anyone had been "inappropriate" with me.

"Look," I said. "As far as I know, nothing weird has happened. No one's been diddling around my hoo-haw or forcing me to suck anything I didn't want to. There's really nothing to worry about."

My assertion didn't seem to help. Morgan's mother took two weeks off work to handle my "issues." When neither drugs nor prayer groups proved effective, my case was escalated to a task force of priests that worked within the local diocese. The exorcists I mentioned earlier (I mean, seriously, what century is this?).

Confined to my little pink bedroom, I was splashed with holy water, yelled at in Latin, fed nauseating foods, played the most discordant, grating music imaginable, and of course, constantly read passages of The Holy Bible. While they prayed to God for me to leave Morgan's body, I prayed for God to strike down these tormentors. In retrospect, I wish that I could have put on a better show: rotating head, projectile vomiting, and the like, but I'm not quite sure how any of that works (the spine alone seems to be a major limiting factor there, am I right?). I suppose they had the stronger case, because my prayers were not answered, and with no end in sight, I decided to go.

With my mind made up, I weighed everyone I knew for a good fit. None were in any way appealing, and I wanted to be as far from this home and that church as possible. I determined not to jump from one body to the next, but to travel bodiless until an enticing new host presented itself.

It was a Sunday night when I slid from Morgan's shell. Mother and Father were in the room, seated beside my bed, their weary heads alternated nodding off and popping up, like two exhausted carousel horses. With us, as always, were Father Humphrey and a couple of the loathsome exorcists. They were doing the chanting thing. Prevented from reading or even watching my favorites: *The Brady Bunch*, *Dukes of Hazzard*, or *All My Children*, I lay there twiddling my thumbs and glaring at each of them. I finally sat up and shouted: "Fuck this!" and left.

Hovering around her ceiling light, I watched Morgan's body flop back down onto her Raggedy Ann-patterned pillow, eyes half open and mouth slack. Mother and Father came to life and rushed to her, slapping her cheeks.

"Morgan? Morgan, honey? What's happened? She hasn't done this before!"

Father checked her pulse. She was still alive; her eyes blinked when her cheeks were pat. But she didn't look quite conscious. Her staring eyes almost seemed to be pointed at me, as if I was visible, so I jumped to the tall dresser and looked back at her. Her gaze had remained focused somewhere near the light. The priests and Morgan's parents tried everything to wake her up before one of the exorcists declared that she had been cleansed of her possessor and would simply need to rest and recover for a couple days. I stuck around to see how it went. I had no urgent business drawing me away, so why not?

Morgan didn't come out of it. Her body functioned at its most basic level, but the girl that was there before was no more. Realizing that my presence must have erased her, I left the following afternoon. I later learned that Mom and Dad didn't accept their daughter's *departure* for quite a while. They returned to traditional doctors, who eventually declared Morgan to be in a permanent vegetative state. She was kept on life support for *years* after that.

It was a fascinating revelation, to think that I had this ability to remove a person from existence. Had I done something wrong in the possessing process, or was this simply the nature of the game? For the sake of better understanding myself, I went on a bit of a spree.

The first was a 55-year old gentleman named Ulysses who was walking his German shepherd, Shiloh, down Morgan's street. Shiloh immediately noticed a difference in her master and began whining and pulling backward against the leash.

"It's okay, girl," I said, and she yanked backward harder, barking at me.

I left Ulysses's body and perched atop a nearby light pole. He just stood there in a daze, the same vacant expression as Morgan. Shiloh quieted and began licking Master's hand, as if to clean a wound. Another one down, as they say.

Entering a large plain building a short time later, I discovered I was in some sort of police headquarters and found my way to a prison-like wing of the place, with men locked in individual cells. I quickly drifted from person to person in this detention center, trying on bodies as if they were sweaters. I didn't linger for long, but I'm certain the aftermath of my visit was quite confounding. A row of prisoners on one side turned to lobotomized skin suits, while the adjacent row remained intact.

With all honestly, that day gave me pause. Was I a murderer of minds? Was this my purpose, to silently expunge consciousness? Did I have a purpose? If I were so inclined, I could have wiped out an entire city of souls in a single afternoon. And the idea of doing just that did linger. Why shouldn't I? I was curious if I was capable of such numbers, and if the results would be universal or if some individuals would remain unscathed. It would be the most efficient way to gather concrete figures. However, I found no truly compelling reason to do so. When one weighs such a philosophical decision—the should or shouldn't—I have found it best to lean toward the side of inaction.

Now, when I look back and analyze this first month of my existence, I recall it with the sagacious mind I currently possess, reprocessing the memories of events and people involved as if experienced by the savvy, practical Frederick of today. But if I were to be honest with you (and myself), I would admit that my true thoughts were not so detached and methodical. Indeed, I was bewildered, and— it pains me to say—more than a little frightened.

* * *

The post-habitation state of idleness—I came to refer to it as a *Fredbotomy*—created an ongoing melancholy among the friends and families of my discarded personas, such that I found little interest in occupying any acquainted individuals, no matter how appealing they'd become. With their lives irrevocably altered, they had ceased to be the fascinating individuals I had come to know. With their sister or brother or parent or child no longer present (in the traditional sense), their waves grew less wavy, and the light in their eyes turned dull. It was decidedly inconvenient for me. I must then roam naked and investigate, observe, study—a lengthy process when done correctly.

Over the years I developed such distaste for the in-between periods that my stays grew longer. The idea of being "unemployed" carried such negative associations that I had begun taking quite seriously the decision to depart a body. I asked all the important questions you would imagine one would ask when faced with such a choice. Have I gotten everything I can out of this life? Is there anything I can do to eke out a bit more? Move the family to Inner or even Outer Mongolia? Change professions, get married, get divorced, assassinate a government figure, have a child, an affair, go to more concerts, get in a car accident? Minor life changes like the aforementioned can go a long way toward reinvigorating a stagnating existence—especially after an entire year has passed.

Shortly after leaving Leesburg, I hopped a pilot to Holland and spent the better part of the decade there. I only spoke English prior to my arrival there, and struggled as I learned Dutch. Another question pops up. Why did I speak fluent English? Was I an "American Demon?" It certainly didn't seem so after six months settling into Rotterdam.

After three years living as a prostitute named Naatje I decided to see more of the world. I do not know if I contracted the HIV or if she had it in there awaiting me, but being sick was not for me, and thus, my departure.

I spent time in Greece, Burma, Southern California. My SoCal friends and I went to Brazil on vacation and I liked it so much I stayed for years, albeit as different people. It was a refreshing change. I had discovered a country where everyone seemed to worry less than even I did. And they were stuck with those lives, well, for life!

Throughout my journeys I perfected numerous trades. I was a travel agent, a thief, a drug dealer, drug addict, concubine, casting director, and thief. (I love stealing.) I lived as men, women, teenagers, gay, straight, transgender. Being transgendered was admittedly ironic: Valerie had become Fabien, and then I became Fabien. I personally identify male, and my name is Frederick, so I must be male at the core, but who knows? I find both genders enjoyable, though must admit to fits of exuberant self-exploration whenever entering a new female. Women's bodies deserve discovery, whereas men are all essentially the same.

* * *

Portuguese became my fifth fluent language just as Brazil began to feel less like a relaxing departure and more of a dull, unchallenging trap. Within minutes of the first inkling of a desire to move on, I was out of my travel agent host Enzo and once more enjoying the simple pleasure of passing through walls. At the airport I found a well-dressed businessman on the way to his gate and checked his ticket. Mexico City. Close enough. So long, Alessandro Cruz.

With only one more body transfer, I flew to the United States, intent on rediscovering my place of birth, Leesburg, after 30 years. And it was like a new world. The white people's overt racism had diminished to the point where slurs were only whispered between close friends and family, and gays were only abused at the voting booth. Progress was rampant!

My host, Javier, stood out like a sore Latino, so I ditched him in the Potomac River and began my rediscovery of Leesburg. I began at the courthouse and the Confederate soldier monument. I would swear the same fucking pigeons were perched on him, busy filling in the few remaining dark patches of exposed bronze. I hovered along the path I had long ago traversed, to the spot where I entered young Morgan. Yes, yes, I know you disapprove of reminiscing about the girl. I wish I could assert that "everyone was doing it" or claim that if I had known what would happen to her that I wouldn't have done it. But that would be a lie, and my actions since then—and with whom they occurred—would vehemently refute such a claim. If I told you about the baby, you would hate me even more. Oops.

Well, there's a reason I've opted to share the story of Joseph Cling above all the others, and you might just think differently of me when all has been recounted. Or perhaps unlike my own resettlement process, one thing cannot erase another, and you will wish you never knew of me. I certainly hope not, because I believe that everyone can learn something from another, no matter how reviled they may be.

It was spring, and Leesburg's abundance of foliage had already blossomed. The white flowers of dogwoods and magnolias and black haw gave the stately bedroom community an air of purity. I observed the families in the cars and trucks as they passed, new mothers pushing strollers, retirees feeding (fucking) pigeons, and found myself struck by all I witnessed. When I'd been there before, my perspective—my wants and needs—were juvenile. Since leaving Leesburg I had experienced dysfunction and danger, connivery and pain, drugs and violence (and that was just in California! Ba-dum-dum!) and I was finally ready for a wholesome environment like this.

Many of you place *love* high on your priority list. Well, I felt I was now mature enough for *love*, or at least ready for the opportunity to swim in its vicarious pool. I set out to scout the neighborhoods for candidates. My very first choice would seem inappropriate for my goals, but a strange fortune it turned out to be.

With little regard for why, I approached a small house with a well-kempt lawn and meticulously pruned landscaping. A shiny new coupe sat in the driveway, suggesting children either had yet to arrive, or had long since moved out. Inside, I found a rotund retiree named Chester sprawled across his leather couch, crumpled newspaper on the hardwood floor beside him. Staring at the ceiling, deep in thought, he sent a plump pinky up his nose and examined its spoils.

"What about *this* weekend?" A woman's voice called from another room.

Chester grunted and replied without pause, "Gotta work on the yard."

I hopped onto the coffee table as the woman appeared from around a corner. Her short salt and pepper locks appeared to be fresh from the salon, her makeup impeccably applied and in surprisingly current colors for her generation. She was visibly annoyed.

"That's *every* day, Hon," she said. "Howsabout you reschedule your oh-so-important weekend work for Monday or Tuesday? We haven't seen her in months."

Chester rotated a finger in his belly button as he frowned with thought. "'Course I wanna see her … It's just, it's forty-five minutes each way … that's gonna bump into weeding 'round the herbs. Plus I was gonna repaint the garage next week."

Uh oh. Her hand went to the hip.

"Your daughter is more important than painting a damned garage that you just painted last year. And she's more important than weeds. Know what? I'm taking it out of your hands. You got no choice: we're going up to Frederick this weekend."

She left the room and Chester sighed, returning to that which troubled his nostril.

I lingered on the coffee table listening to Chester's constant phlegmy wheeze. I wasn't sure if I was troubled or simply intrigued to a degree I had yet to experience. Less than an hour from my birthplace there was a *town* called Frederick? How exactly did I miss that? Was it simply a coincidence? How exactly did I know that I was so named in the first place? It was one of many enduring questions. I just knew. It was sitting in there along with the English language and some knowledge of history and basic mathematics, and a desire to inhabit a human body. I would be joining Chester and the missus to this town.

In the meantime, I would explore their house and coax out its secrets. Everyone has secrets. And most often it is the *ordinary* of the world that harbor the darkest secrets of all.

But the Demottes didn't have a surprise sex dungeon in the basement, and the best thing I found was no secret at all. Instead, it was the framed photographs hanging from the walls and sitting atop doilies on practically every wooden surface.

2. Introductions

I don't understand people who can sit in silence with another person. I had learned over a couple of days that, for the most part, Chester and Claire Demotte enjoyed each other's company and spoke without pause when eating together, or even when watching the TV.

"Is she the one from that other show?"

"No, she's the one from the movie with that Sandler fella."

But sit them down in a car and the lips stick as though glued. Half the drive to Frederick, Maryland was spent in utter silence without even the relief of background music. I was tempted to enter Claire, switch on the radio, and then leave her slumped against the passenger window. I had been around them enough to perfectly mimic either, but I had no interest in a prolonged stay with a long-married couple. Nor am I so callous. I may not care about people's lives, but I don't wipe people out of convenience. Well, not often anyway. Either way, stop dragging me into your judgmental thought process. I'm trying to explain this new leaf I was turning over. Remember that whole *love* thing I mentioned? Forgive me for my impatience, but I was eager to see this town called Frederick and meet its most fascinating citizen: the Demottes' unmarried, 34-year-old daughter, Melanie.

Back at the house, every wall or horizontal surface was like an altar to this only child. She was a radiant thing with big, curly auburn hair, freckles, and enviable eyelashes. She had a chubby period from I would say 8 years until 13 when she began to sprout. The more recent photos revealed she had kept the poofy mop, occasionally wore glasses, and opted for tight-fitting sweaters in winter. And always that beaming smile. In only a few pictures had she actually looked into the lens, her gaze instead focused upon another person in the room, or on whoever held the camera. She was no model, but wore the shine of someone relishing life's every day, and that radiance gave her a beauty I hadn't thus far observed. But those were only photographs, and without the benefit of meeting her in person, I filled in the blanks of her personality with my fantastic imagination. The woman was utter perfection, I tell you.

We arrived well before lunch, pulling into an apartment complex with a brick first floor and paneled uppers. Chester parked in a covered spot despite Claire reminding him that the visitor spots were uncovered.

"Let them tow me."

I followed behind them, bouncing around like an over-caffeinated toy dog. Up a flight of stairs to the second floor, round a guardrail, and here was Melanie's apartment door: #222. She had some potted succulents on the rail and a little plastic table with a hibachi grill. I hopped onto the barbecue and eagerly waited as they knocked. It was exhilarating, keeping myself in suspense like that. I could have simply passed through the door, but opted for the high of delayed gratification. Chester's posture improved and his gut reduced in size by two percent. Claire bulged her eyes repeatedly, apparently in an effort to appear fresh-faced, and coaxed her double chin to retract.

The door opened and my Melanie finally appeared. A singsong "Heeeyyyy" passed between mother and daughter. Tight hugs and lipstick prints. I locked on that face from the pictures, the one with apparently luminous warmth. I couldn't understand what I saw, though. Her waves were common and dry. Where was the Melanie I knew so well? She certainly looked like herself, physically, but something was missing. Had I built her up so much that anything would have been a disappointment? I stopped myself right there. We were only just saying hello on the doorstep and I was already predicting the doom of our nonexistent relationship. I decided that all that anticipation warranted a measure of patience.

"M'dear," Chester said with tilted smile and furrowed brow. She squeezed him hard, raised her shoulders, tucking her face into his armpit as if snuggling with a warm blanket. She closed her eyes as she inhaled his deodorant—a fond scent from her youth. Her body relaxed into his. He patted her back while scrutinizing the apartment through the doorway. "Still have that cat, do ya?"

Melanie's muffled voice: "You ask that every time, Dad. Yes." It was the first of many adorable Melanie moments.

We moved inside and they all sat down on the couches in the living room. The apartment was a good size, open with an adjoining dining area and kitchen. Beyond, a sliding glass door without curtains or blinds. The balcony had room for two chairs, a little table, and a mountain bike. I snooped into her immaculate bedroom with attached bathroom. Melanie had prescription drugs, but nothing exciting. Tampon wrapper in the wastebasket by the toilet. Wholesale jugs of shampoo and conditioner, as well as the understandable bottle of detangler. No sex toys in the nightstand, nothing lacy in the underwear drawer. The secret stash of neatly rolled black and red panties sat in the back of the drawer, where they could always be found.

As Claire began her apparently traditional recounting of Chester's list of recent mistakes, I moved on to the kitchen and checked the cupboards and fridge. Melanie liked yogurt and fruit. A couple Lean Cuisines sat in the freezer. She possessed the kitchen tools of a home cooker, not an eat-outer. Spices of every sort. A well-worn mixer and new food processor. No illicit drugs in the kitchen either.

Having found no potential dealbreakers, I returned to the living room and listened in while the cat shot me an accusing glare. He apparently didn't like me on his cat tree. He didn't like me, period, but that was nothing new. Animals and me don't get along so well.

"And how old is this postal worker?" Claire asked.

I felt like a hawk overlooking its prey as I watched Melanie's demonstrative face and mannerisms. She didn't appear to mind the question, but there was definitely something wrong—something weighing on her.

"You two would like him, I think. And he's not a postal worker. I mean, he works for the Postal Service, but he's not a mailman or whatever. He investigates ... *things*. She flipped a hand, apparently unsure what it was he actually did. "And ... he's in his early forties."

"Don't feel like that's a little old for you, Mel?" Chester said. "I mean, just think ... when you're in your fifties, he'll be in his sixties. Big difference there, you know."

"I'll keep that in mind, Dad," She said it with good humor. "Not really thinking about marriage at all. He's nice and everything ... I don't know. Trying not to get all wrapped up in all that at this stage. Either way, he's only seven years older than me. And very active ... you know, he's been to Antarctica."

"What the hell was he doing there?" Chester asked.

"It was a college thing. Maybe you can ask him yourself when you ... well, I guess *if* you meet." She paused a beat and changed subjects. "So tell me how *you* two are doing. Anything new in Leesburg? Any whispers of scandalous misdeeds?" Melanie's eyes flashed a little with this, but it was an act. Claire could see something was wrong, too, though I wasn't sure if she already knew what it was or simply didn't wish to pry.

"We're well," Claire said. "Trying to keep busy. Working on an RV trip with Pat and Steve if I can get your father to leave the landscaping for a few days."

"Not gonna happen," Chester murmured.

Claire went on, "Also, your uncle has gained some weight back, so that's good."

"That's good," Melanie nodded. "Any new words?" She didn't seem all that interested, but was being polite.

"No, same words, but he's sorta been making eye contact for the past few months. Never did that before. Could be nothing, but you know, any change like that is a good sign. The therapists say it means Dom's still in there somewhere, even after so long."

What was this? Talk of a relative in some sort of vegetative state? A strange twist … I wondered: a remnant of my wild-oat-sowing early days? I had yet to observe one of my *leavings* after an extended period and was not aware of any actually speaking again. There were certainly enough similarly stricken people in the world for this uncle to have had nothing to do with me, but these folks were from a small town where I had left a rather sizable trail. The odds seemed to lean in my favor that this person was one of mine. And if so, I was intrigued that there had been changes over time, and signs of progress like eye contact. In contemplating this, I was not seeking relief of guilt, if that's what you're thinking. No, I had none to relieve. My interest lay solely in understanding myself, just as you wish to understand yourself.

I also wondered what had initially drawn me to the Demotte home. The fact that I instantly learned of my namesake town from them. That they had birthed a marvel like Melanie, to whom I felt more drawn than anyone before or since. And now, the revelation that they might be related to a shell through which I had long ago passed. The coincidences were stacking up, but while it may sound as though these were the thoughts filling the stage of my consciousness, they were, in fact, merely background dancers. The star performer consuming my attention was Ms. Melanie Demotte, seated in a cushy loveseat that in no way matched the rest of her unmatched furniture. A simple flit of the fingers when speaking, the way she played with the V of her V-neck shirt. My initial disappointment and concern evaporated with each passing second in her presence.

Looking back, that first thirty minutes in Melanie's apartment were perfect, a brief period which I could never effectively relay. The best I can do is to explain that I am voyeuristic by nature. Every one of you possesses secrets and odd habits, personality quirks; some have kinky fetishes or shame-ridden desires, painful memories, deep-rooted fears, ambitions, hopes, dreams. There are aspects of every one of you which no other soul would ever know. In the absence of some kind of mind-reader, many of your fascinating characteristics would remain sealed within your consciousness, traveling with you to your grave.

Think of a celebrity. Someone you have seen on a tabloid cover, but not on a reality show. No, one of the private sorts for whom the paparazzi must straw-grasp to form a story, and take pictures with telephoto lenses. Now, imagine being a fly on the wall of that person's home. The most mundane practices become captivating! What TV shows do they watch? Does he absentmindedly scratch his crotch when no one is around? (Probably.) Is she a slob? Who calls him on the phone, and what do those conversations sound like? What does she grab from the fridge or pantry when craving a midnight snack? How does he masturbate? In what order does she scrub when showering? Does he stare at himself in the mirror, studying the details of his face and body and deepening lines, plucking gray hairs, popping zits, trimming nose hairs? All of this is humdrum shit when applied to your spouse of a decade or two, but insert the name of said tabloid superstars and now we're talking, right?

You are *all* celebrities to me. The fly on the wall scenario is the sole advantage of my naked phase. It is when I get to see and hear the things you do when you think no one is watching. I imagine that long ago most people were more mindful of what they did in private, believing that God was always watching, but in my experience, when you are alone you seem to feel secure in your privacy.

This is why the period between bodies can be enjoyable, but it does begin to feel *wrong*. Not the invading of privacy—no, that's fine—but the sensation of being loose. It starts to feel as though I could drift apart or fade away. The best way to describe the equivalent sensation would be *starvation*. This begins three or four days in. The longest I had gone without a body was six days, and that was a horrible, terrifying experience that made me question my perceived immortality. A story for another day.

My point is that I was relishing this moment, observing Melanie—getting to know her. This meeting was like our first date, albeit somewhat one-sided. But she would meet me soon enough. That much I had decided the second she snorted her father's armpit. I wanted to be loved like that. I wanted to have positive feelings associated with my presence. I wanted my smells to evoke memories of wonderful times.

The conversation returned to this postal worker, and you may be able to guess why he was a subject of my interest.

Melanie said, "Joey says the same thing. He thinks I should quit and do art full-time, though he says it half-jokingly. I haven't even—"

"Hard to make a living in art, I'm sure you know," Chester interrupted.

"Not necessarily," Claire said with a glare in Chester's direction. Turning back to Melanie, she said, "And you used to focus so much more on your creative outlets—photography, painting, music. When's the last time you painted?"

Melanie glanced up to an oil portrait on the wall—an old black man with sunglasses, a small dog on his lap, staring at me. Not knowing much about art, it looked pretty damned good. I recalled the Demottes' cluttered walls, thinking at the time that at least there were a few decorations that weren't Melanie, but now I realized they were all Melanie's paintings. The odd few black and white landscape photographs there were surely hers as well.

"Years, Mom. I'll pick it up again. And I still write songs from time to time."

"But you're too tired."

"Maybe …"

"You do too much. You always have. I like this Joey already. When do we get to meet him?"

"I don't know. I'm …" There it was again. The sadness. Her shoulders fell almost imperceptibly, and the shine in her face dimmed. Maybe Joey wasn't such a suitable host after all … "I'm in a weird situation. Have to figure some things out … you know, with work and stuff …"

Claire didn't wish to pry. She pressed her lips together and lowered her brow.

Chester had no such restraint: "What situation? Just spit it out."

Melanie shook her head. "No, I'll figure it out. Nothing big— nothing for you guys to worry about."

"Fine, but what's the situation?"

Claire frowned and put a hand on Chester's knee, "Hon."

Melanie shook out her face and put on a smile, "So … you guys hungry or what? I have a new recipe I've been dying to try, but you know, no inspiration to be a gourmet cooking for one."

"Oh, no, sweetie," Claire said, standing. "You do enough without having to slave over a stove for us. Let's just go out to Kelligan's. Your father loves their beers."

They went back and forth with "it's no trouble, really" and "you need to relax." I just wanted to know more about this "situation" and to meet Joey the Postman.

I accompanied them to dinner at Kelligan's Brew House where Chester stuffed his face and watched baseball on the suspended televisions. Claire and Melanie discussed life's banal affairs. The triviality of the conversation did not dissuade me. I observed Melanie simply matching her mother's preferences for chitchat. But I was quite relieved when Mom and Dad gave their departing hugs during the extended good-bye ritual back at Melanie's place. Chester went off to get the car while Claire tried to hammer down Melanie on a date for meeting Joey.

"We'll figure something out, okay. Love you, Mom."

"Noncommittal, but I'll take what I can get. Last thing I want is to be a part of your stress."

"I'm not stressed, Mom. There's Dad. Go before he honks. I'll see you soon, 'kay?"

Alone at last.

We adjourned inside and Melanie plopped down onto the couch, rolled to her side, and pulled a throw blanket over her shoulder. I sat on the coffee table, her face so close I could feel her breath passing through me. She was staring blankly across the room, but I moved into her line of sight until her gaze fell directly on me. We were looking into each other, sharing a moment. People don't just sit and stare at each other like this unless playing a game. But Melanie and I held this for a few minutes until her eyes eventually drifted away.

A lot on the mind, this one, but I would have never guessed the source.

* * *

Our first evening together began enjoyably enough. Melanie had eventually fallen asleep on the couch and I watched her dream. Her eyes rolled around behind her eyelids as the sides of her mouth twitched. I moved atop her chest and inhaled her exhales (such as I can, being a non-corporeal entity), then "kissed" her pouty lower lip. I wanted to suck on it, but all in due time. Her subtle tics turned to the grimaces and shudders of a nightmare, so I backed off. Watching me from the third tier of his tree, the cat leapt down and hopped onto Melanie after I had moved away. I gave him the invisible evil eye in return and lurched forward threateningly, to which he responded with a flinch and low growl. Melanie stirred, but did not wake.

"She might be yours now, my friend, but not for long. Joey the Postman is allergic to your dander, didn't you know? He didn't want to bring it up to her in the beginning, but there it is, fucker."

She woke to her cell phone ringing a few hours later. I looked at the screen before she grabbed it. Andrew Kalestian from Melanie's work, Frederick Medical Center. She looked at it and sighed, contemplating whether to pick up. She answered on the third ring.

"Hey."

I slid close to her ear to listen in.

"I miss you," said the deep voice of Mr. Kalestian. He had a faint Eastern European accent. "What are you doing right now?"

She swallowed and said, "Just getting my place together … laundry and stuff … getting ready for the week."

"Mm-hmm. Sounds like activity best accomplished on a *Monday* night. I'm coming over."

"No," she snapped, caught herself, and continued slower, "Not tonight, okay? I'm pretty tired and—"

"Have a headache? Come now, gorgeous. I *need* you right now. I need to see those eyes, smell the neck, be *inside* you. I don't think you understand the intensities of what you do to my brain. You're in there all the time."

Who the fuck is Andrew Kalestian, and why is he trying to seduce my woman? I wanted to zip into that phone, come out the other side, and scramble the intensities of his brain like eggs.

Melanie's free hand went to her stomach and clutched a roll of skin.

"Andy …" she attempted.

"I'm leaving now. Clear the laundry off the bed, my dear."

"Andy, no, I'm serious." But the phone had gone silent. She looked at the screen and saw the call had ended. Her body slumped back into the couch with a loud exhale. She wasn't happy, but I was disturbed to watch as she attempted no callback. She stared off with desolation for a minute before growling to her feet, grabbing shoes off the floor, tidying the kitchen bar, then darting to the bedroom.

I was stunned that she was letting this happen. I was infuriated with her, and contemplated simply leaving to go find another. Every fish in the ocean was at my disposal, so why get myself embroiled with some cheating whore? Well, she is *not* a whore, and I'll kindly ask you to refrain from such vulgarity. I stayed. I stayed and watched the whole gut-wrenching act.

Andrew was in his fifties, obviously worked out, and regularly shaved what would otherwise be a dense thicket of black chest hair. The ID in his wallet said he was an orthopedic surgeon. The thick, silver ring on his finger and the laminated photos on his key ring said he was married, with kids. He smelled of food. I thought I detected grilled onions and cinnamon, and guessed it was a meal his wife had just cooked for the family.

I sat on Melanie's dresser beside the bed, feeling for the first time a strange, buzzing pain. I watched his ass cheeks flex rhythmically, her feet in the air on either side of him. He slapped her breasts to make them shake, his eyes fixed upon her chest the entire time. I studied her face, searching for anguish. I wanted to see the expression of a rape victim, or at least some sign of dissatisfaction with him, but even as he grew more forceful—slamming into her with what seemed to border on violence—there was neither. She appeared to enjoy every moment. He finished on her belly before collapsing beside her, a gasping sweaty mess after just seven minutes (7:23, to be precise, not that I was timing them).

And then it appeared. The face I wanted! She was distraught and possibly a little disgusted. He lurched forward to slap her ass as she shuffled out of bed toward the bathroom. He laughed and didn't see the dirty look she shot his way. I watched him lay there a moment, to see what sort of post-coital man he was, but all he did was stare at the ceiling while lazily playing with his retreating, uncircumcised penis.

I hurried to the bathroom, hoping to find Melanie in tears, but she was cleaning her belly with a wet towel. She gave herself a quick look in the mirror, eye to eye, searching herself, or perhaps judging, before returning to the bedroom and throwing on a big shirt. She sat down on the side of the bed, not looking at Andrew.

"What time is it?" He asked as he looked at his watch. Melanie didn't bother answering, aware it was rhetorical. "Oh shit, didn't realize!" He said and rushed to the bathroom to clean up. He splashed water on his crotch then lathered it with hand soap. When finished clearing evidence from the obvious places, he pulled a towel from the rack, moistened a corner, and corkscrewed it up each nostril, removing the latent scent of sex therein. How thorough. Returning to the room, he scrambled to get dressed.

Melanie played with her toes while she sat. The moment was dreadfully clichéd, and she seemed to be acutely aware of this fact. Even when Andrew leaned down to kiss her neck and provide the obligatory tit squeeze, she smiled politely.

"I missed you so much," he said, holding her chin so she looked in his eyes.

"Yeah, me too," she said. "I'll see you at the office tomorrow morning?"

Andrew thought for a beat then replied, "Yes, about eight-thirty. Be sure to get the monthly order out to McKesson before ten, and see if Dr. Picker can trade Tuesday afternoon for me, okay?"

"Sounds good."

"You are the best." He actually winked.

He led himself out.

Melanie flopped backward on the bed with a deep sigh. It was an endearing habit of hers, I had noticed, punctuating moments with big, collapsing motions. She lay there, staring absently at the ceiling for a moment before deciding to finish what Dr. Kalestian had started. I watched, but without enjoyment.

She showered him from her body and put on some short boxers and a tank top. An adorable outfit. I wondered if she felt she needed to lose ten to fifteen pounds, or if she ever exposed her cellulite like that when others were around. The Melanie I crafted from her parents' photos wouldn't have given any of it a thought, but I was no longer sure I knew the woman before me.

But I stayed, didn't I?

It was the scandalous behavior I would normally appreciate witnessing—enjoying the surprise of it, if nothing else. But I felt betrayed. How could I ever trust her, once I had become her boyfriend? Without the ability to observe her in secret, she could be engaging in all manner of salacious acts and I would never know! I am truly perplexed by how you people do it, this blind trust.

She placed a glass of water on the nightstand and slid under the covers. A twist of the lamp switch. Phone ringer set to silent. Alarm set. The cat came padding into the room and hopped nimbly onto the bed, but upon spotting me on the extra pillow, hissed and ran out. Melanie tried to call him back in, but he had opted for the living room.

She rolled like an alligator for the first ten minutes before settling into a *hare's sleep*, as we say in Holland—waking from the slightest sounds. I imagined what it would be like to be in a body lying beside her like this. I could spoon her, wrap an arm around her waist, dig my nose into her hair—but not for too long! Unless she *liked* hot breath on her neck. I supposed I would know soon enough.

Yes, despite myself, I still wanted to be with her.

For how long, I did not know. My idealized version of her had indeed been ruined. Before, she was a vibrant, hopeful, virginal maiden, just waiting for someone like me to introduce her to what life had to offer. Now she seemed to me a bit used, a bit older, a bit broken. That was how I felt while I watched her sleep that first night. Unsure, demoralized, judgmental. Both of us had suddenly become very human.

* * *

You know when your mouth is dry and you know you won't be getting any water for a while? How about sinus headaches? Constipation? I had reached the fourth day of dishabitation, and it feels like all of the above. That's the closest comparison I can make anyway. Especially the part about being constipated—it's like going a full week without taking a crap. But I still needed observation time with Joseph Cling. I went to work at the medical center with Melanie, hoping she'd receive some correspondence from him, or for her to contact him to meet up that night. Though I could find a temporary body to bide my time, it was a practice I tried to avoid. A sudden suicide or accidental death in the news would not necessarily rock the city, but in smaller towns, people took such things to heart, and who knew who was related to whom or were friends from high school? Melanie was already depressed and I needed her focus to be on me.

Each time her desk phone rang, she looked at the screen with anticipation. I did the same, and we were both deflated by the discovery of work-related callers. I knew that she was waiting for Joseph because she repeatedly went through his text history on her phone, smiling at his little jokes or emoticons. After lunch, she opened her contact list and her thumb hung above the CALL button beside his cell phone number.

"Do it!" I beckoned, but she ignored all of my silent pleas.

When Dr. Scumbag wasn't around, she perused Facebook, liking and commenting on several friends' posts and photos. And then it happened. A popup on the screen.

The instant message was from Joseph Cling, and it read:

> **Guess who's back and thinking about you and hoping your free tonight and misses you?**

With deep anguish, I noted his inability to differentiate "your" from "you're."

She wiggled a little in her rolling chair, the shine in her face slowly returning. Her fingers hovered above the keyboard as she contemplated her reply.

Ummmmmm ... my mom? But I just saw her!

Oh. Nevermind then.

Shut up, you miss me?

Maaayyyybe ...

Maybe I miss you, too.

The semi-adolescent dialog went on for a few minutes until they settled on a time—fortunately, that night. He would pick her up at 5:45 at her apartment, and she was to bring a raincoat, her camera bag, hiking shoes, and her sleeping bag with cushion roll.

The glow of my beloved Melanie returned, as if her dimmer switch was controlled by a man typing somewhere, unseen. I liked that this man planned surprises for her. She seemed genuinely excited at the thought. I knew that I, too, could be the sort of mate that surprises, and certainly better than whatever Joseph had in store for her.

Joseph had set a wonderful precedent for me, and unlike other men, I would not tire of such activities or become less thoughtful over time. Melanie would be my one and only focus, so she would always feel special, desirable, funny, sexy, surprised, and whatever else I observed to be a need. I don't need empathy to observe actions and reactions, pleasure or displeasure. If I detect a sign of discontent, I adjust accordingly.

Here is the thing, and I'll say this to you only once to keep from sounding like an arrogant asshole. There is a right thing to say in every situation, be it with a man or woman, personal setting or professional. After a few years observing different types of people and personalities, one can quickly *assess* and then *respond* accordingly. And I am not simply referring to placating. By the "right thing" I mean that which the other person wants to hear, but also that which gets me what I want. Conceptually, it is embarrassingly simple, but I have taken the practice to a level far beyond. When I so choose, I *always* say the right thing. This is why I am successful in what I do. It is a rare circumstance where I find myself unable to assess and respond. It is also why I am a mind-blowing lover.

Yes, I said it.

On the flip side, there is also the perfect *wrong* thing to say.

Those words which will bite the deepest and leave a permanent scar. Women tend to be naturals at this practice, but when so inspired, I too can devastate the coolest, most confident person on Earth. It can be as simple as casually telling a thin person they're fat ("Keep at it, hon … you'll lose the rest of that."). They laugh it off at first, but soon I am a voice in their head.

But why think of such detestable cruelty? I had a date that night, and I was ever so excited to meet him.

3. Surprises

M elanie skipped out of the office fifteen minutes early, rushed home, and began throwing together an overnight bag. She pulled two battery packs from her camera bag and slapped them into the charger. She grabbed her sleeping bag and air cushion from the closet shelf and threw them to the front door. She fed the cat and scooped the litter box. She picked out clothes for the night and jumped in the shower.

I had become so comfortable with the idea of being Joseph that I truly felt as though her intense grooming presaged a night out with *me*. She paid special scrubbing attention to certain areas of her body, as though imploring me to later provide equally intense consideration to said areas. She would be stunned and enraptured and awestricken by me, rendered defenseless by her ecstasy. I envisioned her expression of shock, of wonder, her face revealing that "… it's never been like *this* before!" If I were in a man's body at that moment I would have erupted in my pants.

She dried and lotioned, deodorized and perfumed, applying only a subtly-toned lipstick, allowing her face's natural beauty to do its job unaided. She selected a bra practical for hiking activities, but packed a prettier one in the overnight bag. With Joey Cling's 5:45 arrival quickly approaching, the bags were sealed and placed by the door. She took a final look around the place and something struck her. Into the bedroom she rushed and stripped the linens off the bed, cramming them deep into the closet.

The doorbell rang.

We both flinched.

Her smile shone exquisitely as she swung the door open. Joseph stood there and took her in for a beat before stepping forward. They hugged tightly before kissing. No words exchanged. They were attracted to each other, but I don't know if it was love I was seeing. There was certainly awkwardness from both sides, even as they kissed. I moved a little closer, studied his style, watching his hesitant lips, eyes, what he did with his hands, pelvis, his breathing. They pulled away a little and locked eyes. It may have simply been his fatigue, having just returned from some sort of trip, but my first impression was that he was depressed.

I moved closer still, but I had crossed some invisible perimeter and had to quickly move away. He was like a powerful vacuum cleaner tube and I was a helpless strand of hair on a hardwood floor! I could see every single wave reaching out from his body, stretching, trying to reach me, like a jellyfish drawing in a tiny shrimp. It had been several days loose for me, but I had never been pulled in like that before. Joseph's body was going to be something special.

"You ready?" He asked. She nodded with a little smirk and wide eyes. "Then let's go. Tell me what to grab."

She almost seemed relieved to be done with the kissing part, but I was self-aware enough to know that I could very well be imagining such things. I didn't actually want her to enjoy herself too much until *after* I took over Joseph duties.

Joseph was 6'1, around 190lbs. His forehead lines were deep, and his hair was thinning a bit at the crown. He had plenty of gray hairs peppering the brown, but otherwise genetics had done him a solid. He looked like one of those fit, rugged guys in a Just For Men hair dye commercial, or in a modern-day western. Yes, I could see him on a horse, a straw of wheat jutting from the side of his mouth. But put that man in expensive jeans and a tight polo shirt. With just a glance, there was no question he was an eye magnet for women. I wondered if he exploited this attention, or remained monogamous, but his tentative nature suggested he may actually be oblivious to his desirability.

Obvious morality issues aside, he was certainly a more suitable mate for my Melanie than Mr. Dr.

They loaded the back of his SUV—an older, yet well-maintained Land Rover. He opened the passenger door for her, and closed it when she was fully settled inside. At the surface, he seemed genuine: a good mate. But I pondered what lay beneath. I wouldn't have as much time with him as I prefer, so much of my studies would be post-habitation. If he was carrying on with other women, it could come back to haunt my budding relationship with Melanie. But I *needed* to be inside him soon. With so many days bodiless, his waves continued to pull at me and I had to put up a fight, like a tug-o-war.

On the drive, I lingered atop the dashboard, as far from him as possible. I listened to his voice and the stand-out words he used most frequently ("dorky" and "ludicrous"). The way he glanced at her when driving. His hand resting casually on her leg. When she retold the humorous parts of her parents' visit, and then an anecdote about them from her youth, he nodded and smiled appreciatively. He only spoke about himself when asked, and not at length, though neither too succinctly. His primary charm seemed to lay in his genuine interest and instant grasp of a story's meaning or impending punch line. I would be superb with this sort of thing, but not so subdued.

Melanie glanced outside at a passing road sign.

"Are we going into Cunningham?" She asked.

"Could be."

"Well, you know it's closed after dark on weekdays?"

"Mm-hmm."

She squinted at him, "Are we going to be *outlaws* this evening?"

Joseph smiled and shrugged. She stared at his mouth and put her hand over his on her thigh.

In just twenty-five minutes I had observed and noted numerous mannerisms and facial expressions he used, word choices, music taste, the fact that he drove the speed limit. I was reasonably certain that sex was on the agenda for the night, and though I would rather be in him while he was in *her*, I needed to see the act before I made the final leap. If everything else about Joseph suddenly changed, but the expressions, words, and sex rituals remained, nothing would seem particularly awry that could not be easily explained.

We exited the highway and took a small two-lane road for several miles before finding the turnout he sought. He parked.

"I love this place," Melanie said as she strapped on her camera pack. "Never been here at night though."

He turned around and told her she could leave the sleeping bag bundle while he pulled on a large, stuffed backpack and stretched a headlamp over his head.

Melanie and I followed Joseph to a break in the treeline—a trailhead with a sign that read: "FALLS – 1.2mi" with an upward-pointed arrow.

"Didn't bring my bathing suit though ..." Melanie murmured. Joseph didn't respond.

We hiked the mile in relative silence until the sound of a waterfall became audible a good distance before the end of the trail.

"I can smell it!" Melanie said.

But when we reached the clearing, only the white tips of the rapids were visible in the darkness, reflecting the minute amount of starlight. Joseph shut off the headlamp. Melanie said it was beautiful, I guessed to avoid highlighting the fact that she would be unable to get any good pictures without *light*. They stood there alongside an invisible river, listening to the harmonics of rushing water. Perhaps they were waiting for their eyes to further adjust to the dark. I thought this was probably as good a view as possible at the hour. Joseph turned around and faced her; he put his hands on her shoulders.

"Do you trust me?" He said.

"I did up until you just asked ..."

"I want you to turn around and sit on this rock with your eyes closed for about ten minutes. That's a long time, I know, but there's a payoff."

"Yeah ... I mean, yeah, but are you going to leave me?"

"Somewhat. I'll still be able to see you, though. Tell you what, I'll sing so you can hear me the whole time."

"Ooh, I don't think I've heard the Cling singing voice. Deal!"

Melanie turned and sat down on the large, smooth rock and closed her eyes. Her smile quivered as she basked in the tense pleasure of the moment. She didn't feel entirely safe, but that seemed to contribute to the enjoyment.

"Okay, now no cheating," he said as he walked off alongside the flowing river. "It'll ruin it if you look before I say."

I stayed with Melanie and watched him set up. He alternated between whistling and singing a discordant version of "You've Lost That Loving Feeling," but by the time he had made it near the base of the falls, we couldn't hear anything. After he switched on the first light, I realized what he was doing, but wondered if there had been too much build-up. His surprise was interesting, but I wasn't sure it would inspire the desired reaction from Melanie. Knowing her as I did, I predicted she would play it up either way. But when he finished and returned to her side, I learned that I didn't know my Mel like I thought I did, and had underestimated my soon-to-be host.

He put his hands gently on her shoulders and kissed her neck.

"Did you peek at all? Tell the truth."

"No way! I sat here and enjoyed the sound of the water and the rocks and bugs. Smelling the cool, moist air … all of it. Butt's a little sore, but otherwise I'm in heaven. The fact that there's something more than this is just icing. Is it ready? Whatever it is?"

"Yes. Are you?"

"I *think* so."

"Then stand up, keep your eyes closed, and I'll help you turn around."

Once she faced the falls he moved his hands to her waist, standing behind her.

"So can I open?"

"Five more minutes."

"Huh-what? Seriously?"

"No, open your eyes."

She opened them and they instantly went wide with surprise.

"Holy shit!" She blurted. "Holy shit! How did you …"

She surveyed the waterfall, now lit with multicolored lights positioned around it. Green, red, blue, white. He had even thrown lights into the basin beneath the falls, making the water glow and flicker on the jutting cliff rocks.

"I can move them if any are placed wrong. Well, except for those two." He pointed to the water.

"No, no way, they're perfect! How did you ... I mean, the power?"

"They're just flashlights. Really bright ones—the LED kind. I got some of those colored gel things to rubber band over some of them. I hope it works ... I thought it would be enough light, but ... argh, I'm a dork."

"No, no ... my God, Joey ... this is too much."

She turned around and embraced him, kissing him with radical passion such that I knew she wasn't faking her reaction for his benefit. He had scored a homerun, as they say, and I made a mental note to schedule elaborate surprises on a regular basis.

Joseph tripped backward a little, perhaps a touch uncomfortable with her level of passion, but still responding accordingly. Another mental note.

She pulled back and looked into his blue, green, and red-spangled eyes, kissed him one more time, gently.

"Can I shoot it?" She whispered.

"Please! Before the batteries run out," he chuckled. "Can I help with anything?"

"No, I got it. I think you've done enough, sir."

"Good, cause I have a water-filled shoe and soaked pant leg. Took a little dunk walking across the rocks."

She laughed at him as she pulled out her mini tripod, setting it up on a boulder, while Joseph tended to his shoe and sock. Melanie adjusted her camera settings, taking several test shots before finding the speed and aperture she liked.

"Oooh sweetie, it's so beautiful! Look what you did!"

He hopped to her and peered at the last photo on her viewscreen: a crisp, vibrant shot one would find in a landscape photography book.

"Hey, I just threw up some lights. You're the artist."

She snapped off a few more pictures then turned around to hug and kiss him again. I contemplated taking him at that very moment, but I didn't know what came next on the evening's agenda, nor had I seen him perform in bed. Well, I knew that if things continued on their current course, he would soon find her legs wide and accommodating. Furthermore, the man had *earned* his final turn with her, and I would have the rest of his lifetime to better him.

Melanie moved her camera closer to the falls, captured several angles, then moved again. In all, she took over two hundred photos from five different positions. She had him remove the colored gels for the last few shots taken from all the way back, and he gathered up the flashlights after that. She asked about the ones in the water and he said he'd come back for them next week during regular hours.

"Unless you want to dive in there."

"Quite all right."

They packed everything up and hiked out, Melanie thanking him in as many paraphrased word arrangements she could muster. The man was almost too humble, even apologetic about it being a little cold out. I began to wonder more and more about him. Even with the awkwardness, how was he unmarried into his forties? Or if he was married and divorced, were there kids somewhere? And what happened to the marriage? In the end, these questions were unimportant. Soon, he would be a new man, and whatever was wrong with him before would become mere reminiscence.

We drove the dark, wooded road back toward the interstate, Joseph reminding Melanie of a conversation between them some weeks prior. Apparently, the Frederick County Tourism Board had put out a notice that they sought the community's photo submissions for an upcoming advertising campaign. Selected photographs would be used on flyers, websites, posters, and other media. Winning submissions would split a pool of $10,000.

"So I thought no one else would be submitting pictures from nighttime."

"You're brilliant," Melanie said. "I wonder, though."

"What? Wonder what?"

"Well, if we were trespassing … I don't know. I'm sure it's fine."

Joseph just gave her a clever look in reply, and passed the onramp to the interstate, turning down a parallel road. I spotted a sign that read "Catoctin Armory" with the swirling embellishments of historical sites. Melanie noticed we had missed the interstate, as well.

"Wait, where now?"

Joseph shrugged mysteriously and pulled onto a side road. We crunched into a gravelly vacant parking lot.

"Our quarters for this evening," he said with a smile.

"A parking lot?"

They chuckled and got out, and Melanie scanned around the area.

"Wait … I came here on a field trip once. This is those ruins, right?"

"Mm-hmm."

They grabbed all their gear and Joseph put on his headlamp. A trail led to a large stone structure that looked like the remains of some old castle. Melanie followed Joseph to a large wooden door secured with an impressive chain and padlock. He placed his load on the ground and searched his pockets, then produced a key which he held up for Melanie to see.

"Okay, now where the hell did you get *that*?" She said.

He smirked and unlocked the padlock, pulling the chain from the thick, metal loops.

"Stay here for a second, okay?"

She gave him a skeptical face and he disappeared inside. I stayed with Melanie and watched her glance around nervously. Joseph appeared to be exceeding her tolerance level for adventure. Another note: surprises, not danger. We could hear him moving things around, planks of wood tossed aside, stone bricks scritching along a concrete floor, sweeping. When done, he poked his face out the door.

"Well, it's not the Ritz Carlton … I … I should have come to check it out first … It's just … I just got the key today, and…"

Melanie gave him a peck on the lips and told him she didn't need a fancy hotel. How sweet. She apparently didn't even need an establishment with running water, power, or basic sanitation standards. We entered the ruins and took in the sights and smells. Inside, it looked like a fortress sacked by the enemy. Whole brick walls had given way, timber supports splintered and split. I suspected the place had been frequented by drifters and drunken teenagers for decades before anyone cared to lock it up. To me, it looked like an ideal location for those seeking a potent dose of tetanus or dormant bacteria. Joseph had cleared a good amount of space on the dusty floor for them, and proceeded to set up candles while Melanie brought in her stuff. I turned to watch her face as she observed the evening's accommodations, waiting to see the feigned appreciation and wonder. But, again, she proved me a foolish assumer, and I realized then that she wouldn't be my sparkling Melanie if I could predict her every reaction or thought. She chewed the inside of her cheek, shaking her head with amazement.

She said, "You are full of surprises tonight, Mister. This is just breathtaking … my God. How you think of this stuff …" She turned to him with clever eyes. "Though I have to say, the key reads a smidgen less criminal than waterfall trespassing."

He continued lighting candles and placing them at different heights around the rubble, the room growing brighter and yellower.

"Yeah, you know me. Can't exactly break the law in my profession. I got permission for a night photo shoot and the key from a friend of mine. Sorry … I hope that doesn't shatter your perceptions of my bad boy nature."

He climbed down from a pile of stone blocks and she said, "What do *you* think?" as she reached around his neck and pulled his lips against hers. He reciprocated for a short time before pulling away awkwardly, and I noted the first hint of frustration in her face.

"Let's eat first," he said. "I couldn't track down a real picnic basket, but just pretend the grocery bags are wicker."

"Oh, perfect!" She said. "I'm starving."

Crestfallen, "Sorry, maybe we should have eaten at the falls?"

"No, no, it's all good. Everything is perfect. You're like a dating professional."

He smiled, but with a little frown—unsure if it was a compliment, perhaps. I wasn't so sure myself. They sat and ate the store-bought roasted chicken with a French baguette and some fresh fruit. They drank chardonnay in plastic cups. Joseph told her about the ruins around them, explaining that up the road lay a blast furnace structure that was used during the civil war and the "armory" we were in was where they would actually produce ammunition. She seemed somewhat intrigued by the tales, but his delivery left much to be desired. If it had gone on a moment longer I would want to shoot myself. I didn't know if he was purposely ignoring Melanie's cues, trying to delay intimacy, or if he was simply an imperceptive moron.

They cleaned up the food, unrolled cushions, prepped their sleeping bags. Teeth were brushed with the aid of a water bottle. Joseph peed outside while Melanie quickly changed into something a little more comfortable. Upon his return, he found her lying provocatively across their bedding. I saw him swallow nervously before turning to secure the door with a wood plank. I pondered his reticence toward intimacy, behavior repeated more than a few times during our brief acquaintance, and then *caiu a ficha*, as we say in Brazil—something clicked in my mind. I imagined that somehow his subconscious knew that to take her would be his final act in this world. That he must avoid it at all cost, lest he be erased.

But then he appeared to succumb, kneeling over her and gently kissing her lips.

She slid up her elongated nightshirt and slowly spread her knees, revealing the absence of undergarments.

Joseph proceeded to kiss her neck—little pecks, never in the same place. He kissed her ear, her cheek, her forehead, the tip of her nose. He brushed her arm lightly with his fingers while his gentle lips explored every part of her body ... from the clavicle up. This went on for some time, and while Melanie made soft sounds and subtly writhed beneath him, I couldn't accept the idea that I could yet again be wrong about her. My Melanie wanted to be ravaged, not pecked and caressed and treated to a prolonged physical serenade of "Your Body is a Wonderland."

She unbuttoned his polo shirt and pulled it off. He began pecking her breastbone. She reached down to unbutton his pants, but he crept slowly back and lifted her shirt, now kissing her belly. Soft, slow, loving, nauseating. But Melanie put up with it. I wanted to jump inside him and show him how it's done! I wanted to get in there and assure Melanie that I wasn't a sexual moron. But at the same time, I knew how important it was to see this. I would need to devise a plan for transitioning her to an erotically literate Joseph.

Joseph whispered things like "You're so beautiful" and "I love every part of you." Melanie hummed appreciatively, but what I heard was "Mm-hmm … let's get on with it."

Finally, Joseph made his move. He glided in to pleasure her orally, but she suddenly—shockingly—put on the brakes.

She said softly, kindly, "Not … still not really … the hike, you know?"

Joseph appeared mortified. I wondered if that was all he had been building up to for a half an hour. That he would have to start over! Thank heavens for Melanie. She immediately grabbed him and pulled him down atop her.

"Maybe you'll make it up to me next time," she said playfully.

He was still shaken, though. It was as though she had told him what *I* would have told him twenty minutes ago! She reached down and fondled him as she kissed him deep.

She pulled her face back from his, looked in his eyes and said, "Can I be on top this time? You turn me on so much." But she didn't wait for his answer, turning him onto his side and pulling down his underwear. I finally got a look at what he had going on down there, nullifying my fear that his inadequacy was due to microphallus or some sort of grotesque disfigurement. He wasn't a horse by any stretch, but he had nothing to be ashamed of. I could definitely work with it.

He let her take over and she guided him home. He participated more than I would have given him credit for, even grabbing and sucking a tit here and there. After a few minutes, she sat up and helped herself out while still riding him spiritedly. She yelped and hunched forward suddenly, beginning to climax. He watched and grabbed her thighs and went with her.

If I had lungs, I would have sighed with relief. It was like bad soft porn, though ended better than one would expect given the lead-up.

She collapsed onto her back beside him, breathless. No attempt to cover up or modestly clean herself. Joseph had a hand over his softening little friend and simply stared at her.

He said again, "I love everything about you."

She replied naturally, but with what I perceived to be carefully chosen words, "You're the best thing that's ever happened to me."

I could hear the doubt that he couldn't. I knew what was going on in her head when she thought about him. The words "...if only..." were definitely in there. The question was, would she overlook a few lacking qualities in light of ten others she loved? Or perhaps it was my own projection that his "style" wasn't up to muster. Maybe she was perfectly satisfied. Maybe she liked the deferred gratification. I didn't think so. And I had seen enough.

I let Melanie get dressed. Joseph slid on his boxers and unblocked the door, letting her out to pee in the bushes. He averted his eyes.

I descended from the rafters and entered him.

4. Settling In

Well, this was unexpected. I had spent the past few days harboring an admittedly creepy obsession with Melanie Demotte, my focus on Joseph Cling wholly rooted in his pre-established access. But Joseph felt like *home*.

Of all the bodies I had inhabited, his fit like it was tailored just for me. There are things you come across in life—technologies of convenience, homes, songs, people—that you didn't know were missing until after they arrived. What I hadn't realized until that moment was that all of my previous bodies had a little too much room, or not quite enough. That their brains worked a bit differently than what felt *perfect*—a concept I would not have thought possible before Joseph. Only in retrospect did each seem a bit Papa Bear or Mama Bear.

Melanie came back inside the dusty armory. Nervous, I tested out my Joseph voice.

"Welcome back," I said, and she smiled warmly.

Joseph's manhood wasn't in the proper mindset for a second round of fornication, despite my own primed state. It was okay, though, as I had a plan forming on how to fix Joseph in her eyes. And I had a list of to-do's, not the least of which was to keep Melanie's boss out of her pants. She had yet to cheat on *me* and I would keep it that way.

We crawled into our sleeping bags and faced each other. She shifted around inside hers, curling into a fetal position, getting cozy.

"I want to see you again tomorrow," I said.

"Wow, yeah, absolutely," she said, but she was tired. Some amount of the fatigue may have been prognostic. "After work?"

"You could play hooky."

She considered the idea.

"Could *you*, though?" She asked.

"For you, I could." As soon as I said it, I felt foolish. The subtleties in her expression told me I had misstepped. It was too much. She should feel no pressure. "I'm kidding," I quickly said. "Just let me know when I can see you again. You know, whatever works."

Her smile returned and she pulled her sleeping bag tighter over her shoulder.

"Are you in town all week?" She asked.

Ah, right. Joseph had a job. He investigated ... *things*, as Melanie had put it, for the Post Office. Unlike past hosts about whom I cared little what lay in place prior to my arrival, I needed to learn everything about Joseph. I could not simply uproot him from friends, family, or occupation without a backward glance. And I had only spent a single evening with him, versus my usual minimum two days of observation. Fortunately, I had seen him enter his phone's passcode, and one's phone these days is a convenient snapshot of a life.

"I'm pretty sure I'm around. Let's talk tomorrow some time."

She nodded, and we cuddled with each other briefly before she succumbed to sleep. I watched her for the first time through real eyes and gently stroked her hair with real hands. I had so much to look forward to and had a predictably difficult time getting to sleep. Joseph's body was ready to slumb, but I busied his mind for over an hour before giving in.

* * *

We woke up early to the sounds of disgusting, harried pigeons above us. We packed up and I drove Melanie to her apartment, mindful of the speed limit, and of not staring at her. We kissed good-bye and I looked lovingly at her bedraggled morning state. She didn't seem to care about the rats nest hair or lack of makeup or puffy eyes.

She hadn't even looked in a mirror since awakening. This was the Melanie I knew from her parents' photos, and it was truly difficult to let her walk away, back to the world's disposal, back to the risk of a car accident, the uncircumcised penis of an adulterous doctor, back to her innermost thoughts and feelings—including, perhaps, doubts about *me*, even though I hadn't yet been given the chance to show her how truly perfect I was for her.

I watched her beautiful, healthy rear jiggle through her yoga pants as she walked to her steps. She glanced back and waved a little wave. I waved back and forced myself to depress the gas pedal. I wished I could go park, leave Joseph's body, and watch her in her apartment—observe her real feelings about the night, maybe even listen in on a call to a girlfriend while she prepared for work. But I had never returned to a body I had left. I didn't know if it was even possible and always feared that *I* would be stuck in that vegetative state forever, unable to leave: the ultimate karmic reprisal for the minds I had wiped. No, I certainly wouldn't be testing the limits of demonic possession on the best body I had ever inhabited, just to spy on the best woman I had ever met. I would be living within the confines of this form and by the rules that came with it. That is a part of the excitement of life, isn't it? To live at the mercy of that we cannot control, eternally appreciative for another day granted without tragedy.

I exited her apartment complex, made a few turns through the residential neighborhood, and pulled over. I put the Land Rover in park and went through the glove compartment. Ketchup and mustard packets, a plastic-wrapped Spork, napkins from various fast food establishments, and a little vinyl booklet. Inside I found the vehicle registration and current insurance card. The address matched the one on Joseph's driver's license. At the bottom of the glove box clutter I found two gun magazines, both loaded with hollow-point bullets. Condiments and ... ammo? Uh ... who are you now, Joey Cling?

I checked around the vehicle for the matching gun, but came up empty handed.

I went through the contacts on his phone, then pored over all of his text message and call history. He spoke most frequently with "Mom and Dad", and texted most often with James Cling, Mandy Cling, Melanie, Scott Lieter, and Kevin Najafi. James was clearly Joseph's brother. Mandy could have either been James's wife, or Joseph's sister. The tone of the Scott and Kevin texts were casual, but definitely business-related. The most recent exchange was with Scott, wherein Joseph thanked Scott for covering for him today, and instructed him to "… try not to get shot."

Scott had crudely replied, "Try not to get AIDS."

Joseph did not reply to this, which I supposed was a good sign. Kevin seemed to be a supervisor of sorts, with messages ranging from "I need you onsite by 2" to "reviewing all new affidavits early tomorrow."

I plugged Joseph's home address into the car's built-in GPS, and the female British voice said "Now mapping … Home." Of course. The address was already programmed in. I apparently lived twenty-six minutes away, accounting for traffic.

"Your destination is on your right."

A handsome, white Colonial matched the address and I pulled into the driveway. A detached garage lay at the end of the driveway, but I couldn't find a remote opener anywhere in the vehicle. I parked and walked up the brick staircase to the windowed door. I peeked inside, wary of trying to enter the wrong house. I rang the doorbell. Something moved inside the house, then I heard the tell-tale sound of dog nails clicking on a hardwood floor. Sniffs and excited whining beyond the door, but no barking. This wasn't good. Like cats, dogs don't like me. In fact, I had yet to meet an animal that didn't consider me some sort of threat. I searched the key ring for house keys, finding a few possible candidates, and hoped the dog would simply run past me. I would then, of course, slam the door behind it and hope it would expediently find itself in the path of a speeding car.

What?

They don't like me, so fuck them! Sure, a dog catcher would be preferable, but with phone number and address tags, they would just call or bring the damn thing home to Master. And Master isn't coming back anymore. It's better for all concerned if the animal dies.

The second key turned clean and I opened the door a cautious crack. A bushy gray, white, and black snout poked out, sniffing and slobbering. He was some sort of sheepdog. I protected my groin and swung the door open wider, but he only just stepped out onto the porch and began a rigorous sniff session around my knees. Not even a growl.

"Everything all right, Joe?" A man's voice behind me.

I turned and saw a bearded middle-aged gentleman in a flatcap standing at the end of the driveway.

"Yeah, everything's fine, thanks!" I pointed at the dog. "Just trying to keep this guy in."

The man frowned and gave me a puzzled smile, "She probably just wants to come out and say hi to me."

As fascinated as I was with this strangely unruffled dog, I just wanted the jerk on the sidewalk to go away. But we might have been friends, so …

"Probably right," I said and stepped out of the dog's way.

The animal remained intent on my crotch, as if searching for drugs.

"Oh, you must have been around another dog, I'm guessing," Nosey neighbor said. "C'mere, Jacksy! No love for me today? Jacksy!"

I stepped inside, Jacksy the dog sticking to my legs, "She's probably just hungry. We'll see you later, okay?"

"Yeah, sure," he said.

I waved and closed the door behind me. I crouched down and let Jacksy smell the rest of me. I took it as a further good sign when she licked my face and ear. I pet her and scratched her around the neck. As much as I hated animals, I found this one to be disarmingly cute. And I vehemently reject any suggestion that I only hated animals in return for their hatred of me. Vehemently!

"Hi Jacksy. You know me, right? Same old Joseph, right?"

She may not have been convinced, but she certainly was happy for someone to be home. I found her tags and pulled them around to see. A dog license, rabies tag, and a bone-shaped tag that read "JAX" along with my address and phone number. The number was different from my cell phone, so that was certainly a good find. So many things to memorize. It dawned on me the daunting undertaking I had ahead of me. The old Frederick would take a body and go have fun. This was going to be *work*.

I looked around the front room. Coat hanger, umbrella stand, key rack with a second set of keys hanging, an impressive, black grand piano, nothing much on the walls—a single decorative painting on the otherwise bare walls, hardwood all around, including the stairs to the second floor. I ambled around taking in the place, Jaxy still at my heels. A doorway led to an under-utilized kitchen. Joseph had a toaster and microwave that appeared to be in regular use, but the oven and cooktop were spotless. He may not have even boiled water in a tea kettle.

I went through the drawers and cabinets, noting the wide variety of glasses—three, to be precise, each with a wearing design: Coca-Cola, Star Wars, Corona. In the fridge, he had orange juice, sliced cheeses, leftover Chinese in take-out containers, all the standard condiments and salad dressings, along with yogurts, cottage cheese, apple sauce, and chocolate pudding. Nothing was expired, and even the Chinese couldn't have been more than two days old.

I found the spice cabinet and immediately spotted the goods on the second shelf. Yes, there were the typical over-the-counter pain relievers, but my, did Joseph have the selection of orange prescription bottles! It was a fairly reliable indicator of an individual that lived alone and didn't do a lot of entertaining. He didn't bother hiding his drugs in some private bathroom cabinet.

What do we have here?

Valium, Zoloft, Xanax, Wellbutrin, Codeine, Percoset, Oxycontin, Promethazine, Vicodin, some others. My suspicion about depression had apparently been right. I read the labels on the ones I didn't recognize and wondered if this was simply Joseph's "as needed" stash or if he had a real problem. About half of them were expired, both recently and long ago. I supposed I would soon be feeling the withdrawal symptoms of any physically addictive drugs, and presumed that my arrival would do away with any mental addictions. In the past, I had occupied a nail biter with the tiniest nubs of emerging nail. I hadn't the slightest compulsion to continue that habit.

I went on with my traditional discovery ritual, examining every facet of each room. There was an extra bedroom filled with boxes and random, unrelated items. It looked like things he no longer used, but didn't want to put in a garage or storage unit. I reclosed the junk room's door and determined to keep it closed. I left the computer in the study alone—that would be its own session later. Internet history, cookies, favorites, saved passwords. These would be the most revealing, especially considering he lived alone and had no cause to clear his history.

I examined his neatly organized wardrobe: even jeans and shorts were hung—t-shirts, too. And then I spotted something in the far corner of the closet behind a series of trench coats. It was in a long, black garment bag. I worried that it might be some sort of freaky patent leather bondage suit with red ball gag—worried not for the intriguing secret fetish, but for the like-minded past associates who could appear at any time, shattering Melanie's vanilla image of her beau. But the bag revealed a past of another sort.

I unzipped the side. Folds of white chiffon slid out. I spun around to look at the closet again, verifying they were all men's clothes, and they were indeed. A second closet in the hall contained a vacuum cleaner and extra bedding—some with a bit of feminine flair. I returned to the wedding dress and searched for a dry cleaning tag or other explanatory labels. There were no tags on the garment bag, but I did find something curious.

At the bottom of the bag I found two boxes, the long flat sort used for necktie gifts or men's socks. The first contained a beautiful white gold necklace with an opal pendant. The second box held a white veil and pair of long, white gloves. Price tags hung from both, revealing that neither had been worn, certainly not at a wedding. More questions, but I moved on to the next phase of my settling in ritual. I stripped down nude.

Now, as I mentioned before, Joseph's body was like the perfect outfit: form-fitting, yet not too tight, supportive in the right places and otherwise relaxed. Typically, when I perform my body examination I find off-putting details like a fat, hairy mole, or hemorrhoids, herpes or worse, a blanket of back hair on a man, a wildly unkempt pubic region on a woman. But as I looked at myself in the mirror, running my hands over my body, I felt no such revulsion. I ran my hands around my neck, shoulders, pectorals. My chest and belly had enough hair to be manly, but not so much that one would believe me to be wearing a sweater. I probed my belly button then reached around and squeezed my cheeks from top to bottom. They were the firm sort that were walked regularly, not those of a desk jockey.

I grabbed a washcloth, wet it and cleaned all around my anus. Turning my back to the mirror, I bent over and grabbed my calves, checking everything out in back. I felt around for hemorrhoids or signs of trauma, but all was in order. I happened upon my scrotum and gave it a once over, like a doctor searching for hernias. This purely innocent probing led to an erection, and I was able to get a better look at my gear. No distinct slant or bend, no heinous scars or overly bulgy veins. The tip was nicely flared. I couldn't wait to use it.

"Don't mind if I do …" I said to myself in the mirror. It may seem odd to pleasure oneself while staring at your own body in the mirror— perhaps a bit homosexual for me, since it hadn't always been my body—but to me it was different. As I mentioned before, I had done my time as man with man, and woman with woman. They were fun, if a bit forced. It was only by experiencing those cultures that I knew for certain that I swung firmly toward the hetero. So please, relax and let me jerk off.

I didn't last long at all, my mind busy with phrases. "This is me … *I'm* doing this … *my* body …" It was a magnificent, uncontrolled orgasm. Almost threw out my back. I cleaned the floor afterward, and then hopped in the shower. I took my time, lathering every inch. As I washed my hair, I felt the thinning area at the crown and wondered if that was something I would want to fix someday. I supposed that would depend upon Melanie.

With shampoo running down my face, I heard my cell phone begin to ring, and quickly rinsed off. It could have been anyone—a telemarketer, for all I knew—but I assumed it was Melanie. I toweled my hair, face, and hands and hurried to the phone, though it had long since stopped ringing. As I reached out, it sounded a voicemail notification. On the screen it simply read **Missed Call** and **New Voicemail**. But it wasn't Melanie; it was Scott Lieter.

His voicemail said, "Where the fuck are you, bro? SWAT is waiting here and you're the one with the fucking warrant. Get down here, quick, before someone calls Najafi."

Shit. My mind raced. Where is here? Warrant? SWAT? Am I an actual cop? I should obviously know all of this information, and I hadn't been planning on quitting anytime soon. I had money stashed in a Dutch bank account, a little more in Brazil, but not enough to last in the U.S. for more than a few months without a job. Did Joseph have money? His house was nice enough, but he could have inherited it for all I knew. I suddenly felt like I knew nothing—that I had ignored everything I had learned over the years. I was angry. Angry at that fucking voicemail and this Scott's attitude, angry at Melanie for distracting me from my process, angry at the dog for staring at me standing cold and naked.

"Get the fuck out of here!" I yelled, but Jaxy just cocked her head. "Go!"

Nothing. She opened her mouth and panted, tongue producing a uvula of slobber that would soon string out and drip on the floor.

I stomped past her and stepped into a pair of boxers I found in Joseph's top dresser drawer. A stack of neatly-folded white t-shirts lay beside the boxers, and I pulled one on. It stuck to my wet back and chest, further irritating me. I despise that feeling. It makes a body feel like I am wearing it.

Finding the email account on his phone limited to a few weeks of personal correspondence and spam, I went to the office computer. I tapped the keyboard and was relieved to see the screen turn on, no password required, and an internet browser already open. He had multiple tabs up, all about the falls and armory. I found his email software minimized and restored it to full screen. Skimming through the subject lines, I found **WARRANT: Case ID 0345391**, and opened it. The email had what appeared to be an auto-generated form letter: **To The Attention Of The Filing Officer: The files attached hereto** …

blah blah blah. But it was dated a week away, and referred to mail theft, an offense I doubted merited a SWAT team. I closed the message and searched for a similarly titled email, finding another from a week prior, different case ID.

Prohibited Mailing Investigation: Arms and Ammunition

The attached file contained a scanned document. There was a date range, starting yesterday and ending a month later. There was an address, a list of suspected contraband, suspects involved, and pages of legalese. At the bottom I found the scrawled signature of the approving judge. I picked up the phone and tapped **Call Back**.

Scott's aggravated voice: "Un-fucking-believable, bro."

"Sorry, bro," I said. "I had car trouble this morning and my phone was dead. Is everyone still there?"

"Yeah, everyone's still here. Get your shit together and get out here before the suspects leave the house and fuck the whole thing up."

"Yeah, I'm hurrying," I looked at the screen again. "It's the Hesperian house, right? Four-two-eight-four?"

Scott moaned, pulling the phone away from his face.

"Bro, you gotta dump this broad if she's fucking you up this bad! Yes, Hesperian. And don't forget your fucking gun and vest. Or … shit … pants!"

"Yeah, I got it. Sorry again, bro."

"Or the warrant!"

"Right!"

I hung up and clicked **PRINT**, the printer beside me beginning to hum and whir. I ran back to my bedroom and searched for appropriate clothes. Lots of hanging polo shirts and khakis. I grabbed a blue polo, but as the shirts parted, I spotted the back of the white polo beside it. On the back, it read *POLICE – U.S. Postal Inspector*. Well, that was lucky, I thought. I dressed hurriedly, grabbed the warrant, and ran downstairs to search for my gun and "vest". I presumed this meant a bullet proof vest, and the reality of where I was about to go hit home. I could be shot and killed. I did not fear so much for my life, knowing

I could simply move on, but I realized that I was afraid of losing *this* life. It had only just begun, after all. Why on earth would someone *choose* an occupation that places in peril this fragile mush of flesh and organs? Every one of you seems all too aware of mortality, and yet you climb rocks and jump from airplanes, work in mines that cave in, swim in waves where sharks were reported just yesterday! Perhaps it is faith. Silly, silly faith.

Flipping through the coat closet downstairs in search of a bulletproof vest, I came across a thin windbreaker with Postal Inspector insignias and lettering. It was something, but still no gun or vest.

The car!

I guessed that Joseph might have stashed his gear in his car before picking me up. I grabbed the keys and ran out to search the Land Rover. Nothing. The situation was sliding into ridiculousness and my heat was rising. I felt my face flushing red with blood. Then I thought back to the second set of keys on the hanger, and the detached garage. I jogged to the big door and peered into one of the windows. Inside, a new white sedan sat among storage bins, bicycles, tool chests and cabinets. I ran inside the house and returned with the keys. Around the side of the garage I found another door and tried a few different keys before the knob turned cleanly round in my hand.

I flicked on the wall light switch and pressed the trunk opener on the sedan's key fob. It popped open in a snappy, satisfying manner. Inside lay sweet relief. A bulletproof vest with *"United States Postal Inspector – POLICE"* emblazoned across the front. A pistol in a shoulder holster. A shotgun locked inside a mount. An assortment of kits. I wasn't sure of the difference between a "Fingerprint Kit" and a "Fingerprinting Kit", but that would be an easier play, should the need arise.

I pulled on the vest then the shoulder holster, and checked the pistol to be sure I knew how it worked. I couldn't find a safety, but tried out the other switches and buttons. The only one that seemed to do anything ejected out the bottom the magazine thing with the bullets. I verified there were bullets in it, and slapped it back in. It was a satisfying feeling, like playing cops and robbers, but I really was a cop.

I could shoot someone if I wanted to! Though the moment the idea occurred to me, reality struck again. That whole shooting thing was a two-way street. Did postal inspectors really shoot people, or was the weapon just for show?

As I jumped in the driver seat, a scenario played out in my head. I get to this Hesperian place, apologize to Scott Lieter, we go do our thing (whatever that is), I see some criminal with a gun, and shoot him in the face. "What the fuck are you doing?" Scott shouts. "You shot him! We can't shoot people! Why the hell do you even have real bullets in there?" The conjectural berating went on as I drove out of the garage and clicked the remote to close it behind me. I had to swerve around the Land Rover, driving over my lawn, to get around it. I would have to remember to park the SUV half-off the other side of the driveway in the future.

GPS guided me to my destination and thank Zeus for GPS! As I drove, I noticed numerous nonstandard buttons on the dashboard. There were switches for lights, and several others I couldn't identify by their white symbols. One in particular caught my attention. It had a megaphone icon on one side and sound waves on the other. I pressed the sound waves side and, sure enough, a blaring police siren sounded outside. Pedestrians (or "civilians" as I decided I would henceforth call them) stared at me as I zoomed past. Behind the sun visors, at the top edge of the windshield, I noticed the light bar extending from the driver to passenger side. As nervous as I felt on my way to this unpredictable situation, I really liked my company car, and was developing an even greater affection for this lovely body and what came with it.

Less than twenty minutes later, I rounded the last corner to the address and spotted a man in khakis and a polo shirt—certainly out of place for this neighborhood—leaning on my white sedan's twin brother. I could feel him glaring at me through his shades as I double parked and opened the passenger side window.

"Welcome to work, bro," he said. I recognized the voice as Scott's. "Sure you don't want to go grab some coffee first?"

"Where should I park?"

He shook his head and sighed. "Back up and put it around the corner back there. I'll tell SWAT we're ready to meet."

I nodded and reversed back around the corner.

I grabbed my vest from the trunk and pulled it over my head. I watched Scott talking to a team of armored officers around the opposite corner. They, too, sent me looks. Fortunately, Scott eased off when he came back across the street.

"Okay, so I ran the meeting and they're going over their entry plan one more time. Are you re—um, your vest is on backwards."

I looked down. "Oh, crap ... sorry, I—"

"Look at you, all flustered. So how was last night?"

"Oh, yeah, it was great."

"Can I smell your fingers?" He smirked. I didn't reply, unsure of Joseph's typical banter-with-men style. "Tell me you got some, bro. This morning bullshit better have been worth it."

I resecured my vest and holster and gave him a noncommittal nod and smile.

"Still such the gentleman, Joey. Admirable, but you gotta give us married slobs some kind of ... what's that called? Where you get the good feeling or whatever out of someone else doing something?"

"Vicarious," I said.

"Right, vicarious. Help a brother out some time, mm-kay?"

"I'll do what I can, bro."

One of the SWAT men gave us a quiet whistle and Scott cocked his head toward them.

"Let's roll," Scott said, and we began to walk across the street. "Wait, where's the fucking warrant?"

"Oh, I have it! I do!" I said and jogged back to my car, grabbing it off the seat.

The leader of the SWAT team asked to see it, and read it over with his head bobbing through the sections.

"Looks good. Oh, and thanks for joining us, Cling. These fuckin' trucks aren't air conditioned, just so you know. Probably a hundred and twenty in there right now."

"Yeah, real sorry." I said.

"I don't think we wanna hear how sorry you are. We wanna hear about fuckin' beer." He said it with a dead-serious face, but a couple of his men grinned, so I smiled in return.

"Oh, sure. I'll buy you all some beer. A ludicrous amount of beer."

Scott snorted. "Careful what you're signing up for there, sport."

"Alright, we gonna do this?" The SWAT team leader said. The name badge on his body armor read *"ORTEGA"*. "According to Cling's affidavit, we got at least three suspects in the residence, all considered armed and likely prepared to use 'em. The inspectors here will assist with perimeter."

One of the SWAT men behind him said, "Finally some action. Last three entries been kittens."

"You *want* to be shot at?" I said.

"Fuck yeah, buddy! Means we get to shoot back!"

The others all laughed. I got the impression there was a specific breed of man that signed up for this unit, and I certainly wasn't that sort.

Helmets on, weapons held tight across their chests, and a few with SWAT-emblazoned riot shields, the team lined up and crept across front yards toward the suspects' house. Scott waited a moment before following, pistol in hand. I pulled mine out as well and remained behind him—my human shield.

As dry grass crunched beneath my shoes, the fragility of this body returned to the forefront of my mind. My vest would keep a bullet from reaching my heart, lungs, and other vital organs, but what of my brain, my eyes, my throat? Who decided the torso was the most important area to protect? The SWAT guys clearly knew it was just one part of a complete breakfast. They were armored from head to toe.

Scott stopped in front of me, hunched and peered around the corner of the neighboring house. In front of us, the SWAT team was lining up at the front porch of the suspects' house while others branched off and crept along both sides, toward the back yard. The paneled walls wore the typical crackling paint and wear. The yard consisted of a few small patches of stubborn grass, a cactus, and a plastic tricycle. I wondered if there were kids inside.

I peeked over Scott's shoulder and saw Ortega at the front door, two of his men holding a battering ram between them. I felt like I was in a movie. He held up three fingers … two … one…

"Police! Search warrant!" He shouted, and the battering ram swung back and then forward, splitting the front door as it smashed open. More shouting: frantic, garbled. A single gunshot, then a string of shots from what seemed to be the entire house at once. Scott shuffled back, shoving me to move as well. It was actually happening! Guns were firing less than twenty feet from me! Ortega had said it was likely to happen but I hadn't thought it was *actually* likely to happen!

"What in heck is going on?" An elderly woman said from the porch above us.

"Police, ma'am," Scott said. "Please stay inside your house."

"Ya'll need to leave that family alone," she murmured as she retreated back into her house.

I heard the echoing shouts of "Clear!" from next door and followed Scott across the cracked driveway. He glanced back at me with a small smirk.

"Guess no arrests today, bro."

"What? You think they killed them all?"

"Not necessarily, but figuring on the odds. Once someone gets shooting …"

"Inspectors?" Ortega called from the front door.

We walked up the concrete steps and stood before him, both of us trying to catch a glimpse inside.

"Two perps dead. One child fine in a back room—CPS, ambulance, and coroner called. Old man in front here. Never stopped rocking in his chair. Female suspect not here. You want us to clear the kid, help you search the premises for the goods?"

Scott turned to me for an answer.

"Ah … what do *you* think?" I asked him.

"Really? Uh … yeah, I guess clear out, Lieutenant. Let's get PD over here to handle the kid and record all this." Scott gave me a curious glance. Apparently I would normally have taken charge, but I admit to being somewhat in shock, and nervous to be surrounded by men with still-warm muzzles. Oh yeah, and entirely incompetent.

As the team exited past us, Scott poked a head in the door. "Old man sure is still rocking. You know who he is?"

I pulled the folded-up warrant from my back pocket and scanned through it to the list of names and ages. Indeed, a seventy-six year old male was on the list of residents, though not tagged as a suspect: Justinian Avery. I had apparently included a note that Mr. Avery's government assistance income was paying for the residence.

With everyone else out, Scott and I walked in. A man in his twenties or thirties lay face-down on the floor, blood dripping from his saturated t-shirt sleeve. At his side lay a shotgun. Besides the blood, the room was relatively clean, albeit suffering from its age. The hardwood floor was separating and warping beneath worn couches and faux-brass tables. The distinct smell of mold dominated the room.

Outside, SWAT officers spoke breathlessly.

One voice in the front yard: "I thought you were gonna fuckin' shoot *me*!"

Another: "Nah, I saw the guy."

A third voice: "You fuckers need to stay low inside when I'm doing a back entry. Fuckin' round hit the water heater right beside me."

I glanced around the rest of the room as Scott proceeded forward down the hallway. Beside the front window, the old man rocked away, his cloudy eyes gazing off toward a spot on the adjacent wall. He had a big, gnarly nose, black raised freckles, and a garland of tightly-curled white hair. He wore what appeared to be a satisfied little smile. The planks creaked beneath him.

"Sir?" I said, and snapped my fingers in front of his face. "Sir, can you hear me? Mr. Avery?"

His expression remained as it was, his breathing did not alter, and he blinked at a regular interval. His behavior was reminiscent of my past refuse—those shells once occupied and then discarded without closure. Even in the haste of my early days, I knew who I had been in and who I hadn't. At least the look of them, and this man wasn't one. He may have been living the simple life of a houseplant, much as anyone else I had left living would be today (in the absence of a sympathetic Chief providing the pillow treatment), but unless there were other demons traveling about the east coast of the United States, Mr. Avery was simply the owner of an ill-functioning brain, or the victim of some traumatic accident.

As my nose hovered six inches from his, I stared curiously into those murky eyes, studied the trench-like crevasses of his brow wrinkles, the dense stubble on his jawline and chin. So many details, so much history and expression for such a—

"Get yo mutha fuckin' face outa my mutha fuckin' face!"

He said it quietly, though in a deep baritone that seemed to come from his chest, and I stumbled backward, tripping over a rug. As I caught myself, my eyes snapped back to him, and I saw that his expression hadn't changed a bit. He continued speaking, though his words were unintelligible.

"What happened?" Scott asked from behind me. I jumped a little.

"The old man … he—uh—spoke."

"Wow. Amazing, bro. Look, I found their stash in two rooms, plus old boxes with our postage. Wanna help me inventory?"

I gazed at the old man, rocking with his subtle smile, and then followed Scott down the hall to record all of the contraband.

After the traumatized child was escorted out by CPS, Scott and I wrapped up the evidence and made our exit. Crime scene photographers snapped shots of the dead perps on the floor and ignored us as we reentered the room. I watched the old man's eyes as I crossed the living room to the front door, half-expecting to catch him in a quick glance at me, but his "attention" remained on the same section of wall as before.

Outside, several members of the local PD stood in the front yard. Scott motioned them in as we stepped out of their way.

"You going to do your job now?" Scott asked me. "Or planning on asking me to check all this in?"

I responded with a prolonged "uh" to which he nodded knowingly and looked away with a strange expression. I couldn't tell if it was frustration or good-hearted resignation.

"Yeah, I got it," he said. "Don't keep this shit up too long, though. I'll start getting all jealous and bitchy."

"Yeah, okay, thanks," I said.

"And I want raunchy fucking details at some point."

I smiled and shrugged.

"Go on," he said. "Gimme the warrant and get the fuck out of here. Don't distract me from doing your job."

I handed him the warrant, patted his shoulder, and walked back to my sedan. I sat in the hot car for a few minutes. I beat back the urge to revert to my habit of fleeing that which was less than convenient or outside of my comfort zone, simultaneously whispering in my own ear that to quit the job and find something in sales wouldn't be all that detrimental to Joseph's established world. It was not as though Melanie had been drawn to Joseph based upon his job. Then again, I still didn't know how they had met. What if Scott or someone else at work had been the matchmaker? In fact, if she knew anyone related to my job, they could tell her I was behaving "out of character"—a portrayal I avoid above all others. And what kind of man was I to whimper away from a dangerous profession? I'd been a (peacetime) soldier in Holland for nearly a year. I had more fun on that base than in any other job. The workplaces I'd justifiably fled in the past were due to pistol-sucking tedium or intolerable superiors, not danger.

I leaned forward and wrestled my vest off, tossed it onto the passenger seat, and glanced outside. Scott was staring at me from across the street with a look of dubious concern. I smiled and waved and drove away.

5. First Date

I f guns and bullet proof vests and dead people set back my confidence in this new life, Melanie's existence reduced the latter to a sighing shrug—a necessary to-do of life like housecleaning or scraping dog shit from my backyard grass.

Now, is it immature to feel triumphant that *she* called *me*? Probably. And I can't take all the credit, only being awake with her for less than two hours, and with little conversation or interaction during that time. I suppose I could give a portion to Joseph for his planned evening. As much as I would like to imagine that, after our parting, Melanie was beset with thoughts and emotions about the *morning* Joseph, I was fairly certain it was the falls and atypical campout on her mind.

"Hey you," she said. There was a distinct giddiness in her voice.

"Hi there," I said, my coffee pot hanging in the air, mid-pour. "I'm so glad you called."

"Me too. Last night was really special. I just wanted to thank you again."

"Yeah, of course. I ... I had a good time, too." My arm began tiring and I finally put the coffee pot down on the counter. Jax was at my feet, waiting for floor food to drop. I had decided she could stay around a while. She wasn't so bad.

"So," she said slowly.

"So, it's your turn to do something over-the-top magnificent for me? Wow, Melanie, I don't know what to say."

She laughed—a raw and genuine outburst of pleasure. I counted it as my first score.

"Okay, that is so …" I could hear the smile in her words. "…weird and great. It's great. I'll call you back, okay? I apparently need to do some major planning."

"Sounds good, but are we talking about tonight or …"

She had hung up at some point before I finished the question. I would just have to wait for her, and for some reason that only increased the buzzing in my head. I just needed to maintain patience with this torturously slow mating ritual.

* * *

She didn't call me that night. Or the next day, or the day after.

I used my time wisely, though, researching what the hell a U.S. Postal Inspector is. Have you even heard of this job? Apparently, because any crime having to do with the mail is a federal offense, the Postal Service has its own police force. These are the folks that deal with crimes against postal workers or anything illegal that takes place on Post Office property, but they also handle things like drugs or weapons being sent via the mail, identity theft, threats, and even terrorism. Joseph's division covered not just Frederick, but Baltimore and many other urban areas. And based upon his frequent travel, I ascertained that his investigations often took him out of state. I also discovered that Joseph was scheduled to begin mentoring a new recruit in a month. Lovely.

I fed the dog, went to work (more on this later), fed the dog. I read Joseph's email threads going back for years, studied his old calendar entries and task lists. He appeared to have been extremely organized— meticulous with case notes and even vacation planning.

I found a thread from two years earlier between Joseph and Gabriella Capps. Gabriella was outlining plans for a big vacation in Jamaica, listing things to do and places to visit in order of priority. I found a revealing word: "honeymooners". There were no more messages from or to Ms. Capps after that thread was concluded. And it didn't seem particularly concluded; Gabriella wrote that she would talk to the travel agent again and get back to him.

I recalled the unused wedding dress in the closet and wondered how this relationship came to a close. Maybe it wasn't all that important, being a couple years back, but I needed to be able to answer questions when posed, or at least have a normal discussion without being evasive (unless that was characteristic behavior). Ah, so much to learn! And I was beginning to feel saddled by the monumental task, overcome by a mean case of the fuckits. I half-jokingly determined that I would develop a personal philosophy of *carpe diem*, having tossed aside all those past *diems*. It would be simple, if a little off-putting for old friends.

"Hey old buddy," a childhood friend says. "Remember that time we went hiking and stumbled upon a secret society performing ritual sacrifices in the woods?"

"Yeah, but that's in the past, old buddy. Let's talk about *the now*."

It could work.

But in reality, I quickly tired of research and halted with more questions unanswered than answered. Instead, I put Joseph's habit of creating lists for everything into practice. I established my discovery shortlist, outlining my top priorities.

1) Do everything possible to keep Melanie happy, satisfied, and committed to me.
2) Learn how to be a postal inspector or find another job.
3) Meet my family and closest friends.
4) Meet Melanie's vegetative uncle.
5) Determine the connection between me and the town of Frederick, if any.
6) Go from there and *carpe fucking diem*.

I looked over the list on the computer screen and frowned, realizing I'd somehow missed a very present and major priority. I added a new 1) at the top, shifting the existing list down one line.

1) Make love to Melanie.

Now the list was complete. I fed the dog, went to work (thankfully, shootouts were not the norm), fed the dog. Then the phone finally rang. It was just after 8:00pm on Thursday. I wanted it to be Melanie, but it was Joseph's brother, James. I debated whether to answer, but decided he was an important part of my to-do list.

"James," I said.

"Joseph," he said. "Am I bothering you or something?"

"No, no, not at all. How are you?"

"No really, what's going on?"

I guessed the brothers had some well-established routine in their communication. And though I had the voice down perfectly, who knew how the two of them conversed? Or if some conversation had been left hanging.

"Nothing, really," I said in a chipper tone. "Everything is going great. Tell me what's going on with you."

"Is someone else there? You're talking … I don't know … *weird*."

What to say to that? A close brother could easily pick up nuances in speech that I may have overlooked. Getting over a cold would seem a trite excuse.

"You caught that, eh? Can't get anything past you, can I? Yeah, a lot on my mind."

"I'm sure. You never told me what happened with Melanie and the falls. Just went silent. And it was your turn."

"My turn?"

He barked back without a second's hesitation, "What the hell is up with you? Yeah, your turn. That's it. I'm coming over."

Uh oh.

"Oh, my *turn*," I said with sudden recognition. "I thought you said 'your dern' … whatever that means." It was pathetic. I laughed at myself. "Honestly, I'm really just spun over Melanie. She hasn't called and it's been days. Literally, *days*."

"That's ridiculous. You didn't think I said 'dern' because you immediately asked 'my turn?' when I said it was your turn to call me. Look, I want to, but I can't come over right now. Taking care of the kids while Mandy's in New York, but I'll see you at Mom and Dad's this weekend and we'll talk." Something crashed in the background and James shouted to Lucas to be careful. I knew from past emails that James had two boys and a girl: Little Joey (never just Joey), Ariel, and Lucas.

Mom and Dad's? I put the call on speakerphone and opened my calendar. Joseph had everything else in his life painstakingly scheduled, so why wasn't there an event slated for that weekend? Shit, there was. 10:00am Saturday to 8:00pm Sunday. The title: "MD". No notes, no other information whatsoever. Then again, why would Joseph need any more than that? He just needed a marker on the calendar. I must have thought it was a doctor's appointment I would intentionally miss.

"You still there?" James said.

"Yeah, I'm here," I said. "Everything okay over there?"

"Yeah, just Lucas knocking things over. So you're not going to tell me what's really happening then?"

"I don't know what else to tell you. Honestly. I'll see you at Mom and Dad's, okay?"

"If you don't show up, I'm going to come find you."

"I believe you," I said, chuckling. "Take care."

"You're still talking weird."

"Sorry. Things have been ludicrous."

There was a brief silence on the line, save for the background hullabaloo on James's end.

"That's it?" He said, again incredulous.

"I'm *really* sorry?"

He sighed, "All right then. *Take care* it is then." And hung up.

Maybe I was supposed to say "I love you." I had no clue what his problem was, but clearly we weren't connecting in the manner to which he was accustomed. I hoped I wouldn't have the same issue with Mel—

Another uh-oh. Melanie was busy planning something— presumably for the approaching weekend. It would be fairly damaging to tell her I now couldn't go, due to prior plans. I mumbled "fuck fuck fuck …" for the next five minutes.

I contemplated wording, then sent her a text message.

Hey there ... so about this weekend ...

I waited and a few minutes later, she replied.

I have outfits all picked out.

Great. Now for the kindest way to suggest she set those outfits aside.

A new text alert.

When are you picking me up?

Odd. Did she think she had already shared her big plans with me? Or *did* she share them, but for some reason I didn't receive them? What if Joseph had another email address or instant messenger or other mode of communication she would have used, but that I had no clue existed? My forehead began to sweat. I figured out a potentially brilliant reply.

Not sure yet. Had we discussed a timeframe at all?

The delay between texts was maddening, but the technology is a lifesaver for someone in this sort of sticky situation. If my conversation with James had been via text, I doubted he would have observed anything out of the ordinary.

Well that was a few weeks ago, but trying to think. You just said they expect us Sat morning. That's all I know.

Ah hah. Joseph had invited her to his parents'. She hadn't been planning anything for that weekend at all, and therefore had no pressing reason to call me. I, on the other hand, should have been in contact with her by now about the weekend. It was fortunate that James called—for a number of reasons. But I couldn't expect that kind of luck to continue. I needed to be on top of things. I couldn't be lazy.

I replied.

Right. Around 10, so I'll pick you up at

I stopped typing. For one thing, I needed to find out where his parents lived. Second, even if there was an opportunity to make love to Melanie at my parents', it probably wouldn't be the sort that I wanted to be my first with her. This was a perfect opportunity to mark off several items from my checklist.

First, I erased what I'd already typed and sent a new message to get the ball rolling:

> What are you doing tomorrow night?

Then I opened up my contacts and found "Mom & Dad Cling". Joseph, bless his soul, had their address in there. I went to my computer and searched for directions from Melanie's to my parents' house. They were allegedly only twenty minutes apart. Then I searched for directions from my house to my parents. The directions said I was only nine minutes away from them. Perfect.

On my phone, a new text from Melanie awaited:

> Washing my hair, packing, other essential tedium.
> Why do you ask?

> I have a plan that could save massive amounts of time, energy, stress, and possibly LIVES…provided your essential tedium can be wrapped up by 6:00pm tomorrow night.

> Well, I'm all for saving lives, whenever possible…

I could see the smirk behind those words, the radiant face and eyes. I envisioned her saying the sentence slow and adorably.

"Then you come to my house. We'll spend the night here, then leave for my parents the next morning."

There was a delay before she responded and I re-read everything said so far, wondering if anything could have been taken wrong. It all looked good to me, and she finally replied.

"Deal."

And that was that.

* * *

In my travels, I learned to cook a number of fine cuisines, though Joseph's convenience store-worthy selection of foods and ingredients suggested he had never applied himself in the culinary arts. So after some debate, I settled on a simple menu for the evening's dinner with Melanie. I went to work—fortunately an office day with Scott. All I had to do was nod and intermittently laugh along with the guys. I stopped at the store on the way home, filling in the massive gaps in Joseph's herb selection, as well as other essentials and the ingredients for the night.

I showered at 5:00, groomed, and went downstairs to get the rice cooking. I premixed the spices, setting the spicy herbs aside in case she didn't do hot. I had all of my other ingredients premeasured and laid out on a cutting board and in little glass bowls. At 5:45 I put on some Bossa Nova music and began slicing limes and pineapple for our Caipirinhas. The night would maintain a strict Brazilian theme, and whether taken as cheesy or not, a man going out of his way with a thoughtful meal, beverages, and music is a man to love.

Just as I was wrapping up the ingredients for the traditional chicken with tomato coconut milk sauce, Jaxy scurried to her feet and ran clicking out of the kitchen. The doorbell rang a few seconds later.

"So prompt," I said as I opened the door. Melanie was more radiant than ever. She had clearly spent time on her hair which hung loose to her shoulders in shining waves. I especially loved the subtle touches of makeup and leg-weakening smile. A small duffle bag hung from her shoulder, little handbag and keys in her hand. Her intoxicating perfume preceded her into the house as Jaxy gave her a thorough sniffing.

"You look great," she said and put her free hand around my waist.

"Look who's talking," I said and gave her a gentlemanly kiss on the mouth—not a peck, mind you. I felt her about to open her mouth, but I pulled back. "Gotta check on the rice. Just toss that anywhere and make yourself comfortable."

"Hey you!" I heard her say in a singsong, talking to the dog. "You're just as adorable as I envisioned! Who's the good girl? You are … yes."

Clearly she'd never met Jax and, I postulated, had never been to Joseph's house. From the kitchen I heard her wedge sandals clocking along the hardwood floor with Jax's nails trailing behind her.

"You decorate well," she said as she entered the kitchen, eyes wandering up and down and all around. I wondered if she was just being polite. I found Joseph's "decorating" to be rather dreary. While I could appreciate order and simplicity, I imagined it appeared thoroughly impersonal to others. Not a single family photograph on the wall or in a leaner frame on a table. In fact, Joseph didn't seem to like placing things on top of things at all. It made dusting a breeze, but the sterility bothered me. I would slowly rectify this. I already knew what the first framed photo would be.

"Wait, are you actually cooking?" Melanie said.

I wiped my hands on a kitchen towel and smirked, "Not usually, but I found a simple recipe on the Food Network website. You like spicy, right?"

"You know I do. What is it?" I tossed the chopped onion, garlic, ginger, and jalapeño into the skillet. It all effervesced in the olive oil and the scent filled the air.

"You'll just have to wait and see," I said.

"Oh my God," she said, putting a hand in the small of my back. "That smells amazing."

"Hang on … I have a drink for you."

I muddled the lime and pineapple in a bowl with sugar as Melanie strolled past the breakfast table and into the living room.

"What's this music?" She called.

"It's Brazilian," I called back. "Is it too dorky? Do you mind it?"

"Mind it? It's perfect!" She reappeared in the kitchen doorway. I handed her the caipirinha in a tall glass with a straw and lime wedge on top. "Wow, look at this … Mmm, that's tasty. I feel like such a … I don't know, *adult* with all this."

I laughed, "Me too. It's weird. It's as though our generation never embraced all this stuff. Or maybe I'm generalizing."

"No, I think you're mostly right. Maybe we just took longer, and men never learned about romance." She put a hand up. "Present company excepted, of course. This drink is *really* good."

As I cooked, she put her elbows on the counter and we discussed other observations, quirks of "our" generation, and the subtle differences between the pop culture of her teenage years and mine. I got so lost in the conversation that I began reminiscing about experiences in Holland, only realizing my slip up after a few minutes. She didn't seem to know any different about Joseph's youth and so I simply segued into serving.

"I'm so sorry, what can I help with?" She said.

"You're fine, you're fine, just grab a utensil roll and pick a seat wherever you want."

She glanced around and spotted the maroon cloth napkin rolls.

She said, "You rolled silverware into napkins."

I popped up my eyebrows and plated her meal, sprinkling fresh parsley on top.

"You know," she said. "You didn't have to go to all this trouble to get in my pants." Harry Belafonte's "Jump in the Line" came on and Melanie began dancing her way to the table. "I love this song!"

I sighed and wondered at that moment if Joseph truly appreciated what he had. Melanie had somehow retained this teenaged spirit, but without coming off as clinging to youth. In my experience, a truly rare find. But why hadn't Melanie been to his house? And why was she succumbing to the pressure of her sweaty, married boss? I wondered how long that had been going on before Joseph came around, and if it was something she had any intention of cutting off, once and for all.

"Wow, Jesus, spicy all right!"

"Oh sorry," I said. "Too much?"

"No way, it's amazing! This was a 'simple' recipe?" She said. I nodded emphatically, my mouth full of chicken and coconut sauce. "I'm going to have to keep you in the kitchen, Mister."

I liked the sound of that.

She had cleaned her plate, as did I, and I took the dishes into the kitchen. I refilled her drink and we adjourned to the couch in the living room. She sat on her feet and faced me. I kept an arm stretched out across the back cushions and played with coils of her hair as she absentmindedly caressed my knee. The Brazilian music streamed from Joseph's excellent speakers over our heads as we talked and laughed. She was so relaxed and confident and smart. The more we conversed, the more I loved her. As eager as I was to, as she said, get in her pants, I had no interest in pushing toward that goal. Just *being* with her—bullshitting about the world—was wholly gratifying. And then she said something I had already forgotten I was waiting to hear.

"You know what … you're really … I don't know, *fun* when you're drunk."

I smiled but realized as soon as she did that I had no drink in my hand. But more present in my mind was the true meaning of her statement: I was *better* than him.

She frowned and said, "You've been drinking, right?"

"Oh yeah, of course. I left my glass in the kitchen. Feeling a bit thirsty again, now that you mention it …"

She relaxed and followed me into the kitchen where I made fresh caipirinhas—her third, my first. I felt her eyes fixed on me as I crushed the fruit in the glass. We were silent, only the sound of a tenor sax solo and clicky mid-tempo rhythm smoothed from the other room. I poured the cachaça over the ice and fruit and handed a glass to her. She curled it in her hand and put her other arm around my neck, her eyelids at half-mast, staring at my lips as she leaned close. We kissed—a real kiss, our tongues awash with alcohol and sugar and citrus.

Her glass clumsily found its way back to the counter as she pressed her hips to mine. I slid a hand down to her thigh and pulled her against me even harder. We kissed and bit lips and I tangled my hand into her hair, holding her face to mine. Our breathing sped up and she slid a hand between us, landing on my very erect manhood.

She pulled away a few inches and looked at my eyes with an odd expression.

"Fuck," she said quietly, and I panicked for an instant. Had she forgotten something? Noticed something wrong? "I want to *marry* you!"

I blinked and swallowed and didn't know what to say. She had caught me completely off-guard with that one. Hell, I would have married her the next day, but she was buzzed and very aroused and so was I. I pulled her close again and snuck a hand under her shirt and up to one of her breasts. Skin to smooth skin, bra tugged down, nipple clenched between thumb and forefinger, her hand rubbing up and down over my jeans ... I nearly lost control right there.

I grabbed her wrist and pulled her away. She studied my expression; hers was an impassioned "how dare you take my hand off your dick" and I pinched her nipple harder. She inhaled a quick snort and put her free hand over mine beneath her shirt, her face now one of surprise.

"Let's go upstairs," I said. "Now."

She nodded a little nod and I took her by the wrist to the stairs. Jaxy followed but I blocked her at the door to the bedroom and closed her out in the hall. She whined a little, but I quickly forgot about her when I turned around to see Melanie facing me a few steps away, shedding her shirt. I pulled mine off as well.

"Candles?" I ventured, unaware if there had been a past conversation between the two of them.

"Don't care," she said.

She sent a hand straight down the inside of my pants and took hold of me. I reached around her arm with both of my hands, unbuttoned her jeans, slowly lowered the zipper. She let go of me and reached further down, cupping. I could still hear the bass of the music through the floor, pulsing a perfect rhythm. I kissed her neck, used my teeth a little. She pulled her hand out of my pants and reached behind her, unstrapping her bra. She slid it out from between us and I finally got to feel her bare breasts against my bare chest. I savored every moment of it, every new contact, every first act.

We pulled each other's pants off as we shuffled toward the bed. I moved to climb in and she stopped me with a hand on my chest.

"Wait," she said and sat down on the bench in front of the bed.

She wrapped her fingers around me, gave me a few gentle pulls, then put her lips around the tip. I closed my eyes despite wanting to see. My head buzzed; I felt drunk despite having swallowed only a couple sips. She took her time, squeezed here, clutched there, glanced up at me with intensity. I saw one of her hands disappear between her legs and her head went back for an instant. I wanted to do that for her, give her what she apparently never got from Joseph: this mouth down there in her hand's stead. But she had put the brakes on that last time, and I would have to wait for a sign that she was ready for it.

The chances diminished as she crept back onto the bed from the bench, her legs closed but hand pulling me on top of her. My plan to briefly kiss her legs and show her that her body was still a wonderland had gone out the window. I had scheduled it as my segue before "losing control" and ravaging her, revealing that I had always been holding back, not the frustrating lover she had come to expect. But it didn't matter. No farce was needed, and things couldn't have gone any better than they were going.

We kissed as she reached down and pulled me inside her. She wrapped her legs around my back and squeezed me in deep. I took hold of her wrists and brought her arms out over her head, letting her know I was more than able to take control. I watched her face, her eyes, her body, all in the full light of the room. Her head rolled side to side on the down comforter as I sped up—not slamming into her like her boss, but still an unrestrained force.

The thump of the music downstairs paused and then resumed with a new song and beat. I sat up and brought her legs to my shoulders, changing our tempo as well. Her hands free, she squeezed a breast with one and brought the other down to join the mix. I let her continue to pleasure herself, watching her face contort. She was getting close. I was about to go myself and slowed down to wait for her. I had to close my eyes to prolong the process, but in my head I was still seeing this whole picture.

She brought her legs down and around me again, reached up with both hands and pulled my face to her chest, arched her back and tensed her legs. I didn't know if she was climaxing, but I couldn't hold back any longer. My body seized, intense heat and electricity burst from my groin and, in an instant, reached every end of my body. I collapsed on top of her and she emitted a quick, brief shriek, as if she had been burned, but the rest of her body quaked and I knew she was there. Her hands moved confoundedly from my sweaty back to her head to my cheek.

"Oh my God, oh my God …" she panted.

I rolled beside her and onto my back, also gasping for air. I turned to look at her face, still rapt. She let out a small laugh and shook her head. I grabbed her cheek, turned her toward me. Our eyes maintained contact as I gave her a small kiss on the lips.

I dragged myself from the bed, into the bathroom and lazily washed up.

Melanie called from the other room, "Bring me a towel, would you?"

I returned with a towel, moist with warm water on one side and dry on the other. She moaned appreciatively as I wiped her down, but then she took over for me. I turned off the lights, switched on the ceiling fan, and climbed into bed beside her, throwing the covers away. She tossed the towel somewhere in the dark and put a hand on my shoulder.

She groggily said, "One surprise after another with you, isn't it?" And then turned onto her side, facing away from me.

I didn't reply, but brought my hand up to her head and lightly stroked her hair.

"Mmm ... I like that," she said and shortly thereafter, she was asleep.

6. Anniversary

When I awoke, Melanie was gone. No sounds in the house. I looked at the clock on the nightstand: 7:07. I pulled on a fresh pair of underwear and khakis and hurried downstairs. I heard Jaxy's tags jingle from the kitchen and walked in.

"Good morning," I said, raising an eyebrow to the scene on the kitchen tile.

Melanie was sipping coffee, sitting on the floor with her legs crossed. Jaxy lay on her back, head in Melanie's lap.

"Busted," Melanie said with a smirk, and I saw the pile of lunch meat in her other hand. "I was just endearing myself to her … creating some positive associations."

"I'm jealous," I said. "How are you doing?"

She shook her head and looked away bashfully, a truly precious smile appearing. She took a deep breath and turned back to me.

"I'm doing really well. And you?"

"Couldn't be better. I mean that literally."

We shared a prolonged look—a look that created a new hum in my head. This was not the sort of feeling I would have expected to experience without some kind of physical contact. I was drunk on *bliss* for the first time in my life, and her apparent agreement only doubled my elation.

"So …" I began. "We should probably eat something before getting ready and heading out."

"You don't want me to feed you turkey on the floor here?"

"How about eggs? I think I can pull off some eggs."

"How about *I* make breakfast, since you did such a great job last night?"

I surrendered the kitchen to her able hands and we played around with each other here and there. We didn't talk anymore about last night, and I rather liked that. To me, it meant we were on the same page. It meant the evening was an absolute. It needed no review or thanks or analysis. Beyond that, it seemed to have cemented something previously uncertain. Witnessing Joseph and Melanie's prior interaction, they looked like a couple dating—seeing how things played out and perhaps making an effort to be a certain *way* with each other. But the unspoken air of the morning felt like a new level had been achieved. This was a new couple, smitten and comfortable with one another. I imagined she awoke to thoughts of me and the future and even trying out the sound of Melanie Cling ... Melanie Demotte-Cling ... Mel Cling ... hmm, sounds like "melting." Mrs. Cling. Yes, I thought she liked the sound of that one.

We ate Melanie's scrambled eggs, bananas, and toast with coffee and orange juice. As we discussed the coming day, I happened upon some handy knowledge. She had known my brother James for years. Before the medical center, she had worked at the same company as him, along with James's wife, Mandy. Mentioning that he had an identical twin brother (news to me!) that was single, James had arranged a blind double-date for us a few months earlier, believing that it was "time" for me. Melanie's expression when she'd said it—

"*... and, you know, how he'd said it was* time *for you ...* "

—implied a sympathy for Joseph's past. After experiencing last night, I couldn't imagine a woman expressing such compassion for a man being left at the altar. That seems an appropriate brow furrow for a first or second date. That told me that Gabriella—the original future Mrs. Cling—had most likely died. This was an interesting realization, if true, possibly affording me some amount of acceptable distance when it came to the past—touchy subjects I preferred to avoid in conversation, a perfect excuse for a "seize the day" mentality.

We cleaned up breakfast, showered, and got dressed for the day. I prepared an overnight bag for myself while Melanie attacked her hair.

While gorgeous when complete, I don't think I would have the patience to deal with that mess every morning.

I put down a few large bowls of dog food and water for Jax, propped the back door open for her, and loaded up the Land Rover. I had memorized the directions to my parents' house and tried to appear casual as I scanned for street signs.

"So tell me everyone who's going to be there besides James and Mandy," she said.

Good question. I knew as much as she did.

"We'll see, I guess," I said. "My parents are so … I don't know … you'll see." Sometimes my ambiguity is masterfully delivered. In my peripheral, I could see her pondering that one over.

A few minutes passed and she spoke again, matter-of-factly, "Part of the reason I ask is because I'm wondering how you'll introduce me to people. And if there are a lot of people and we're ever apart, how I would introduce myself to others. Just want to make sure we're saying the same thing."

I glanced at her expression. It was straight and clinical.

"You're looking for some definition," I said. "As in, 'what are we?'"

She bobbed her head side to side, "I guess, but not like that. Not for me. Just if anyone asks …" she considered for a moment. "But yeah, I guess that's a good thing to discuss anyway. It's kind of weird to bring it up like this, and I swear it wasn't my intention. I was just trying to avoid awkwardness at the—"

I interrupted her semi-ramble, "My hope is that you would allow me to call you my girlfriend."

She smiled and nodded, "Yeah, yeah of course, that's … perfect, I guess. I mean, what else would I be, right?" She laughed a little.

"They're kind of weird terms for anyone over thirty, I think, but no one's bothered to invent better words. Though I'd be happy to be your manfriend, if you like," I joked. "Or maybe partner. Or domestic partner."

"How about lover? You don't like lover?"

"My mother would love that, yeah." I made the last turn onto my parents' street. A sign read NOT A THROUGH STREET so I hoped I'd made the correct turn.

"Sexual slave?" She continued and put her hand over my crotch. Funny. I'd once been a sex slave for nearly a year.

"Oh lord," I said with a smirk as I spotted the private driveway that lead to the house. "Can you please *not* give me a hard-on before I walk in my parents' house?"

She giggled and I drove under the vine-covered archway. The driveway was long, taking us along a tree-lined road to a white Queen Ann style house. It was large, but not so as to appear extravagant. The yard was too big to define as such. It was of a size one would refer to as "acreage." Grass covered a good part of it, a brick well, rose garden, an overgrown, perhaps inoperable fountain, and at the far back lay a patch of dense woods. There were six to eight cars scattered around an expansive paved area in front of the large detached garage. I spotted a few more expensive vehicles along with newer, mid-range SUVs and sedans. I guessed there were fifteen to thirty people in the house.

"Watch it, Joe," Melanie said as I parked, and I looked up from the gear shift.

Two little girls in light, flowery dresses weaved between the parked cars, laughing in a game of chase. They disappeared around side the house.

"Whose are they?" She asked, but I feigned busyness getting out of the car. The reality of what was about to happen took hold. She was asking how I plan to introduce *her* to my family, but the real question occupying my mind was how the hell do I introduce *my family* to her? If we were attacked at the door, I would be put on the spot before a gaggle of nameless faces. Ideally, we would glide in, find James (and that was a whole heap of scariness in itself—*twin* brothers? Did we have to be twins?) and his wife, who already know Melanie, and she could maybe pair off with Mandy and be introduced around. I would listen in to these introductions while James ... well, while James observed every minute detail about me that was different from the person he knew. There was really no way to win.

"Come on," Melanie said. "We can bring stuff in later. It looks like everyone is already here!"

Oh goodie.

A female voice in the house called out, "Joey's here!" as we walked to the concrete steps. The door opened and two older women stood front and center to receive us. I saw other people down a hall beyond them walking toward us in the doorway. I heard "Joey" several more times as one of the older women reached out to hug Melanie.

"You must be Melanie!" She said and squeezed her. I received an approving eyebrow from the woman that I ascertained was my mother, Leilani Cling. Her hair was short yet stylish, coming to long points beside her jaw. She wore blue eye shadow and her teeth were even whiter than her hair.

The other woman scooted past the two of them in the door and extended her arms to me with a pouty smile.

"Come to me, darling," she said. She looked similar to my mother, but her hair was gray and wavy and she wore a flowy white blouse with a subtle floral pattern.

"So good to see you," I said as we hugged. She pulled away and peered down at my abdomen. "And I see you're still keeping fit, unlike your brother. I asked him when his due date was." She winked.

"You're mean," I said with a smile and my mother shoved her gently aside to hug me.

"Outa the way, Annette," my mother said.

"Pushy wench," Annette said, and my mother rolled her eyes as she kissed my cheek.

Faces appeared behind them, shuffling ever closer to greet us. I spotted James among them, a mimosa in his hand and looking at me stoically. He did have a bit of a paunch, and his face was rounder than mine. His hair was essentially the same, kept short, a bit of gray over the ears. He looked like he was dressed for work at a big box retailer. His khaki pants were wrinkled; his blue polo shirt had a little white logo on the breast pocket. Upon closer inspection, it was the Intel logo. Mind you, I was not judging his choice of attire for an anniversary party, but rather I was surprised by his extra pounds and personal style, having expected a mirror image of myself. I had appreciated that Joseph's clothes all fit him very well, and that they were all neatly pressed. James, on the other hand, seemed somewhat of a slob. Okay, I guess I was judging him.

"You look …" my mother began in my ear, "*alive*," she whispered. She grabbed my cheeks and gazed deeply into my eyes. "I haven't seen this face in a while." I saw her eyes had begun to moisten and her tight-pressed lips quivered ever so slightly.

"Let them through, you jackals!" A gruff man's voice said from around a corner. "Let 'em breathe! Where's my favorite son?"

"Stephen!" Mom scolded.

"No offense," the man said as he appeared in the congested foyer. "You didn't hear that, Jamey."

"Yes I did, Dad," James murmured. "For about forty years…"

Dad looked a lot like me, but with forty extra pounds and a bushy black moustache. His hair was black as well, and with an inch of telltale gray roots. He cut a meaty hand between my mother and the other woman, made eye contact with me and gave me a very firm handshake. "Son," he said. His eyes shifted right to Melanie. "Miss."

Mom rose onto her toes to Dad's ear and said, "You see your son, here? Look at him."

Dad looked me over. "Hm-mm … yes."

"So glad to meet you, Mr. Cling," Melanie said as they shook hands.

"And you …" Dad began.

"This is Melanie," I said, and then had an idea and repeated louder for all to hear. "This is my girlfriend, Melanie, everyone."

A chorus of "Hi Melanie!" and she was absorbed into the crowd. I, too, found myself walking through a gauntlet of "good to see you" and "congratulations" until I ended up in front of a stiff James, eyeing me from head to toe. His wife, Mandy, slipped between us and gave me a warm hug. She was beautiful, though not my type, if I have a type. Thin, blond, giant breasts, perfectly tanned legs stilting out from the bottom of her bright blue dress. James must have landed this one while he still looked like me.

"So I'm guessin' things are goin' well with ya'll?" She said quietly with a sly smile. She had a Southern accent—I guessed Louisiana.

I smiled back with genuine pleasure. A cocker spaniel navigated its way through a forest of legs and sniffed my shoes and pant legs. I knelt down and pet its head and floppy ears. Yet another animal not attacking me.

"I told you, didn't I?" James finally said.

"Oh, you don't have to 'told you so' him, hon," Mandy said to him. "Since when are *you* the big brother, anyhow?" An interesting question, and somewhat telling of my relationship with him. Apparently, I was the dominant one between us.

"I'm just saying," James said with a shrug. "You were worried, too."

"Can we not talk about this anymore?" I said lightheartedly and stood up. "I can't seem to find my *girlfriend*."

The two of them laughed and I finally saw James for what he was. He had this gloomy air about him, even when allowing a smile to sneak through. It seemed to me that James tried to emulate the gruffness of our father. I had been intimidated initially, but no more. If he was accustomed to being the "little brother" I could use that to my advantage.

"Where's Jaxy?" Mandy asked.

"Oh, she's at home," I said.

"You left her at home?" Mandy said, flabbergasted. "She okay?"

"Yeah, she's fine," I said. "I left her tons of food and water."

"Wow, *okay*."

I heard James behind me ask her what was happening and she said "He left Jaxy at home" to which James replied with equal shock, "What, why?" So I supposed that was a bit of a flub on my part. I wouldn't have thought it acceptable to bring a dog to a party.

A hand pulled at my shoulder and I glanced back. Two more strangers with big grins awaited their chance to say hello. I felt like a celebrity among this group, but then again, we were all still saying our hellos, and if I knew these people, I doubt I would have had that impression. Regardless, I felt loved and welcomed and part of a family. It was all new for me.

A few minutes later, I had found Melanie. She was stuck in a conversation with an older couple. Or not so much a conversation, but a story. The man was telling her about how I had won every spelling bee from first to sixth grade. I caught Melanie's eye and she reached out, pulling me to her side.

"Your Uncle Brian and Aunt Coral have just the most wonderful things to say about you," Melanie said.

Aunt Coral reached up to me, put her hands over each ear, and pulled me down for a big kiss.

"Jesus," Uncle Brian said. "I think that was adultery right there! Right in front of my doggone face."

Coral smacked him on the arm and he exaggeratedly massaged the "wound" as she wagged a finger at him.

"It's so great to see you both," I said. "We'll talk, okay? After all ... *this.*" I waved around at the crowd and they both nodded and motioned us off.

"Joey," my mother called from the kitchen, right off the foyer. "Did you guys eat breakfast? We still have waffles, we've got fruit, cottage cheese ..."

"We did, thanks though. We ate." Melanie nodded beside me. Her hand was wrapped around my arm.

"... cereal, I think there's some bacon left, biscuits, I could make some more eggs ..."

"Lani, for Christ's sake, they ate," my father blurted.

My mother scowled as she closed the refrigerator and muttered, "Not sure why we need to invoke the name of the *Lord* about breakfast..."

"Thank you so much for the offer, Mrs. Cling," Melanie said, putting a hand on her shoulder. "It sounds so great, if we weren't so full—"

"*Lani*, please, sweety," my mother said. "You won't be 'Mister' or 'Missusing' anyone in this house, you get me?"

From a hallway I heard an unfamiliar voice say, "Joey didn't bring Jaxy."

Fantastic. Was the fucking dog going to be the talk of the town?

The crowd slowly filtered back out into a large family/TV room and a formal living room with classical dark wood and cream sofas, matching ornately-carved tables and tasseled lampshades. I saw small and large kids stream past a sliding glass door at the back of the sunken family room. Beyond them, a motionless swimming pool followed by flowery bushes, rock garden and statues that ran the gamut from charming to whimsical (read: tacky).

There were cousins roughly my age, and some younger. Our introductions were more casual: "Hey, man," and "How you been?" I briefly entertained the idea of daring a few wallet pulls to gather names. Crowded rooms are embarrassingly easy, but I held off as names continued to present themselves in conversation. There was Edgar with the goatee and his girlfriend or wife, and then Winona and her awkward female "friend", Roberta.

I know, pickpocketing family members would seem a brazen, unnecessary risk, compounded by having to return each pulled item. I'm proud to say, however, that in thirty-plus years of stealing, I'd been caught once. Fear not, though, I kept my hands to myself. But if I so desired, I could have had every necklace, earring, and bracelet in that house, and I certainly wouldn't have been caught by Edgar, Winona, or Roberta.

Oh, and don't worry, you don't need to remember any of these people or their names. Besides James and Mandy, my parents and their friend, Annette, none of them are important to the story. I don't even remember the names of the scampering kids except for James's three, and little "Rocco" which, for some reason, stuck. But you don't have to remember him either.

The guests resettled into conversations old and new—old as in, "Where was I? Oh right, listen to what a jackass my boss is..." versus new: "Why do you suppose Joey didn't bring Jaxy?"

I thought I had all the names of adults catalogued and matched up to faces, but the children were a different matter. There were no wallets to lift. I slipped out back where most of the kids were still running around. I noticed one child, a boy of maybe six or seven years, alone in a peach tree. His sandy blond hair hung in front of his eyes. He had a squirt gun at the ready, but the kids playing chase kept failing to run into the range of his weapon. I moseyed over to him with my hands in my pockets.

"What you need is a garden hose," I told him.

"Hey Uncle Joey," he said. "We can't use the hose. Gramma said it's 'cause'a the mud last time. You wanna come up here with me and help?"

I smiled and looked at the little tree, already filled with only the little boy in it.

"As much as I'd love to, you're such a big boy, I think the tree would break."

"Not if you're careful," I loved his matter-of-fact tone. Even when he said, "Watch out, the girls are coming," it was flat and seemingly unemotional.

Indeed, four girls flew by in a blur, giggling. The boy's stream struck two faces and resulted in satisfying whines and cries of "Joey!"

"Good job," I said to Little Joey as I leaned over a low branch.

"Thanks, but I was aiming for Ariel."

"What are the names of the other three again?"

"You mean Sianna, Emma, and Ella?"

"Right," I said as the girls rounded a giant oak in the distance and started back toward the house. "Which one is which, again?"

He identified each by their shirts, thus naming Ariel by omission. I asked him where his brother was and he pointed out Lucas in the pool with some other boys.

"He doesn't want to play with me," Little Joey said.

"That's just because he's not as clever as you, hiding in a tree like this."

"That's true," he said with an earnest nod. "He's really bad at hiding."

I wished Little Joey luck in his mission and excused myself to the restroom. Back in the house, I observed some of the framed photos on my way to the bathroom. More than anyone else, the twin brothers appeared, always together, usually in some sort of physical contact. I couldn't tell them apart, but in the teenaged and older shots, one always had an arm slung over the other. I guessed that was Joseph, a protective wing over his "little" brother. If not for the faded, yellowing photos and dated clothes, any one of the shots could have been of Little Joey. Two Little Joeys, shirtless and tanned with a shimmering river backdrop. Ten-ish years old: at Disneyworld or –land, another with them asleep in the back of a car, one's head rested on the other's shoulder. An old, crease-damaged photo of the babies, lying in the same crib, one asleep, one awake with a penetrating gaze into the camera lens. An extra wide shot of ten-plus children of various ages, most of them laughing, making silly faces, or looking away. I leaned close and found James and Joseph, perhaps seven years old, just like Little Joey. One was lifting his shirt and poking a finger into his belly button, the other appeared serious, pensive, and echoing the intense stare from the infant photo. I wondered who was who in these younger shots, neither appearing more dominant than the other, just very different personalities.

I had thus far dodged having to tell Melanie anyone's name that I hadn't already caught, but there were a number of tricky questions or comments which I had to deftly maneuver.

"Where's Jaxy?" Over and over and over again. I started making up a story about her not feeling well, but for some it had a reverse effect to what I had intended. I guessed I would never hear the end of this dog thing. But there was more than enough other awkwardness that day.

"Hey, thanks again," Cousin Edgar had said to me at one point with a quick elbow to my arm.

"Sure, no problem," I replied. He seemed satisfied with that.

The oldest woman at the get-together, my mother's aunt, Bibi, with a thick Polish accent pointed at Melanie from across the room and asked the person next to her "Is that Gabriella? Looks like she gained weight." Heads snapped my way as I did my best to feign uncomfortable bemusement. Melanie, seated at my side, had heard it, too, and her sudden grip on my arm told me she knew exactly who Gabriella was. Someone bent to Bibi's ear and corrected her, but she was defiant rather than ashamed, and helped to very loudly confirm what I had suspected.

"Well, how do I know? No one tells me someone dies. They don't tell me someone's born, they don't tell me someone dies!"

"Sorry, Joey," Winona said with a mournful face.

I brushed it off and avoided eye contact with anybody.

"Yeah, real sorry," a male cousin said. "Never got to call you or anything, but we were thinking about you when we heard about the accident …"

"Okay, I think that's quite enough of *that*." My mother had appeared in the family room from the kitchen. "Melanie, hon, how are you in the kitchen?"

Melanie looked at me, as if for permission. I snapped a "go for it" nod and she stood up from the love seat.

"I think I can hold my own," Melanie said.

"Good," my mother said. "'Cause we're a bit traditional on some things in this house." She helped Melanie up the two stairs and then addressed the room. "But the men are *always* on dish duty."

Groans and chuckles.

"Come talk to me," a voice behind me said. I startled a little, though recognized James's voice. I hadn't noticed there was a door behind the couch that led to the formal living room.

"Yeah, sure," I said and stood up. "Excuse me, everyone."

The pitying looks had remained on their faces. I was pleased to get away, though more than a little nervous talking to James one on one.

I followed him out the front door, down the steps, and past the cluttered fronts of cars parked too close to the house. We walked around the corner to the shaded side of the house, away from the quickly increasing heat of the summer sun. Patchy grass struggled to grow between assorted flagstones and well-packed soil. James halted and turned around to face me, expressionless. In the distance behind him, children fled screaming from a rule-breaking garden hose attack by a teenaged girl. James glanced quickly back—a father's reflex—observed no one injured, and turned back to me.

"Ariel almost got soaked there," I observed, pleased to demonstrate my familiarity with his daughter.

He ignored my comment and looked me in the face.

"Have we met?" He said.

It sounded like a genuine question, one you would ask a stranger in line at the grocery store.

My mouth opened, but I had no words. I tried to shape my face into whatever expression Joseph would have made if accosted with such a question from his brother. My usual verbal dexterity had taken a coffee break.

"I ..." I hung on that for a few seconds, tried to think. I looked past him as if the mischief occurring beyond was equally interesting. "Is that a joke ... your version of the old 'who are you and what have you done with my brother' thing? If so, I promise you I'm just trying to keep it together. This girl ..." I thumbed behind me.

James interrupted, "You're just not *you*. I don't get it. I could tell you a hundred things you're doing, not doing, or doing different. Where's the kiss on Mom's right cheek? Where's the dig at my gut? Why did I have to pull you outside to talk? I feel like if I didn't say something, you would have gone on through the day and the night and tomorrow as if I was one of *them*."

I shook my head and shrugged apologetically, pretending everything was about Melanie. "I'm so sorry, I really am. But you need to be happy for me. This is a big deal, I don't have to tell you. Don't give me a hard time for falling in love."

"That's not ..." he stuttered, blinked rapidly. "You can't say that this is all just that! You had already been seeing her for weeks and nothing changed. We talk every fucking day for forty years and that just stops? When is the last time we missed a day, let alone two, let alone five? You tell me what changed? Are you saying this is the new you? I lose my Jojo?"

He sounded like a dejected child. I reached out to him, took him by the shoulder with a paternal hand, "No way." I smiled. "Never. This is just a weird few weeks. It's hard to explain, but you ask what suddenly happened? I'll tell you what. It got *real*. I don't think I was ever really *in it* before that. And the same thing happened for her. Did you see her? She's glowing. It's like we went to some level that neither of us has been to."

"I've heard that before," he said. I was feeling better with every word, though. It was becoming a brotherly heart-to-heart versus an interrogation. "But this is something you would have told me the second it happened. Before, you would have put a finger up in her face, told her to hold on, and walked outside to call me. Did *she* tell you to back off with me or something?"

"No, no way! Melanie loves you guys. Just keep it together. Don't freak out on me. This thing is so important to me—really life-changing. I'm thinking and feeling and seeing things I never have before. Mom told me I finally look *alive*! That she hasn't seen me like this in a while. I need *you* happy for me, too, not acting like a spurned lover."

His face snapped back like it had been slapped.

"I ... I can't believe you just said that."

"Come on, you know what I mean!" I shook him and tried to brighten the mood, but he was so down and hurt and confused with a flurry of thoughts and emotions stomping all over his face.

"I think I do," he said, grief-stricken eyes rolling about slowly, searching my face.

"Well good," I said. "It doesn't *look* like it right now, but you'll see. Everything's going to be great."

"Uh huh."

"So let's get back inside," I said as I patted him on the back. "You have to protect me from Bibi, though, okay?"

He walked beside me, quietly, as we turned the corner back to the front of the house. I felt his look, though, and snuck a glance at him. His eyes were big and probing and seemingly affixed to me. I didn't like it. It was exactly what I had feared going into this day. Fortunately, though, his problem seemed to be feeling cast aside in favor of Melanie. He felt like he was losing the brother he knew, which, I guess was true. But this was the new Joseph and he needed to get used to it.

I climbed the stairs and James finally spoke behind me.

"Gondag shlupfine winthuh wheels, nah?" At least that's what I heard him say. It was a big string of gibberish.

I stopped and turned back, "What's that?"

His face was blank again, "Nothing."

* * *

A couple of the families left before evening—long drives and wanting to avoid night driving. The rest of us sat down for dinner at a long table in the formal dining room. Kids were sequestered at a smaller fold-out against the wall. I was placed toward the middle of the table with Melanie on my right and Mandy on the left. James sat beside his wife. We hadn't spoken since our discussion outside. I tried to avoid him without being obvious, engrossed in this conversation or that. I felt his eyes on me at various points, and noticed Mandy asking him what was wrong more than a couple times. He had brushed her off each time.

My mother sat at one end of the table, my father at the other. Every so often, Mom would tell a funny story or share a complaint about Dad of which he would only catch the tail end.

"What was that, Lan? You're not telling them about *that*, are you?"

"No, no, dear. Just bragging about your golf scores." She winked at him.

"Right," he said, a playful, untrusting expression on his face. I liked their relationship—roguishly loving, and still very much alive. That was what I wanted for Melanie and me.

"And how did we come to meet each other," Annette asked Melanie from across the table. Annette was the woman that first greeted us at the door. She was not technically an aunt, but a childhood friend of Mom's that was very much a part of the family. She had been present at the birth of James and Joseph, and was apparently the first to hold my body as an infant. She cradled me in the hospital room's corner while the doctors struggled with James. Earlier, in front of the pool, she shared the story of James's highly complicated birth. He had almost died in the process. She had joked that he was a "stubborn son of a breech" to which Mom had groaned and said "That one ever going to get old for you, dear?"

In response to Annette's question about our meeting, Melanie swallowed her mouthful of spinach lasagna and said, "I used to work at Johns Hopkins with James and Mandy. They introduced us."

"Ah," Annette said and turned to James. "So we've *you* to thank for this new Joey?"

James choked and brought his napkin to his mouth. He tried to say "excuse me" but the food was apparently still in his throat and he turned away, hacking. The table quieted and everyone's eyes were on him. Mandy slapped his back, but he raised his hand to his side and shuffled away, out of the room.

"Jesus," Dad said. "He okay?"

"Go with him, hon," Mom said to Mandy.

Mandy nodded and hopped up at once, "He just tried to talk with his mouth full and something went down the wrong pipe."

"Let that be a lesson to you, kids," Dad called to the kids' table. "Manners aren't just for being polite! They keep you alive, for Christ's sake."

Mom shook her head at Dad's re-invocation of Jesus. Annette spoke up to fill the silence.

"Let me tell you about that boy," Annette said, referring to James. "At one point we thought he was going to end up a recluse or a serial murderer."

"That's an exaggeration," Mom interrupted.

"No, not really, darling. You might look back different now, but I remember all the problems you had with him. Joseph here was the angel and James was ... well, I'll say it ... the *demon*."

An ironic twist.

"He's not even at the table, 'Nette," Dad said. "Can't even defend himself."

"There's nothing to defend!" Annette shouted. "He's a doll now! Been a doll since before Junior High! But *before* that ... ugh ... do you even remember the things he would do?"

Mom looked uncomfortable and more than a little riled by the subject. "Yes, Annette." She said the name with bared teeth.

"You used to call me in a panic! How many times did Jack and I take the boys off your hands just to give you two a break? So I know *exactly* the sort of nonsense he was up to. Hiding in the shower when I was—"

"Annette!" Mom barked and shot her friend a death glare.

Annette was stunned, but then looked around the room at all the averted eyes and hovering forks. She snapped out of it in an instant and her poise returned.

"So sorry, love. Forgot myself there a moment." She pushed her wine glass away an inch, blew a kiss to Mom, and turned to my father at the opposite end of the table. "Stephen?"

"It's fine, 'Nette," he said. No harm."

Eating resumed and James returned with Mandy. He forced a smile, grabbed a new napkin from the counter, and sat down. He and Mandy briefly fielded the "Everything okay?" questions, and smiled pleasantly at someone's obligatory "You know swallowing works best if you *chew* first!"

After dinner, many of the guests returned to the pool, the warm water steaming into the night air. My parents' backyard was stunning at night, the landscaping enhanced by underlighting and paths lit by strings of lights. The dancing glow of the swimming pool played in the leaves of the white oak trees.

I sat in a lounge chair beside the pool and had a nice long chat with my father. Actually, I said very little—simply listened to him expound on forty-five years of married life (the subtext being that he was trying to encourage me in that direction, swaying any lingering fears I might harbor), and how it feels good to not worry as much about his boys. He said that he and Lani had weathered these massive swings throughout their children's lives. The fear of losing James to an unspecified medical issue his first year, then the behavioral issues to which Annette had so publicly alluded.

I caught a hint of the turning point with young James—though Dad didn't out and out link it to him directly, but it seemed that there was a big health scare in town, followed by a year when many friends moved away. Dad said that it had essentially scared James straight, brought the family closer together, and led to a glorious period—our teenaged years; the subject of so many of those hallway photographs— followed by a short time in empty nest depression.

"It's like a Christing rollercoaster," he grumbled and sipped from his bottle of beer. He raised one eyebrow and peered over to me, a clever smile hidden beneath his bushy moustache. "But a rollercoaster every person should get on. She want kids?"

"Melanie?" I said. "Yeah … well, honestly, we haven't had that conversation yet. But she seems to love them. I know she'd be a great mother. Guess we'll cross that bridge, you know?"

Having kids with her had crossed my mind, but in a far off, distant future sort of way. Dad brought the idea into sharper focus.

"Yep, yep," he said, gazing across the pool to Melanie and Mandy, seated around a glass table beneath a lit, orange umbrella with some other women. "Not trying to rush you, Jojo. Not my intent at all. But hurry the fuck up."

We laughed and clinked beer bottles.

"Happy Anniversary, Dad. Sorry I didn't bring a gift. Been really—"

"Hey, quit it," he interrupted. "We said no gifts and we meant it. I don't know what it is with people and gifts. Who's it for? Is it for me or you? Me? Well, I don't want anything, so what the Christ?"

I smirked. "Right. Just respecting your wishes, sir."

He snorted a little, "Now go tell your brother to do the same. I don't know what the hell that massive thing wrapped up in the house is, but I figured he was trying to outdo you for once. Little did he know, eh?"

I shrugged.

"Well go spend your time with him. I know you don't want to be sitting here tied to an old man all night. That's why I made two of you. Surprised you even sat here this long."

"No, I really enjoyed it. Seriously."

"Well … good." He looked touched. That made me feel warm. I felt a closeness, an affection for him that I had never felt with a man before. "But I don't remember the last time I saw you and him apart for more than a minute so track him down and do your … *twin* thing."

That wasn't likely, but I loved this family, and if I could give James the sense that I was still that same old Jojo he knew, perhaps I could have a similar sort of intimacy with him. If only I had known what he expected out of me. I supposed that twins, sharing the same crib, being dressed the same, having so many experiences from essentially the same perspective, created a bond unlike a typical brother. For all my mastery of imitation, improvisation, and reading people, I didn't know how convincingly I could simulate forty-one years of shared history and constant contact.

I found James in front of the house. He was sitting on the hood of a beige sedan, his feet on the bumper. He heard me coming and glanced back, bristling when he saw who approached.

"Stay away from me," he said and stood up, on guard. "Go back inside."

"Dad says I've been ignoring you, and I completely agree. Can we maybe—"

He cut me off, "Don't call him that."

"Sorry?"

"Don't call him that. *You* don't get to call him that."

"But you do?"

He looked a little stunned by that question. He glanced toward the front door then back at me. "I don't know, maybe. Just stay away from me. I don't want to see you. And …" he was stammering, flustered, "… and stay away from Melanie."

I put my hands out, palms up. "Look, I don't know what the problem is, but whenever you feel better … whenever you're ready to talk, just let me know. Text me, call me, whatever you like."

He snapped a nod and said, "Right."

I walked away, agreeing to keep my distance. What the hell was going on? At some points it seemed like he *knew*—somehow knew exactly what I was. Why tell me to stay away from Melanie? Why say

I don't get to call our father "Dad"? And I had really begun to love this new life. It felt more real than anything I had ever experienced. I couldn't let one person bring that down. He may have been the most important person in Old Joey's life, but he obviously wouldn't be that in mine. That position belonged to Melanie, and as long as he didn't do anything to jeopardize that, I would just have to deal with his existence in the world.

* * *

Later that night, Melanie and I showered and changed into PJ's. We had a nice, bathroom-attached room to ourselves. We lay in bed on our sides, facing each other and quietly sharing our experiences of the day. She asked me questions about how this person was related to that person, and which one was Edgar, and raved about how much she loved my parents. I had learned most of the answers to her family hierarchy questions that day, but sidestepped others I hadn't.

She asked me why I didn't bring Jax. She asked why I hadn't brought an anniversary present for my parents. She asked what was going on with James.

These were all awkward to navigate, but I was preoccupied watching her lips, touching her skin, smelling her scents: shampoo, soft floral perfume, mouthwash, a vanilla hand soap, dryer sheets from her clothes.

My hand wandered down her waist to her hip and then down between her legs. I could feel the minute details of her shape beneath her yoga pants' blend of cotton and spandex. She stopped talking and looked down at my hand as I toyed about. She inhaled a quiet gasp and looked up at me.

"Would you ..." she whispered. "... in your parents' house?"

"I suppose I would ..."

"What if someone heard?"

I shrugged and moved my hand from outside her pants to inside. Her shoulders rose and she rolled onto her back. I sucked an earlobe as

I continued working down below. A hand slapped down over mine and I looked up at her.

"Is the door locked?" She whispered. "And can you turn on the TV?"

I got up and obliged on both counts. The 11:00 news was on—a shot of a helicopter hovering over an overflowing river.

"No, change it," she demanded. "Not news. Something non-distracting."

I switched to a Spanish language soap opera and turned up the volume.

"¡Olivia!" A man shouted. "¿Por qué?"

"Are you kidding me?" Melanie exclaimed in a hush. I grinned and threw up my shoulders. "Fine, whatever. C'mere."

7. Details, Details

I turned off the coffee maker, filled my travel mug, and spooned in heaps of sugar. I like it sweet. Kiki, the cat, snaked between my feet and curled his tail around an ankle, marking me as his territory and reminding me that he had yet to be fed. I heard the shower turn on upstairs, revealing that Melanie had awakened. I let Jax back in from the yard, fed both animals, and grabbed my keys to head off to work.

The preceding paragraph is mind-blowing in its banality. It may merely be an account of a typical American morning routine, but as my government-issued car reached the end of my driveway, and as I waved at my neighbor, Dusty, walking his Labradoodle, "Pogo", and as I congratulated myself for remembering to take out the garbage bins the night before, I couldn't help but laugh. A decade ago I was a normally-timid woman named Soe, wearing a strap-on, screaming as I pumped away at a certain Southeast Asian country's corrupt, murderous leader. He was screaming back, begging for me to stop.

My GPS directed me to the day's surveillance location. I was meeting another member of our taskforce, Brad Rojas, from U.S. Customs. Brad was a—what's that? What about the strap-on? Oh, that's not relevant to the current story—I was just illustrating the vast difference between my previous lives and my life as Joseph. It's just funny how priorities change, you know? I appreciated my new ordinary existence, though those *were* good times. So what was I saying? Right! Brad Rojas.

Brad Rojas, and several others from U.S. Customs, DEA, ATF, and FBI were members of a joint taskforce with my division of the U.S. Postal Inspectors. Our team's mission was to make a dent in certain drug trafficking operations.

What I had learned at that point was that local PD and those other agencies were having a devil of a time with prosecution and sentencing of non-violent crimes. They might catch someone making millions off selling drugs to kids, but when it came time to send someone to jail, the dealers would essentially receive a slap on the wrist. Local prisons were so overcrowded that they were being reserved only for violent criminals. That's where my department came into play. If we could find a way to make the crime a federal offense, appropriate sentences could be handed out, and more importantly, adhered to. Otherwise, all of these agencies' work was a waste of time. The guys on the team like to compare their current work to Al Capone eventually being taken down by tax crimes.

I was meeting Brad at a parking lot outside Baltimore to stake out a suspected cartel distribution house. I enjoyed these surveillance days. It reminded me of my between-body periods, snooping around, watching people without them knowing, and not being arrested for being a peeping tom. It was my *duty* to peep. Customs couldn't go through a citizen's mail, but Postal Inspectors can. It's the simplest way to find out who really lives in a particular house.

Now here's one of the fun things I learned about my job. Customs might intercept a package from Colombia, open it up, and find five pounds of cocaine inside. Who gets arrested for this? The person whose name it's addressed to? But they haven't even received it yet. We need to let the package be delivered, insure they opened it, and *then* arrest them. But this is a touchy thing because you're a federal officer, knowingly allowing contraband to be delivered to a suspect. So you have to be ready to take them down the second they open it. We have some clever tools to accomplish this and they made me feel like James Bond.

Brad and I sat in his minivan for several hours that day, watching the suspect, Riley Packard, come and go. Packard was in his mid-thirties, huge, and with a braided blond goatee that made him look like a Viking. Every so often he stepped outside the house for a chat on his cordless phone, looking down the street as if waiting for something. The mailman, perhaps. Precisely the mailman, in fact. We had Riley's package of cocaine secured in an evidence locker, and it was therefore two days late. The original label had been hand-addressed to a fake name: Robert Johnson.

Mr. Packard's face was red and shiny as he chain-smoked and paced up and down the sidewalk every time he came outside in search of Mr. Johnson's package. His stress level was swelling.

"You satisfied no one else lives there?" Brad asked me at the end of the day.

"Yup, and I don't think *he* even lives there," I said. I had been going through mail addressed to the house for a week and hadn't found a single bill or personally-addressed letter.

"When do you think we can schedule the delivery then?"

I shrugged and perused the schedule in my phone. It appeared that Thursday was clear, just a couple days away, so we agreed on a time.

Thursday rolled around and we had our entry and arrest team meet at a city park down the street from the suspect residence. Brad was the lead, fortunately, so he briefed the team on the plan. Scott Lieter helped me to wire the package so it would signal us upon opening. That would be everyone's signal to move in. In these situations, Postal Inspectors pose as mail carriers to deliver the package. Scott, who was only there for the bust, volunteered me. I thanked him and got changed in the park restroom.

Thirty minutes later I had the box in hand, walking toward the front door. I knocked on the security screen.

"Yeah, hold on, comin'!"

Packard opened the door, but kept the screen shut.

"Got a package for Robert Johnson," I said. A fan in the room blew his stink across my face. He smelled like a wet ashtray perfumed with B.O.

Packard looked at my face, then out at the street. "Yeah, just go ahead and leave it on the porch."

"Signature required, sir. You Mr. Johnson? Otherwise I gotta take this back to the office and someone's gotta come pick it up." I admit I was more than a little nervous, but the adrenalin rush kept me focused. I stepped back a little, feigned impatience.

"Fine, yeah, that's me, just gimme it." He unlocked the screen, signed the delivery receipt, and I thanked him.

The screen slammed behind me, followed by the door. I walked back to my little mail truck and drove around the block. Within seconds of pulling away, the receiver in my pocket rang out and Brad's voice blared through the walkie-talkie in the center console.

"Package breached, package breached! Move in, move in!"

With my role in the bust completed, I rounded the block slooowly. No need to rush back to the house while guns were still drawn. Besides, this was a Customs gig, so my job was truly done.

The walkie-talkie cracked again, "Stand down, stand down, suspect in custody. Property cleared."

I moseyed back to the house to see Packard in cuffs, sitting on his front lawn. Brad, Scott, and some of the others stood over him, chuckling. I got out of the mail truck and walked to them just as Packard rambled, "… mailman dumped the thing on my porch didn't sign nothin' didn't accept nothin' cause it ain't mine and I ain't goin' down for some bullshit clavicle error 'cause some fucktard mailman …"

Brad spoke over him, "Oh, there you are *Inspector*. Good job earlier. You want to go join them inside on the search?"

I could hear the dogs inside the house barking maniacally.

"… ain't searchin' shit without a fuckin' warrant fuckers better get the fuck outa my fuckin' house 'cause I got the first fuckin' amendment on my side and I know my fuckin' rights …"

But the officers inside didn't need my help. A lank DEA agent I only knew by her nickname, Wits, stepped from the suspect's house, onto the porch. She had a beaming smile across her face and gestured for us to come inside. Local PD stayed with Packard while we followed Wits into the house.

Brad said to her, "Are we excited or fucking excited?"

"Holy-fuck-fucking excited," Wits said as she led us to a room from which loud crashing, pounding, and cracking sounds emanated.

"Don't play with my emotions, Wits," Brad said.

Everyone piled into the room where DEA-jacketed agents pried sheetrock from an inner wall. Being last, I craned my neck over the shoulders in the doorway, trying to get a peak. All I saw was the cloud of dust and white powder in the air, then the mess of sheetrock littering the floor. People were happily swearing and high-fiving as the dogs spun in circles, twisting up their leashes. The word "holy" was used repeatedly and without reservation. Holy shit. Holy fuck. Holy God, even. I shook hands with those nearby and mirrored the elated smiles around me. All this before I had even seen it.

What would later be called the "wall of shame" or "snow wall" was only the tip of the cocaine iceberg in this house. *Every* interior wall contained hundreds of five-kilogram packs. It was the biggest bust of already-in-country drugs that the Postal Inspectors had ever seen. The DEA and Customs folks had seen bigger caches, but this house was definitely in their top 100 seizures of all time.

My boss, Kevin Najafi, showed up around the same time as the other senior officials. Everyone wanted to see the megabust in person and insure their agency's contributions were properly evangelized with the growing press presence on-scene. Scott and I stuck around as night fell and pizzas arrived. We eavesdropped on the various high-ranking officials as they moved from spotlight to spotlight, reporter to reporter, like carnival booths where every game is the same. Then I started hearing a concerning phrase thrown around … a lot.

Anticipatory search warrant.

"Thanks to the US Postal Inspectors who were able to obtain an anticipatory search warrant based upon the contents of the intercepted package …"

I began to feel my throat tighten and seal up around cheese, pepperoni, and garlic-parmesan-infused crust. I had not submitted any paperwork for some special type of warrant. I did not even know how to request a regular old warrant, thus far finding a way to skirt it until I could observe the process firsthand. Sweat beads erupted from my forehead. Someone would eventually ask me for this non-existent warrant. Could Scott have obtained it? He hadn't been involved in this case until today. I thought back to a couple days ago in the minivan with Brad Rojas. He had asked me, "When do you think we can schedule the delivery?" What he was really asking was, "How long will it take you to get a warrant?"

I couldn't swallow. I was going to look like an idiot. I was going to be fired. I obviously still didn't know how to be a Postal Inspector, but I sure as hell knew that without a warrant, anything found during our search would be inadmissible. Could we even take the drugs from the house without the warrant? I couldn't imagine—even with a fuck-up this monumental—that all of these agencies would have to simply drive away, leaving millions of dollars' worth of drugs with the suspect. But if it was an illegal search in the first place, how could we take anything from the house? It didn't matter, and I'd never have to worry about it again. All I could do was sit and wait for the inevitable while the sounds of laughter and back pats and congratulations continued to fill the air.

I felt like an ass for not thinking of it sooner. At the office, we used the word "warrant" as frequently as "mail." At the same time, I felt pathetic and weak. A short stack of papers and ink, a scrawled signature, colleagues' confounded words, incredulous expressions on their faces. All infinitesimally small *human* concerns—the fodder of excruciating whining from mortal beings who dedicate their terrifyingly short lives to a particular career and family. Why did I care if I fucked up? I had done far worse things in my life than keep police from legally seizing a fraction of a quarter of a billionth of the world's drug supply. It wasn't that I worried what Melanie would think, or my family—that this would somehow result in my "cover" being blown. That would be a far more bearable excuse for me to feel as I did. Instead it was personal pride, embarrassment, failing.

A wise demon would say that such matters of consequence are inextricably linked to all the pleasures of living as a human. Joy of love: fear of losing it. Rush of danger: risk of injury or death. And I would tell a wise demon to go fuck himself and shove his Yoda wisdom up his wrinkly green asshole. But by choice I had been sucked into this world—this life—and I felt compelled to live by its rules.

It was around 9:30PM when Najafi approached me on the pink cinderblock wall dividing Packard's yard from the neighbor's. Half of the drug packs had been loaded into armored DEA trucks while more walls were being emptied. DEA agents were now tearing up the attic and pulling up floorboards in search of more stash. At the end of the night the house would be a square frame with a roof.

"I need you to go get a bunch of copies of the warrant made," Najafi said.

There wasn't a hint of doubt in his voice. The warrant's existence was an absolute to him. But my guilty ears heard another sentence. "You *do* have a warrant, don't you?" I had already worked out how I was going to play it—how to avoid an incompetence tag, or worse: to admit ignorance to a policy or procedure Joseph had likely followed thousands of times.

"Sure, no problem," I said. "I have it in my car."

I stood up and moseyed across the street, hands in my pockets—the picture of nonchalance. I lifted the plastic file box from the backseat floor and extracted a red manila folder from among the others. I carried it unopened back across the street and presented it ceremoniously.

"Why you giving this to me?" Najafi asked, as if I had placed a baggy of dog shit in his hands. "I ain't making your fucking copies for you."

I slapped my head and reached for it back, "Oh, sorry, I thought you wanted to look it over before I go. I'll just go …" But he pulled it back and opened the folder, rotating to allow the street lights to shine on the papers within.

"Hang on, let me just look it over before you go," he glanced up, sly smile, winked. The rare good mood would soon deflate. It started as a confused frown. I watched his eyes scan the whole first page, then back up to the top … almost there …

"Cling," he said. "Did you even look at this?"

"Did I …"

"Wrong case. This isn't it." He slapped the folder against my chest. "I know it's late, but don't scare me like that. Go grab the real one. Now I *have* to see it to bring my blood pressure down."

I opened the folder, began breathing heavily, swallowed as I tore through the pages.

"Cling ..." Najafi said. "Don't fucking play with me, man. That shit's not funny, man." His normally-repressed South Indian accent was peeking through.

"I ... I ..." I stammered. I looked up from the pages, locked panic-filled eyes with him before allowing my gaze to drift across the roofs of the neighborhood.

"Don't tell me," Najafi said. He put his hands on his shiny bald head. It got Scott's attention and he walked over.

"What is it?" Scott said as he rushed over. "What happened?"

"I ... I think I forgot ..." I began, and went on to explain how I must have mixed up two cases—thought the affidavit I had signed was for the Customs case, not the porn warrant in my hands.

We all looked over at the DEA truck still being loaded with drugs. Scott stared at me in disbelief as Najafi began to pace in the patchy grass.

"It's fucked?" Scott said, shaking his head. "How do we ... What do we tell *them*?" He pointed a thumb toward all the other giddy agents ambling around.

"Nothing!" Najafi finally said. He'd stopped beside us. "You don't tell a fucking soul. I'm going to see what I can do."

"What about all the drugs?" I said. "What if you can't ... they're still loading ..."

"It's contraband, regardless," Scott said. "It's seized either way."

I obviously should have known that.

"Of course," I said. "But they're going to want to leave with a warrant."

Najafi cut in. "And it was supposed to be in the hands of the fucking suspect before anyone started searching anything. But we'll get to all the other fucked up parts of this cluster later. Right now, I'm going to see if I can't save your ass and our office's reputation."

He gave me a menacing scowl and strode off to his car.

"Un-fucking-believable, bro," Scott said.

8. The Middle

Have you ever heard the phrase *Too big to fail?* Well, that's what the Packard bust was. The law apparently only applies to less significant cases. This is the decades-old war on drugs, after all. We don't accept losses in this war due to little administrative legalities.

I wasn't punished at all. In fact, due to Najafi's help with "finding" the misplaced anticipatory search warrant—the one that, as it turns out, was taped to Packard's front door the whole time—my boss was not only complicit in this conspiracy, he was the primary conspirator. All I had done was forget to submit for a warrant. Najafi forged a back-dated affidavit and had a motivated judge approve and sign a warrant. In the days that followed, all Najafi gave me were subtle flashes when discussing cases. He wanted to threaten—to say "if you fuck this up …" or a more cleverly-worded warning, but that would be discussing *it*, and we would never again discuss *it*.

Work actually grew easier for me thanks to that screw-up. I now had a top five things-to-remember list drilled deep into my skull. As long as those particular details were handled right on every case, I would be fine. I finally felt like a genuine United States Postal Inspector. However, there are certain things that can happen in one's personal life that can also affect one's job, especially when one is in the law enforcement field. But I'll fill you in on that later. Right now, allow me to bask a bit longer in the relief of not blowing a multimillion dollar drug bust, and in the brain-buzzing elation of my relationship with Melanie.

In fact, the next few weeks were unquestionably the best in my demon life. Blissful, fulfilling, and *real*. Melanie and I spent every free moment together. With a toothy self-satisfied grin I'm pleased to inform you that we each had clothes and toiletries at the other's place. After a week of juggling locations, we began spending more time at my house, and she brought her cat, Kiki, to stay at my place. Jax had a friend during the day, and Melanie didn't have to feel bad leaving Kiki alone with a mountain of dry food for days at a time. It had been my suggestion—one step in a clever ploy to have Melanie unofficially move in with me.

"Is this a clever ploy to have me move in with you?" She had said.

"Not sure what you mean," I had replied.

I still think it was clever.

She continued to get breaks at her apartment—doing laundry, cleaning, enjoying a night to herself. She had spent the past fifteen-plus years living alone with full freedom and privacy, so I definitely didn't want her to feel a jarring adjustment to coupled life. I was fine with the breaks. I didn't need any myself, but it broke things up for her and made our reunions that much sweeter. We fell into a good rhythm for both of us.

One night off, my cell phone rang. It was James. We hadn't spoken since the anniversary party. I grimaced, took a deep breath, and answered.

"Hi there," I began.

James interrupted, "Gregor?"

"Sorry, who?" I replied. "James?"

He was quiet for a few seconds before hanging up. I figured out he must have called the wrong contact in his phone. Awkward. More so for him, really. Like accidentally calling an ex.

I pushed the jarring moment from my mind and decided to go over the priorities I had listed on my computer. I was doing well! Melanie and I were like sex study lab technicians, trying out new things, mixing it up, and had come to see each other's bodies as personal playgrounds. There was a level of comfort with each other that, at least for me, was unprecedented. I preferred to believe the feeling was mutual and that whatever cloudy memory I had of her with anyone else was in fact a silly misfire of my loaner brain.

I continued my "on-the-job training" as a postal inspector, even participating in a few more home raids, and while still nerve-wracking, I found them quite exhilarating. Melanie loved the stories I told after days like those. I was some sort of authority figure. I got to carry a concealed weapon with me whenever I wanted. I had yet to have any use for it off the clock, but at times, falling asleep, I dreamt up fantasy hostage scenarios where someone needs rescuing, I happen on the scene, blow away some scruffy, clichéd dirtbag, and carry the weeping victim to safety. Melanie found the idea of me walking around the mall with a gun in my pants sexy. There's surely a twinge of phallic symbolism in there somewhere.

I had met my family and friends and looked forward to more time … with most of them. I would ignore the James situation as much as possible while hoping it wouldn't affect my relationships with my parents. Yes, I'd deal with it when the time came, but until then I was happier pretending nothing was wrong.

Melanie began writing songs. Sometimes I would come downstairs and find her on the ottoman facing out the sliding glass door, strumming chords and singing about love or surprises or dreams. My favorite was a song she called "immortality", and not just for the irony of the title. It's about *me*! *She* wrote a song about *me*. Can I share the first stanza with you? I think she's ridiculously talented. I'm just sorry you can't hear her singing it right this second. There's a recording of it. Maybe it can be included in the audiobook version …

It's all been said but never said right
Write a love song, pull strings
String me out, my life a line
I wish it was elastic, stretched out tight
Bunched-up ends, all middle
Hours of day, minutes of night
A little tug from my man
An endless hug from my man

Wrapped around so tight
All I can do is breathe.

See what I mean? I know, right?

She started painting again, too. To me it meant she was at peace with me in her life. She was inspired by me. I may not have given her the creative talent, but I knew it was me that put her back in the emotional space to create.

She brought her easel and some canvases with us on a weekend getaway to Chesapeake Bay. It was a little too cold for swimming but I let Jaxy play in the little waves while Melanie experimented with painting landscapes. Jaxy found a dead pigeon in the sand and peed on it. My affection for my dog escalated to pure love.

We took our time driving back, stopping in little towns and browsing quaint shops, buying odds and ends and challenging each other to find odd items or to spend less than a certain amount in one place. Melanie found a unique oven mitt. Printed on both sides was a woman's hand. Painted fingernails protruded from the tips of the fingers, and a massive embroidered diamond ring rose from the ring finger. It even had a "gold" bracelet around the wrist. She paid real money for it. I found a porcelain trivet painted with a cartoony run-over cat, its zany bloodshot eyes asymmetrically pointed. Its elongated tongue stretched several wavy inches. Dotted-line flies circled above the flat carcass. Despite Melanie's pleas, I did not buy it.

In the evening we stopped at an outdoor shopping center near Georgetown for dinner. We settled on a crowded Mediterranean café and sat outside beneath a large awning.

While Melanie praised the unknown inventor of the outdoor space heater, I watched the early Christmas shoppers stroll the brick-paved court with designer label-emblazoned shopping bags. I don't know if it was my demon nature or the acuity of a fellow thief that spotted them. A pair of well-dressed men with eyes too keen for their clothes. Leaning against the brick walls of a thin alleyway across from us, I could see the never-washed creases in their patterned button-downs, the folds at thirds in their new khakis. I guessed that some fellow of like size had set down his Banana Republic bag and found it missing an instant later.

The thieves were using their phones as evidence of innocent loitering, their eyes flashing up at passersby every few seconds. They were on the prowl for sure. One had a buzz cut; the other wore a shiny slickback.

"Just an iced tea, please. Joey?"

I looked up at the waiter. "Same for me, please. Thanks."

I followed Buzzcut's lingering gaze to a very well-dressed man with silver hair.

"What's so interesting?" Melanie said.

I took the opportunity to show off.

"See the two guys in front of that walkway?" She searched then found them. "They're about to pickpocket the wealthy gentleman chatting over there."

"What? Him? How do you know?"

She leaned up and stared a little too obviously. I put my hand on hers and motioned for her to settle back into her chair.

"Just watch. The guy has no bag to snatch, but there's a lump where his wallet is. It's in his coat."

Melanie was concerned but also fascinated. She whispered for no reason.

"How do you know? What are you going to do? Will you arrest them?"

Oops. This was supposed to be entertainment, not a bust. I couldn't say "I'd love to help but I'm not on duty." Not to mention I still harbored a feeling of kinship with thieves of this sort (if they were good, that is). But Melanie was now fully engaged in this situation and my initial unsympathetic perspective simply wouldn't do.

"I don't really have any jurisdiction when it comes to this stuff. I mean, I could detain them while waiting for the local cops. Wish I had brought my gun though … who knows what they're carrying …"

"Oh, no, you can't do anything!" She whispered. "I don't want you to do anything, okay? Let's just tell the waiter to call security or something."

She had a practical solution. But as the man with slicked back hair began to weave through the crowd on a course toward his mark, I had an idea. I was still showing off, you see.

"Quick, let me borrow a pen," I said.

She dug in her purse and handed me a pen. I scrawled a short note on my napkin and folded it into my palm.

"I'll be right back," I said. "Just relax and try not to stare. Oh, and order me the falafel plate when the waiter comes back."

I exited through the little swinging gate and slipped into the crowd of walkers. Buzzcut was still wall-leaning at the alleyway, his phone screen illuminating his face. His eyes moved constantly as he watched for security and tracked his partner on his final approach. I passed Melanie and gave her a reassuring smile. She was doing well at playing unconcerned.

I squeezed between families and strollers until only a few yards from the thief with the slicked back hair. I saw his left hand disappear into his pocket. It came out as a fist a second later and he tripped on nothing. Change sprayed out in front of him, striking the legs of his mark and the young women with him. It jingled and rolled and startled the whole group.

"Oh, shoot!" The thief said as he dropped to his knees and began picking coins from between the group's feet. "Sorry guys... so sorry ..."

The gimmick was clever in that it didn't depend upon the altruism of the victim. It's one thing to ignore a person picking things up next to you, but a whole other level of jerkdom to either let them retrieve their fallen items *around* you, or to move away without helping. The silver haired victim didn't bat an eye though. He was all too happy to help, crouching down with the thief and plucking nickels and pennies from the pavement and handing them to the clumsy stranger. The crouch also made his coat fall to his side, away from his chest. I passed them and looked into the window of the neighboring candle shop. I continued to watch in the reflection.

"Thank you so much," the thief said. "Was just picking out quarters for the meter ... appreciate it ... oh hey, you mind grabbing those quarters for me?" He pointed and the two watching women turned around. And there's the grab! The brown leather wallet glided from the man's inner coat pocket. The thief stood up and turned, looking around at the ground. The wallet was gone from his hand. I didn't see where he had stashed it.

"Hey, thanks guys!" He said as he stood up. "Appreciate it."

He returned to the throng of shoppers, continuing away from his accomplice. I peered over the crowd and spotted the other thief just as he slipped away into the alleyway.

Good. Only need to deal with one.

I quickly caught up with him and saw the long wallet jutting from his back pocket. A nice pick, but amateurish follow-through. I moved closer, waited for his right foot to reach the end of its stride, just before it would rise from the ground for its next step. The pants crinkled and reached their loosest state around the right buttock. I pinched the exposed end of the wallet, lifted slightly, and dropped the napkin in behind it. The thief's right leg did the rest of the work for me as it advanced forward. I stopped, wallet in hand, and he continued on without a backward glance.

I joined the wide lane of shoppers walking back the other way. The oblivious silver-haired victim was ambling my way, laughing with his companions. I passed him, caught Melanie's eye back at the table, and gave her a just-a-second finger. Her neck craned and I saw her about to protest, but I stopped and ran up behind the mark.

"Sir?" I called. "Excuse me, sir?" He glanced back at me as I jogged up holding out his wallet. "I think you dropped this."

He frowned and patted his coat. I handed him the wallet, smiled at the ladies, and walked back to the café.

"What did you do?" Melanie asked after I had sat down.

"I gave the guy back his wallet."

She rolled her eyes. "Yeah, I saw that. What'd you to the pickpocket guys?"

"I let them go with a warning."

She studied my face, her eyes accusing but intrigued. She continued on about the thieves as our food arrived. "So wait, they teach stuff about pickpocketing in Postal Inspector school?"

I clumsily dodged, "Diverse instruction set," and remained elusive. I could tell it turned her on.

"Well, what did the note say at least?"

"'Busted. Don't come back.'"

"Seriously? You know they're just going to go somewhere else."

"Or they might take the act of good will to heart, thank God they weren't arrested, and go on to lead productive lives. Who can say?"

She shook her head and smirked. "I don't understand why, but you are beyond fucking sexy right now."

Our sex that night, back at my house, is none of your nosey business. Though I do need you to try and grasp the *love* that I felt for her. It's an intolerable cliché to say I loved her more every day, but this is what happened. It's the truth. I loved her so much that I needed her to be in my life for the rest of our lives. And so—naturally—I fucked it all up.

9. Uncle Dom

I met Chester and Claire for the first time at a restaurant in Leesburg. Melanie presented the hideous oven mitt to her mom. Claire couldn't wait to show it off to friends and watch their faces.

Claire loved me right off, but Chester undermined me at every opportunity with ham-fisted subject changes.

Claire said to me, "It sounds like you've accomplished the goals you originally set for yourself, but still have new ones to strive for."

I began, "Yes, I think it's—"

Chester said to Melanie, "Honey, when are you going to play us some of your new songs?"

He was a tough nut to crack, but I held my own, planted some seeds, and knew our next meeting would surely seal the deal for him (whether or not he would admit to it).

My old checklist still present in my mind, I had hoped someone would have brought up Melanie's catatonic uncle, Dominic, during the dinner. He had become a much lower priority—in fact, had left my mind all together for a time—until I had seen him lingering unchecked on the list. Claire didn't say anything about him, and I certainly couldn't weave him into the conversation without adopting as inelegant a manner as Chester. All I knew about him was that he was Claire's brother, that he had spent time in jail at some point, and that he was in a semi-catatonic state. He could apparently eat what was fed to him, maneuver with assistance from bed to chair, chair to toilet, et cetera.

The one time I mentioned him, Melanie had shrugged and gone aloof. I guessed they hadn't been all that close. Regardless, he was on my list. And while it would have been simple enough to highlight the line and hit DELETE, I had decided I would feel better with a checkmark.

I brought him up not long after the Leesburg dinner night.

"Hey, do you ever visit that uncle of yours?" We were at a burger joint downtown.

She swallowed the bite down hard and sucked some soda through her straw.

"Dom?" she said, grimacing.

"Is that the one that's catatonic?" I said.

Her eyes went wide, pointed down, remained there as she wiped her fingers on a napkin, "What about him?"

"Do you ever see him?" I persisted.

Her hands remained in her lap, "No, not really. Haven't seen him for years, why? What made you think of him … now?" Her tone had turned a bit defensive, cold.

"I don't know, I guess just thinking about family. I feel like you know the bulk of my crazy pack, and I've only just met your mom and dad."

She continued nodding absentmindedly, her eyes traveling all over the table. "Well, I don't visit him unless my parents drag me along. There's not really anyone there to visit. He's just a big … *body*, with a gaping mouth."

Yikes. Talk about cold … she was beginning to sound like me! But I could tell there was more to it than that and ascertained that she had tried to block out the thought of him. They had to have been close when she was growing up, or she wouldn't care either way when his name came up. I would challenge her like a good mate should and push her to address those compartmentalized feelings. Well, that's how I justified it in my head. I really just wanted to know if he was a leaving of mine or not; get the old bastard off of my shrinking list of open items.

"Well, I want us to go visit him," I said with conviction. "Even if he doesn't bat an eye. It's the right thing to do. He's family."

She looked at my eyes, vexed, and perhaps a little sickened. She clearly didn't want to do it. "You're really going to push this?" She said.

"It's decided," I smiled. "When's visitors day?"

She threw up her hands and slid out of the plastic booth.

"Mel, come on! Where are you going?"

She pulled on her coat, slung her purse over her shoulder, and marched outside.

Great. What the fuck happened to "assess and respond?" I had ignored every blatant cue.

I cleaned up the table and brought our fountain drinks outside with me. Melanie was on her phone, pacing on a grassy strip across the parking lot. I started to cross, but she saw me coming and threw up an adamant forefinger. I stopped and watched as she walked in lines and figure eights, talking and listening and crying. I couldn't hear enough words to sort it out or determine who was on the other end of the call. I just stood there, feeling like an idiot. Who would she have called? What if it was Dr. Kalestian? What if I pushed her back to him? What if she had never stopped with him?

After a while, she slowly calmed, said "thanks" and "bye" and put her phone in her purse. She took a deep breath, blotted her eyes with her sleeve, and turned her head toward me. I had been in the same position for ten minutes: standing straight, eyes on her, condensation-soaked cups before me, dripping water over my fingers. She saw that I hadn't moved and blurted out a little laugh, sniffing up a runny nose. She walked to me, shaking her head.

"Are you okay?" I asked. "Who was that? Was it about—"

"I'm fine, babe," she said. "Gimme those before your hands freeze." She took the drinks and nodded me back toward the grass. "That was Mandy. I had to call her."

James's wife? What did *she* have to do with it? What had I missed? Melanie set the cups on a weathered old picnic table and sat down. I remained standing.

She peered up at me, dabbing the residual tears from her face. "All is good now, though, babe. I just thought of something 'cause of what you were saying and she assured me that I was wrong, and so like I said, all's good."

I looked at her dubiously and waited a beat. She pulled out a compact and checked out her eyes in the mirror.

"So that's it?" I said. "I don't get to know what it was you thought about whatever it was you were thinking?"

She snorted and looked up at me, shaking her head. "Yup. We're not having *that* conversation yet."

I didn't like that sentence at all. Not only was it a secret, it was information being consciously kept from me and not others.

"Tell you what, though," she went on. "I'll think about that visit to my uncle. It might ... *ugh* ... it might even be a good idea. I don't know ... I just need to sleep on it, okay?"

We agreed, and I drove us back to my house. She left right away in her own car, back to her apartment. She wanted to sleep there that night.

* * *

Dominic Cammerich (Claire's maiden name) of Leesburg, Virginia. 49 years old, formerly married to Lailah Todd-Cammerich (divorced), corrective lenses required. His driver license had been suspended twice, once for traffic-related warrants, and the second time for DUI at age 24. Now he was "medically ineligible" for a license at all.

His criminal record was interesting: public intoxication at 22, indecent exposure at 27, the notes for which indicated that he was caught masturbating in his car outside a high school yard—worse, apparently, because he had driven there with a suspended license. He seemed to calm down after that bust for which he'd spent three months in County. He wasn't on the convicted sex offender list, so I guessed that the American laws around that were instituted after his offense, and he either kept clean or wasn't caught doing anything through his thirties and forties. Then again, perhaps his shenanigans had ceased when his brain was turned to mush.

I did some math and figured out that Dom was about 17 when I took my original, bullish stroll through the china shop that was Leesburg, and he wasn't in jail until years later. That eliminated any responsibility I might have had in his mental impairment. But I still had a restive curiosity for catatonics, so as long as whatever had triggered Melanie's emotional breakdown was back in its secret dungeon, I would use the opportunity to have a look-see. But *she* would have to bring it up again. And she did.

I got home from work the next day and Melanie's car was in the driveway. Inside, Jaxy came and greeted me at the door with a thorough crotch-sniffing, and I heard pots clang in the kitchen. Melanie, hair tied back in a poofy ponytail, walked to me and gave me a kiss. Green onions and carrots and other vegetables littered the counter. A pot of boiling water steamed on the stove.

"How was your day?" she asked and returned to the cutting board.

"Ordinary. No arrests. You?"

"So-so," she said as she sliced the green onions into tiny rings. "My boss is transferring departments and insisting I go with him. The doctor replacing him is known for being really cool, too, and he's not bringing an assistant with him."

"So what are you going to do?"

"I don't know. I want to stay in my department, but my current boss has a lot of say with the bigwigs. We'll see. I sent a private email to one of them letting her know I like where I am and would prefer to stay."

"Me too," and I would love for that fucker to be in another department away from my lady. Who knew what sorts of things he still tried to pull with her? Occasionally, images of his hairy, flexing ass slamming into her would flash into my head at random moments.

Melanie dumped a box of bowtie pasta into the water and began stirring a pot of cream-colored sauce. It smelled of garlic and parmesan. I wrapped my arms around her waist and kissed the back of her neck.

"Mm …" I said. "Salty."

One of her hands continued mixing while the other crept around to my groin for a quick hello.

"Okay," she said with a cute little smile. "Now get out of here and let me slave over your dinner."

I poured us each a glass of wine, placing one in her hand.

"Anything happening this weekend?" She asked.

"Drycleaners for me, housecleaning ... No real plans. Adventure time?"

"Not really, but we could go see my parents if you want." I nodded affably. "And if you're still interested, and if *I'm* feeling up for it, we could go visit my uncle at the home."

I shrugged it off as completely up to her, suggesting no persisting interest of my own. "Whatever you want. I'm still working on earning your father's blessing, so the more interaction between him and me, the better."

She laughed, "You don't have to worry about his approval. And be careful with evocative words like 'blessing', lest people get the wrong idea."

I lifted an eyebrow and smirked at this. The idea wasn't wrong. I would have married her that weekend.

* * *

A Dominican caretaker in a white uniform led us to Melanie's uncle. He sat in a wheelchair in a bright sunroom, staring outside at the facility's garden and autumn-leaved trees in the distance. There was no one else in the room, only white wicker furniture and assorted magazines on glass-topped tables. Fake trees with dusty leaves bookended the sofas. The caretaker rested a hand on his shoulder, leaned over and spoke to him as if he could understand.

"Mr. Cammerich, your daughter is here to see you."

"Niece," I said, and the woman offered an apologetic face and corrected herself to Uncle Dom before leaving us.

I sat down on an aging ottoman in front of him while Melanie remained standing a few feet behind him. I nodded her toward the wicker sofa but she shook her head and gnawed on a thumbnail. She was entirely closed off—an arm across her chest, one leg in front of the other.

I turned to Dom and looked at his face. He was a big man, but not fat. His condition afforded him no exercise, though—not even facial muscles—so his skin hung as if barely attached. He had no visible jawline; his cheeks melted down into his neck. Even several feet away I could smell his sick breath, as if his insides were slowly dying. This was the scent of not-quite-dead. It was also like sitting face-to-face with the embodiment of a lifelong nightmare. What if I were one day trapped in a body such as this? Able to see and hear the outside world, thoughts clear, but completely paralyzed and viewed as a vegetable by others? That's a hell worthy of a demon, is it not? It would seem like kismet for it to all end that way.

I leaned in front of him and looked at his eyes. They didn't seem the same as the rocking man in the house. These eyes had nothing behind them, no small movements. While residing in a body I could hardly see the waves of energy emanating from people, but they were still there like a subtle aura, stronger in some than others. Dom had nothing. He was empty, and therefore nothing for Melanie to fear.

"Dom?" I said. "Hi there. I'm Joseph … Joey. I'm your niece's boyfriend. We came here to visit you." No response, of course. But I wanted to show Melanie that as he was, he would always be (and that I was a really good guy). "Melanie is here. Would you like to see her?" I gestured for her to come around him, but she glared at me and shook her head.

I moved to the sofa beside him, a short distance away, and looked out at the flowers and occasional falling leaf. I sat there in silence and wondered what that looked like to Melanie, standing back there. Two heads, still and facing away from her: one belonging to a person she once knew and loved, the other the most important person in her life. That's truly what I was to her, I decided, and the contrast before her must have only highlighted that fact. I was alive, real, wonderful, now.

I suddenly spotted her in my peripheral. She was slinking slowly around Dom's wheelchair, a keen eye on his face. Standing there for a beat, brow locked, she gazed at Dom's unchanging face. Then she leaned over, slid the ottoman directly in front of him, and sat. She adjusted position until her eyes met his. I turned my face away as if I wasn't watching, but kept my eyes on them. After a moment, she spoke.

"Hey."

She waited, apparently verifying he wasn't going to respond. She took another deep breath.

"It's been a long time. You probably have no concept of time, but I haven't come here for years. And before that, just once or twice with my mom. I ..." she paused and looked past him down the main hall. Other residents floated past attached to walkers with tennis balls on the feet. She lowered her voice to a whisper. "I don't *care* that I haven't been here."

Well, that wasn't the sentiment I had expected.

She went on, "I don't think about you. I have an *amazing* life."

I swallowed and turned away, for real this time. This was a moment. A major, real-life event for her. I couldn't simply sit by and watch it, analyze it, bask in the revelation of it. It was touching and heartbreaking and real.

I glanced back at them. Melanie took a deep breath, formulated her next thought, leaned a little closer, "You didn't leave a mark or—"

"I-ON-ASEE!" Dom's right hand had suddenly raised off his knee and he spoke in a deep, throaty voice. Spittle flung out from the sides of his mouth, droplets striking Melanie's face at the same time as his voice. She recoiled and screamed, and I jumped, too.

Dom's hand dropped and began clutching his knee like a stress ball, as he slowly repeated every few seconds, from deep within his chest, "I-on-asee! I-on-asee!"

Melanie and I had both stood up, she with her hands curled before her mouth, backed up against the glass wall. She was still in his line of sight and so she stumbled sideways to escape his view, sliding against the glass several feet. Dom's vacant eyes remained where they had been. His hand slowed its repetitive motion and his chant lowered to a quiet murmur as drool streamed down to his collar.

"I need to get the fuck out of here," she said and charged out of the room.

I stayed for a moment, observing Dom. Within a minute, he had entirely reverted to his inert state. I wondered what had set him off—if it was Melanie's presence, scent, her words, or did we just happen upon a randomly timed outburst that would have occurred with or without anyone in attendance to witness it. I knelt in front of him, his wide irises oblivious to the burning sunlight pouring in.

"What did you do, Dom?"

* * *

I found Melanie outside smoking a cigarette next to the Land Rover.

"I didn't know you smoke," I said.

"Haven't for a decade. I bummed one from a landscaper. Don't fuck with me about it, either. It's just one."

"I wasn't going to say anything more about it. And I'm not going to ask you if you're okay. That would be stupid. And I don't expect you to tell me what he did to you until you're ready … if ever. All right?"

She managed a small, appreciative smile, twisted her sandal over the cigarette butt, and we got in the car.

We drove back toward Frederick, silent, Melanie staring out her window. My mind returned to Dom. I thought again about what might have triggered him back there. If he were truly the shell of a person—the machine without the driver—would he not be truly lifeless? But then I thought of all the other animals in the world, and how most of which have no such sentient "driver" either. They are animate heaps of digestive and sensory organs. They typically sense danger or environmental changes long before people, unburdened by the distraction of human thoughts or feelings. To these creatures there are events, perceptions, actions. That is all. For a human, to turn off the conscious brain is to become a lower beast...but with millions of years of species-specific instinct. I think human instincts seem to be fairly limited these days, sequestered behind much louder logical thought, but primal instincts developed millions of years ago to insure their species' very survival. And my theory is they're still in there, despite evolution and ages of enlightenment, manifesting in interesting ways.

I hypothesized that Dom was indeed an unconscious shell, but that his instincts were still intact. He sensed Melanie's presence and his body had come to life. His grasping hand, in my theory, was squeezing a breast or ass; his droning gibberish, "i-on-asee" sounded to me like a toddler chanting "I want to see." It was like a leftover prehistoric command: female close ... attack! The caretaker hadn't seemed to inspire this reaction, though. If I were to draw conclusions from the man's criminal record, Melanie's words and behavior, and my own supposition, the obvious assumption would be that he had at some point molested her.

I wanted to put a hand on her leg, but I was too afraid that she'd jump and close off and form some sort of horrible, subconscious association between her uncle and me. *Shit, what if that's exactly what I had done?* I thought. I kept my hands to myself and my mouth shut until I followed the interchange onto eastbound Highway 340 and Frederick's road signs began to appear.

"You want to stay at your place or mine?" I asked.

She took a deep breath and looked about, reentering the world around her. The sun had set behind us and car lights shone in our faces.

"I want to be with *you*," she said. "You, and you alone. I don't care where."

She put her hand on my leg and I crossed my arm over hers and did the same. I can, to this day, recall no more gratifying words than those.

10. Threats

In the middle of the night my phone vibrated somewhere beside me. I blinked and groped for it in the dark. Beside me, Melanie moaned like she was having a bad dream. I found my phone and brought it to my face. On the display, a foreboding alert:

Incoming Call - James Cell.

I tapped ANSWER and slunk out of bed, hurrying toward the bathroom.

I whispered, "Hello? James?"

"What are you doing?" he asked. His tone was flat, almost depressed.

"I was sleeping, like the rest of the people in this time zone. What are *you* doing?"

"Mandy told me that Melanie called the other day, upset. She was asking if either of us had told you about her uncle."

I was still foggy, trying to wake up. I closed the door behind me and sat down on the closed toilet lid.

"And what did you say?"

"Mandy lied and told her we haven't said anything. I was supposed to call you that night to make sure the three of us were on the same page with that. But ... I didn't."

"Oh, okay, right," I said.

"But you have no idea what I'm talking about. So it doesn't really matter, does it?" Now he truly sounded low, defeated.

"Why wouldn't I have ... ah, whatever. So why are you calling me now? At one a.m.?"

"I need to talk to you. Meet up somewhere."

"All right, sure," I said. "Just tell me where and when."

"You're not even *trying* to do his voice anymore," he said.

Fuck.

"I don't know what you're talking about, James. Like I said, I'm trying to sleep here and willing to meet—"

"I can't believe you've had sex with her."

"Excuse me?" I said.

"That's like rape, essentially."

"You are way out of line, James. Keep this up and you are cut off for fucking ever, you hear me?"

"Same thing as me showing up and seducing her, pretending to be Joseph. Some stranger off the street in a very convincing Joseph mask. No different."

I wanted to hang up more than anything. I was clutching my phone so hard in my hand that I heard the bezel begin to crack. My pulse throbbed in my thumbs. He actually *knew*. How the hell would he know?

"Why haven't you hung up on me?" He finally said.

"I'll let you dig your grave as deep as you like, James. It hurts me to lose you, but a person can only take so much abuse."

"That's funny," he said with a weak little chuckle. "Listen ... I want you to leave. I want you to leave him and never come back."

"Really."

"Yes. He'll have a pretty lengthy memory loss, and things will be tough for him for a while, but amnesia can be explained by medical issues ... trauma. Just ... just go now. Every day you stay will make it harder for him to recuperate."

I wondered, did James have some knowledge of demons and their workings? But it occurred to me that he didn't actually have a clue what I was or how I worked. If he was thinking of a demon at all it was of some caricature plucked from the old school mythology. Some wily, horned servant of Satan. Evil spirits and exorcists. He thought I could simply leave and all would be well in his world.

"Sorry, James, still not really sure what madness you're talking about, but I'm not going anywhere. This is my home and this is my life and if you're not in it, so be it. Night."

I hung up. I washed my face with cold water. I went downstairs and outside into the back yard with Jaxy and looked up at the stars and Milky Way. Jaxy peed while I went over the whole conversation in my head. Then my phone vibrated in my pajama pocket.

It was a text from James: Baker park. By the carillon. Tomorrow morning at 10.

* * *

I found James sitting on a bench, arms crossed and staring at the bell tower memorializing Baker Park's namesake. Beyond the small, fast-moving white clouds, the autumn sky was an intense blue. He squinted up at me, his face scrunched with seeming apprehension. A thin wall of comb-over hair rose and fell as the wind broadsided his head. Beyond him, a marathon of curled, brown maple leaves skipped and tripped over each other like nimble little starfish.

I waited for him to speak.

"You have no guilt, do you?" He said. I stared at him. "You have no fear of facing me because you don't believe you've done anything wrong."

"I have no fear of facing you because this ... *problem*, whatever it is, is yours, not mine."

"You basically just answered 'yes' to my question."

I sighed. "I'm not going to stand here and listen to you drone on. If you want to talk, let's talk."

He smiled with a nasty little sneer and snorted, shaking his head at me.

"You certainly are a piece of work," he said. "So who am I talking to?"

I looked at him and tilted my head.

He went on, "Fine, you don't want to answer that one. As you're clearly determined to avoid confirming anything that you and I both already know, I'll simply speak the facts and tell you a little bit about myself."

"Sounds like a plan." I said and sat down at the end of the bench. He scooted a few inches further from me.

"When my brother and I were kids, our school took us on a field trip to a courthouse in Leesburg, where Melanie is from."

Oh, shit.

"There was a girl in my class that I liked … and she liked me. She was the closest thing to a girlfriend, I suppose, that a kid that age could have … had known her since kindergarten or first grade. Her name was Morgan Lampey, and I witnessed firsthand when a lost spirit—a daimon—entered her body." His eyes remained keenly focused on my face as he spoke. I maintained a straight face, but the voice in my head said *shit, shit, shit, shit* … He went on, "We were 'buddies' and so we were holding hands like everyone else had to. But for me, and maybe for her, we were secretly holding hands because we were a couple." With a small smile his eyes moved with the rolling maple leaves. "But suddenly, walking along a paved path in front of the courthouse, she squeezed my fingers so tight it hurt and I yanked my hand away. When I looked at her, she was standing still and tense—the sort of posture you'd see from someone just drenched with a bucket of water over their head. She looked at me, then to a kid in front of her who had said something. And then she spoke. She spoke with the voice of another person. She sounded like a boy with a marble in his mouth. I couldn't even tell you what she said because I was so frightened."

At first I stared at him as if it was the first time hearing this story, but then realized that Joseph would have already known it, only from a different perspective.

"Right, sure, go on," I said.

"A few weeks later, the daimon left her body, leaving her comatose, vegetative."

'Day-mon' … Why does he pronounce it that way?

"It was obviously a big thing all over town, this girl that had some 'accident' and was brain damaged. But me and Joseph, the other kids in our class, our teacher, had all seen the changes in her after the field trip. Her parents had pulled her out after that, and I didn't see her again for years."

"But you did see her again?" I blurted. James looked at me, smug.

"Yes, when we were sixteen. Her parents had kept her alive all that time, hoping that she'd miraculously come back. When I saw her she looked nothing like herself—nothing like a person, even. She looked like that painting, *The Scream.*" He zoned out for another moment, that image clearly on his eyes, before resuming. "A few months later, for some unknown, uninvestigated reason, she died."

I swallowed. I was never proud of Morgan. I never said I was proud of Morgan.

James took a deep breath, glanced around, and resumed. "Anyway, about the time that Morgan went from possessed to catatonic, a clerk at the Library of Congress named Ulysses Tselikas was, remarkably, stricken in the exact same manner as Morgan. He was found face-down on a sidewalk near Morgan's parents' house, unresponsive. And then there was the detention center."

He shook his admonishing head at me. I wasn't pleased with his recounting of my wild, youthful phase. For some reason, when *he* talked about it, it sounded awfully sinister.

"Needless to say," he went on, "this sort of thing happening in a small town—hell, happening *anywhere* in this country—it gets a lot of attention. Everyone in Frederick knew about the comas and panicked about the next round of afflictions. 'Who's next?' was all anyone was thinking. Parents kept their kids home from our school. The Sheriff's office was evacuated, closed down for over a month while they searched for chemicals—some sort of toxic contaminants in the water supply. A lot of families left Frederick. We had some good friends move away, out of state even."

So *I* was the big town health scare my father had told me about at his anniversary party! *I* was apparently the reason James had stopped worrying our parents. He had seen me in person, in his friend, Morgan—scared straight, as Dad said. Now he knew I was back.

"This was a pretty life-defining time for me, as you might imagine. I spent good portions of my teenage years and twenties studying, reading everything I could about entities like you. And I figured out you must have just been starting out back then, considering the trail you left. I know you flew to Holland—the pilot whose last flight left from Dulles a couple days after the Sherriff's office—but I couldn't find a trail beyond him."

I sighed and questioned the point of continuing to play innocent. He knew everything and had no doubts whatsoever. And to acknowledge that which he already knew ... well, perhaps I *could* learn something from him. I could use his lack of firsthand knowledge to raise his defenses. Subtly introducing the threat of possessing his wife or one of his children could keep him neatly in line and out of my business.

A young couple with a dog approached and we were silent for a moment. As they neared, the dog started flipping out, barking at us. I guess I wasn't completely free of that issue. They yanked the animal back and apologized. I turned back to James.

"This is a great review, James, but I'm still struggling to find a point ... or what it is that you want?"

"I want you to leave!" He shouted, stabbing a finger out in the air. "I want you to fucking go! Give me back my brother before too much time has passed! Before you've ruined *everything* about his life!"

I made up my mind.

"James, listen to me. This is going to be very difficult for you to accept." I waited for him to look me in the eyes. "Your brother is gone, and will never come back. You're under the false impression that a ... *being* ... such as me can arrive, can ... *take over*, and then leave without serious ... *complications*. This simply isn't the case. Those people you mentioned—the catatonic ones—they are the inevitable remains of being occupied. There is no graceful departure. Your brother was dead the second I got here. I'm sorry."

He stared at me, uncomprehending. It was a harsh reality to accept and he sat there, stunned for a moment before closing his eyes and shaking his head and rubbing his forehead with his palms. He mumbled quietly and then suddenly popped his head back up.

"No!" He yelled. "No! What you're saying is bullshit! You're trying to tell me that this … this supposed 'inevitable' result of possession is just 'the way these things work' but I'm not buying it. That's your *choice*, to leave like that. You just don't *want* to leave, I get it! You're in love with Melanie and you have every intention to stay in Joey's body until you tire of it. But I'm telling you that you don't have a fucking choice! You leave, and you put my brother back!"

I shook my head, "I wish that was the case, but it's not. Once in, there are only two endings. Stay until the body dies, or leave and the mind is left empty. I think I know this a bit better than someone who has read a couple books written by those without first-hand experience."

The skin on his face slowly drooped and morphed into an expression of utter despair. Reality appeared to be setting in. He looked like someone just informed of a loved one's passing. Well, I suppose that's precisely what had happened. Tears welled up and his mouth hung open.

"You … no … you don't even know. Never cared to learn… I …" He spoke quietly as the tears rolled down his cheeks. The clouds continued to roll by, intermittent sunlight shining down on us. Finally he said something coherent: "Do you even know what you are?"

I snorted a little. "I'm reasonably certain I know better than you. But it doesn't matter. I told you it wouldn't be easy news. I'm going to go now." I stood up. "And do keep this conversation to yourself. You most definitely do not want to share any of what we discussed with Melanie or anyone else."

He shot up onto his feet and moved close to me, spat his words around gnashed teeth, "I'll tell her if you don't go! I'll tell her everything!"

I smiled. "As I said, you definitely don't want to do that. Let's leave it there." I turned to go.

"She'll believe me!" He shouted. "If I tell her when it happened! She'll remember all the changes! I'll tell her what to ask you that you wouldn't be able to answer. I'll tell her about the little girl you destroyed, the library clerk, all of the others—countless people I don't even know about!"

I sighed and turned back to him, speaking calmly, "You don't want to do that because you've already lost your brother. How many other loved ones would you be willing to lose just to have me go, leaving the shell of your brother's body to live out a non-life as a vegetable? Because if I do go, James ... I'll *have* to make a few brief stops on the way out of town."

"You ..." he was beyond incensed. His body quaked, his jaw clenched so hard it looked as though he would smash his teeth. He whispered, "You truly are evil. You are the fucking devil on Earth."

I had to laugh at the histrionics. He was rightfully upset, but his threats had put me at arms.

"That's just silly, James," I said. "Evil is the product of ancient shamans and modern storytellers. It isn't actually a real thing."

"It is absolutely real, and to see it standing before me is truly chilling."

"You're distraught and don't know what to do with your emotions. This is very normal. But don't let our interaction today nudge you into some nonsensical superstitious realm. To call me evil is a bit dramatic, and the very concept ... so old timey. This person tenting their fingers, strumming them together as they plot dastardly schemes. I would think that to be *evil*, that archetype, a person would have to say to themselves, 'You know what? I'm going to be evil today.' And that simply doesn't happen. People will always justify their actions to come out right in the end. And that's not evil, just selfish."

James had calmed a bit but his voice still quavered. He took a step closer to me. "Dieter Manbach defined evil with a diagram of a sliding scale. 'Evil' on the left side, 'Good' in the middle, 'Pure' on the right. The scale slid based upon motives: self or others. Balancing one's motives between for-self and for-others is *good*. Entirely for others is *pure*. Entirely selfish...not a single act or thought of another person...well, that's the epitome of *evil*."

My brain stumbled for a beat, but he was wrong, "I do things for other people all the time."

"But really for *them*? *Really*? In the end, who is the act actually for? Think about it … when have you ever, in your life, done something for someone that wasn't, in the end, for yourself?"

I had no answer. I was certain there were countless examples, I simply couldn't access any at that moment. He had me second guessing every single thing I'd ever done. My silence gave him the impression he had "won" our argument, and he turned and walked away, still irate, yet self-satisfied.

I sat back down on the bench cursing James for assaulting my consciousness with these sorts of thoughts and self-doubt. I scoured my memory for every instance of my good, if not *pure* acts, while maintaining convicted reassurance that none of it mattered anyway. I am a fucking demon and this is what I do.

11. The Doctor

Melanie was particularly raw after our visit to Uncle Dom. Quiet and pensive, distracted and not completely there, she wanted only to be near me on the couch watching TV, to be spooned in bed. I obliged her every need and focused on this time being for her and not for me, all the while denying that James's suggestion had any bearing. I was not an *entirely* selfish being. James could not rile me, I insisted. I would not allow him in my head. But merely thinking this confirmed the opposite. He had become a giant enflamed taste bud, scraping against my teeth whenever I relaxed.

And then Melanie wanted to spend more time alone, at her place.

I wasn't pleased with her absence and was truly concerned. But with my evenings empty, I used the rare opportunity to accept Scott Lieter's repeated invites to after-work drinks with some of the other guys.

We left our cars at work and walked to an Irish pub in Downtown Frederick. It had a dark atmosphere, sticky floor, and smelled of spilled beer, urine, or both. They spent the first half hour "giving me shit" and buying me reckless quantities of alcohol.

Joseph was not a drinker, I discovered—the most I had drunk in this body had been two glasses of wine, at home with Melanie. And as I later found, Joseph *never* went drinking with the boys. Scott and the others quickly seized upon my uncharacteristic willingness to not only drink, but drink whatever was put in front of me. I was thoroughly sloshed in short time, made to play numerous, shamefully poor rounds of darts for the entertainment of all present, and then sent on a number of dares involving innocent patrons of the bar.

I was made to ask the bartender for a maraschino cherry, return to our table, then go back for another, then another, one per minute for ten minutes, until his good humor turned to annoyance. He pulled out the jar, poured me twenty cherries with juice into a glass and said, "That's all your cherries, boss. I'm fucking working, awright?"

This was a real hoot for my group. Next they sent me for a slice of lime. Fortunately, the bartender laughed, shook his head as he dropped the wedge into my palm, and I had the good sense to turn down Scott's order to request a second.

"Okay, Joey. Joey, Joey ... Joey. Joe." Scott said in my ear, loud, but with a tone as if whispering. His arm draped over my neck, he pointed with his pint glass. He repeated my name countless times before I looked him square in the eye. "Hot young thing near the taps. You tell her you're a cop. You show her your gun. Then you tell her you want to protect her tonight."

I nodded. The request sounded reasonable at first, but then some small sober part of my brain got hold of it and I laughed in his face. "That's fucking stupid!" I laughed.

"No," he replied, almost hurt—shocked at my dismissive response to what was surely genius at work. He just needed to tell me slower. You know, so I would understand. "Joey. Listen. You tell her she's a cop ... no. You tell her *you're* a cop and that you want to *protect* her. I'm fucking serious, bro."

"Oh," I said dramatically. "Now I got it. Yeah, that's fucking brilliant. Watch my moves." Scott smiled his relief as I stood up from the table and focused on walking straight and sure. My vision wasn't spinning, but it felt like my brain was definitely doing so inside.

As I neared the bar, the woman in dire need of my protection came into clearer view. She was sitting next to another young woman—both appeared to be in their early twenties. I stopped a short distance behind my assigned target and checked myself out. Shirt tucked in, fly zipped, shoes tied. I was a good-looking man. I wasn't sure what my goal was.

Moreover, I wasn't thinking about Melanie, or how my behavior would appear to her or anyone that knew her.

"I beg your pardon," I said, and the woman finished speaking a sentence to her friend before turning around and looking me over.

"Yeah? Hi," she said. She was indeed cute, playful. Bleach-blond with thin streaks of black. Her loose top hung off one shoulder.

"I was wondering if anyone was sitting here," I said. I was trying to sound respectful and charming, but I suspect it came out very stiff and official, because she responded in a deep voice with pursed lips and a frown.

"No, sir, there is no one sitting in this seat. Would *you* like to sit in this seat, sir?"

"I believe I would," I said in her tone and both girls laughed.

I sat down and introduced myself, though not as a police officer, and not as Joey, or even Joseph.

"Nice to meet you, Frederick," she said. "That's funny they named you that. Bet kids fucked with you nonstop. My name's Isis. This is Savannah." The friend waved, clearly a little irritated by my presence.

"How old are you?" Savannah asked me.

"Alarmingly old," I said. "But I'm not trying to hit on either of you, so don't worry."

"Really?" Isis said with an intrigued smirk. "What *are* you trying to do?"

"I'm trying to escape from my so-called friends who won't be happy until I have alcohol poisoning and am spewing all over the place."

They laughed, Savannah relaxed, and I noticed Isis giving me another look, as though reassessing.

"You have a funny accent," Isis said. She had gorgeous eyes framed by impossibly long eyelashes. "Are you European or something?"

"I've lived all over, but I'm from around here. Where are you from?"

"Upstate New York," she said and swallowed the end of her cosmo. "Where I'm headed back tomorrow."

At some point, I noticed that Savannah had disappeared and it was just Isis and I talking. I bought Isis a number of drinks and eventually we started on relationships. She had a boyfriend—pretty serious, or so she said. They had tried "playing house" for several months before both of them sensed that they needed space apart. And last week, Isis's father called from New York.

"I've been working at the Smithsonian," she explained and handed me her business card. Isis Meier – Museum Specialist. "And he runs the museum up there. They've had tons of artifacts pouring in from this big Viking find in Rhode Island—you know, the thing on the news—and now that I have real experience from down here, he can't get bitched at for nepotism if he brings me in. It's where all my friends are anyway …"

"So you're moving?" I asked, and she nodded. "And what about your boyfriend?" She shrugged, looked down at her empty glass, and then back up at my eyes.

"You wanna get out of here, or what?" She said, grabbing her purse off the bar and looking around.

I wasn't expecting that. I had sobered up a bit and was simply enjoying speaking with an attractive young woman. Not to mention continuing to dodge the nonsense that was happening at the back of the bar. My coworkers had grown progressively louder for the past hour and several glasses had been broken.

Now, to be completely honest, I had developed a sudden raging erection. Isis stood up off the bar stool, brushing against me, and I stood up after her. It seemed almost involuntary. My hand in her wrist, we walked outside into the chilly November night. I tried to think clearly; I tried to resist the blaring howl of the primitive cavedemon inside.

"Isis, hang on a second," I said. Her arm stretched out from me as she continued to walk, but I pulled her gently to stop. Her body flung out, almost tilted over into the gutter, then landed back in my arms. She kissed me with a loose, sloppy mouth, and her hand found what I had hiding in my trousers.

"Oh shit," she said, giggling. "Someone's ready." Her eyes were closed, but she faced me as if looking directly at my face.

"Isis, just a second. Where are we going, exactly?"

She frowned and opened her eyes. "Yeah. Right!" She curled her mouth into a contemplative scrunch and looked around. "You live around here?"

"Not really," I said, keenly aware that she was absentmindedly stroking the bulge in my pants as she looked around. It made it difficult for me to focus.

"Well, my boyfriend's apartment is one block up, one block over."

"Are you serious?"

"Yeah, he's not around. His parents took him and his sister on a cruise. They're halfway to the Bahamas right now. It's safe. Let's go."

And then I was sober. I pulled her hand gently away from my crotch, kissed her on the forehead, and said "Goodnight."

"Wait ..." She called after me, but I had no desire to turn back. "Fred?" Had I really told her my name was Frederick? Was her tongue really just in my mouth? I had come so terrifyingly close to having sex with another woman that I began to sweat beneath my polo shirt in the sub-forty-degree night air. I don't know if it was guilt at that point, but it was most certainly fear: fear of losing Melanie. There was zero reason for me to do anything with anyone else, and every reason for me to remain faithful to her.

I spotted a white DC cab dropping off a passenger in front of an apartment building and ran across the street to block its path. The driver leaned out his window and said "Help you?"

"I need a ride to near Hood College, on your way out."

He waved me in and took me home. It only took a few minutes to get there, but it felt much longer. Worse, I began to panic that Melanie would be at my house, waiting by the door, asking where I'd been, whose perfume is that, or that she'd instantly reach down my pants and somehow detect conclusive evidence of a recent hard-on.

Her car wasn't in front or in the driveway, but who knew? What if she'd gotten a ride? What if she parked around the corner for some unprecedented, illogical reason? I was paranoid until I'd checked every single room. Jaxy followed at my heels the entire time. She smelled Isis on me, that was certain. But she wasn't judging; she just wanted her goddamned dinner. It was 1:30am. She must have been starving.

Jaxy fed, clothes dumped straight into washer (pocket coins, receipts, and all), I walked naked from the laundry room up the stairs to the shower. My head still buzzed as I vowed never to drink again. How many times have people made *that* particular pledge? And I wasn't even lying on the cold tile, embracing a toilet full of vomit.

In bed I lay nude and sweating, chaotically bouncing from moment to moment of the evening's events. Drink after drink, Scott's wicked, scheming expressions, young Isis kneading me like a roll of dough. As if she was there in the bed beside me, I found myself once again at attention. I was compelled to get it out of my system. Perhaps a manual release would purge these evil deeds from my mind and body. I worked at it for a couple minutes, but my mind began to race again.

I conjured Isis's face inside my eyelids, her sloppy kiss, my hands on her waist, creeping up to small, perky breasts I never made it to ... or did I? Her lips that never made it down to join her hand over my slacks ... or did they? Button unbuttoned, zipper unzipped, she looked up at me with just her eyes, and then her eyes became Melanie's, and my pubic hair turned black and bushy. She was Melanie and I was Dr. Andrew. She was depressed and falling back on an old routine. And why wouldn't she? She knew I wasn't the real Joseph, the one she truly loved. And into my head came the real memory of the doctor slamming into her like a pile driver. Melanie's enraptured, hair-entangled face. The doctor's hairy back and ass, flexing, pumping.

I soon noticed that my erection sat shriveled in my hand like a deflated balloon. My stomach gave me a subtle warning—a mildly stinging sourness. I rolled on my side and my gut counseled me to get to the toilet at once. I barely made it, but all vomit found its way into the bowl, and soon I found myself there after all, curled up around the base of the toilet, my naked body relishing the coolness of the tile and porcelain.

* * *

I awoke to Kiki the cat sniffing my lips with his cold nose. I once heard that they do that to see if you're dead, the next step being to take a bite, shortly followed by consuming you, their beloved owner. I suppose if this was the case, all those reclusive cat ladies found dead in their homes would have been skeletonized, but perhaps they simply don't publish those grisly details. I pushed the cat away from my face.

My neck and back were stiff and warped, my head vised with pain. I walked downstairs with one eye cracked open, put on a pot of coffee, and winced back upstairs into the shower.

I forced down some dry toast with coffee, drank a full glass of water, fed the animals, and rushed to the downstairs lavatory for a startling bout of explosive diarrhea. I fell back asleep on the couch in the middle of a fortunately-DVR'd forensic drama show.

Rising again, far less zombie-like, I discovered half of Saturday had passed. I switched yesterday's clothes into the dryer, found my phone on top of the washer, and checked my texts and emails. Nothing from Melanie. In fact, nothing from Melanie in three days. My stomach suddenly hardened with a new dread. I thought back to her last words to me: "I just need some time alone." I had taken it at face value: she wanted to be alone at home for a couple days. It had nothing to do with me. I was the understanding boyfriend saying "take all the time you need!" But how often did women say things to their men that were intended to be taken at face value? I estimated this to be the case about eleven percent of the time. What she was really saying was "I think we need some time apart," and I essentially agreed, sending her the message that I wasn't happy either, because women mistakenly assume that eighty-nine percent of their men's words have a deeper meaning!

Isis and her boyfriend had decided to "take time apart," a charade of an agreement that means one or the other or both are too afraid to break up, and likely have someone else in mind they've been wanting to fuck. Good God, I thought, I've left her with that message for three straight days!

I immediately sent her a text message, "How are you doing, my love? I miss you."

Several minutes passed, and I finally received a response: "I'm OK. Can't talk right now."

That's the message she sends after three days of nothing? I tried to calm myself, speculate on legitimate reasons why that message could be wholly benign. I had made the first contact, and now it was on her to get back to me. She could have been scrubbing a floor, about to get her hair done, at a movie. I reread the message in her cheerful voice and suddenly my anxiety was silly. But then I read it again in the most foreboding, cold voice I could muster for her.

I got dressed, grabbed my company car keys, and blasted out the door to go stake out her apartment from the street. The sedan was so nondescript that it would blend with the random blur of cars which lined the streets around her apartment complex.

Ten minutes later I found a spot behind another newer white sedan. I parked beneath the shade of a sunset-toned sugar maple and reclined my seat back. From my vantage point I could see her second-story front door, and that her car wasn't in her carport. She rarely worked weekends. I grabbed some ibuprofen from my glovebox and dry swallowed it.

I remained there for the rest of the day, alternating between playing on my phone and blankly staring at a couple loading their rented truck with an apartment's worth of furniture. Melanie showed up just after dusk. She took in a couple small bags of groceries and a few plastic-draped outfits from the dry cleaner. I wondered how long it would be before she texted me back, or even called.

I got hungry around 7:00, starving by 8:00, and left to go get some fast food. I hadn't planned out how long I would stay, but decided that midnight would work. I'd go home at midnight. Melanie typically got tired around 11:00.

Nothing interesting happened (that I could see, anyway), nor did she call or text me. I drove home at a quarter to midnight. Once in bed, I lay there stewing, purged of all guilt about Isis. What was Melanie up to, and why was I suddenly a mere annoyance? How had I become so demoted in her heart and mind that I was unworthy of even a text message?

I got only a few hours of sleep, rose with the sun, and by 7:30 found myself in the same parking spot outside her apartment. It began raining at some point before noon, bucketing by 1:00. My only glimpse of Melanie that Sunday was when she came out in a tank top and pajama bottoms, carrying two white trash bags to the communal dumpster. She wasn't wearing a bra and the rain quickly drenched her clothes, sticking them to her body. As she shuffled back to her stairs, clutching her arms against her chest, I suddenly felt a great sinking despair. If I were in her apartment when she came in looking like that, I would have seen her and instantly ravaged her body. I lamented the fact that I hadn't until then seen her in clothes and soaking wet.

The thought occurred to me that I could simply go and knock on her door right that second. Say, "Hey, I've been worried about you, how are you … oh my, look at you …" and then we would make insane love, climaxing all the more powerfully for our lull. But this idea was quickly naysaid, replaced by the image of her perturbed face at the door. She says, "What are *you* doing here?" This is the imagined face that stayed with me as fat raindrops plopped on my windshield from the enormous tree above.

In the early evening, I went to a drive-through. I soon returned to my street parking and ate, the food making me feel as bad physically as I did mentally. A couple hours later, a very expensive sports car pulled into the complex and parked in a visitor spot near Melanie's car.

* * *

I watched Dr. Andrew Kalestian, in his trench coat and shiny shoes, splash across the lot and up the steps to Melanie's door. Panic struck hard. How long had she been carrying on with him again? Had it just restarted or never stopped? Could there be some other reasonable explanation?

I grabbed my phone and tapped out a text. When I looked up, he was stepping into her apartment and she closed the door behind him. I had written: "Melanie, I'm still worried about you. Been waiting for you to get back to me. Can I come over now so we can talk?"

Five agonizing minutes passed and I opened my car door, stinging rain blasting from above. I had to go confront her. I had to stop whatever was happening. My phone chirped and I slammed the door.

"Not tonight," she'd written. "Let's talk tomorrow, ok?"

My face and neck began to burn as I crumpled into my seat. The fact that she'd written me back at all suggested they weren't doing anything yet, but her words told me she considered herself unavailable for the evening—that she couldn't even *talk* to me. I stopped trying to soothe myself with absurd notions of sensible explanations. That man would be inside her tonight. The question was what would I do about it?

A thought suddenly occurred to me. If that asshole didn't pursue her, she probably wouldn't seek him out. I witnessed firsthand her reticence and reluctant placation. I wished I could erase him and return to my body, but I wasn't willing to risk it. The thought crossed my mind that I could simply kill him, but I'd never murdered anyone before ... technically. Besides what I knew from television and movies, I had no clue how to do it cleanly and avoid becoming a suspect. It wasn't as though he was a complete stranger to me. Even assuming I could somehow leave no forensically detectable traces, cops always look first for people connected to the victim. If a single other person knew of his affair with Melanie, that would put me very much in the lens of a detective's magnifying glass. Then there was the James factor. I could see no way to get away with it.

Ah, but I do not accept defeat so easily, and the woman I loved was in the process of being aggressively fucked no more than one hundred yards from me. The relentless rain pounded on my car and I wondered if my work gear in the trunk was safe and dry. My work gear ...

I began to plot the perfect crime. I had already sent a text message to Melanie stating my desire to come over. My text history showed I had been trying desperately to reach her. I decided to just go to her place, but when I got there, I saw a man exiting her door. No, better! I heard the gut-wrenching sounds of their lovemaking through the door, went back to my car, distraught.

I cried there for a short time before I saw the man leave her apartment. I followed him home and confronted him as he exited his vehicle. He admitted to having an affair with her, and in a blind rage I beat him with my steel baton. I didn't mean to kill him! I couldn't control myself ... in fact the memories of that night are fuzzy and distorted. Temporary insanity plea wins.

I wanted very badly to search the internet for Maryland's laws on the matter, but that would be in my history as well, and show premeditation. I knew it had to appear entirely spontaneous. Hopefully, the doctor didn't live an hour away.

Roughly thirty minutes from the time he entered, Dr. Kalestian exited Melanie's apartment. This timing was consistent with their previous relations I had witnessed. He closed the door behind himself, with no sign of Melanie in the doorway. I guessed that she was in the bathroom, cleaning his leavings off of her legs or chest or face. As he pulled out of the lot, all organized thought of my scheme left my head. I followed him, but I was not playing the part of the jilted, jealous boyfriend. I was simply raging, infuriated, and had nothing else in my mind but his blood pouring from his devastated face and collapsed skull.

Few cars drove the shining wet streets, so I followed him from a distance. We turned onto the highway for a few miles and exited on a little-used road. Of course, the man lived in one of the most expensive areas around Frederick, where a private drive leads through acres of land before even seeing a house!

I saw his brake lights far up ahead and I shut off my lights before his disappeared to the right. I drove up closer and saw a tall brick wall bordering his property, the dark crowns of treetops overhung a wrought iron fence along the top. I got out of the car, quietly closed the door, and fetched my expanding steel baton from the trunk. Fortunately, he wasn't so pretentious as to have a huge, monogramed gate at the driveway entrance. I craned my neck around the corner and saw his lights shine across the face of a large white house before the car came to a stop.

I ran, splashing through puddles in his curving driveway, then sloshed across a grass field on a direct path for his car. His headlights and taillights shut off and I saw his door open and the lights inside his car cast him in silhouette. The battering rain masked my approach until the last second when he opened an umbrella and shut his car door. When the umbrella moved up over his head, he found me standing in front of him and he jumped, a precious startled look on his face.

"Who ... who the hell are you?" He blurted, and patted his coat as if in search of something.

"You should have stayed the fuck away from her," I said and flung the baton out to my side to extend it.

"Who?" He stammered. "Who are you talk—"

I swung wide and struck him with the knobby tip, right on the back of his arm. He cried out and dropped the umbrella, clutched his arm, swore. I raised the wand again, this time looking for a nice face shot, and brought it down hard towards his cheek. He dodged backwards and I missed the tip of his nose by a few inches.

I recovered from the missed swing and took a step back to prepare another shot. As I did so, his face turned from anguish to stern focus, and he shifted sideways into some sort of martial arts stance. He spread his legs wide and he moved into a low squat, one hand before him, the other lost somewhere beyond his torso. Fucking perfect. The guy was probably a black belt in kung fu or jujitsu or who the hell knows what.

I wasn't going to wait for whatever move he was setting himself up for, so I aimed a quick blow at his outstretched arm. He snapped the arm back to his body, shuffled backward, avoiding his car, and then lunged forward. It was exactly what he had awaited—perhaps even set me up for. My baton arm had crossed my chest at the end of the last swing and I was hunched over slightly, the side of my face a big open target. He connected with the butt of his palm, smacking my jaw and sent me falling back. A second later, a knee smashed into my chest. Another second later, a foot swept my legs out from under me, and a blinding series of punches and kicks pummeled my head and back.

He started yelling at me, "Yeah, you fuck! How about that, you fuck? How's that feel, you fuck?"

I curled up into a ball, hoping he would stop for a breath—stop for *something*. Even with stabbing pain from numerous locations and new blows striking all over my body every second, the irony of the situation did not escape me. In that much pain, and the outlook for this body so bleak, I knew there was only one thing to do. I'd done it before, countless times without a second thought, and couldn't understand why I was hesitating. Not only would it stop my pain, but I would have the opportunity to enter that fucker's body, walk him into his house, upstairs, and straight out the third-story window. Who cares how it would look to an investigator? Joseph had clearly been beaten senseless and sustained permanent brain damage. Out of guilt, the good doctor offed himself. Justice fucking served.

Even today I don't know if the choice I made was the best option, but an apparent ninja master was beating me to a pulp. I was able to catch a good breath of air, held it in deep, and tried to feel my hands. I squeezed them into fists and found that my baton was still in the right. "Swing it back!" I commanded my body, and my body obeyed. I don't know where it struck, but the kicking, punching, and "you fucks" halted.

I glanced back cautiously and saw through blurred eyes that he was stumbling, his hands over his face. I wiped the water and perhaps blood from my eyes, labored to my knees, and gave him the most powerful shot I could muster to the shin. He shrieked and dropped at once and I wasn't going to let him up again. I managed my way onto my feet, dizzy and physically exhausted, and pounded wildly at his back with the baton. He cried out with agony each time, yelling "Stop! Please, stop!"

He lay writhing on the ground as I stood over him. A cut in my scalp was bleeding, oozing into my eyes with the rain. All he needed was a good shot to the back of the head and he would be done. *If* I wanted to kill him. I wasn't so sure anymore. I was obviously not happy with being thrashed, or his gratified ramblings between strikes, but he'd put up a fight. He wanted to *live*, and I couldn't fault him for that. Then again, I didn't need to fault him for that; he had fucked the love of my life no less than thirty minutes ago.

He dared a glance up at me just as I brought the baton down at his head. A ghastly crushing sound.

A light suddenly shone from the porch up the stairs and a woman's voice called out "Andy? You all right?"

I took off running down the driveway. I heard her scream behind me and then garbled words intermixed with "Andy!"

I jumped in my car, fumbled in my pockets for the keys, found them, and promptly dropped them in the footwell. My eyes nearly swollen shut and clouded with blood, I blindly felt around for the keys. I wiped my eyes on my sleeve and felt around exactly where I'd heard the keys fall. Not there. I cried out swearing. I finally found the keys. They were trapped in the cuff of my slacks. I was infuriated by the cuff in my slacks.

I stabbed the key into the ignition, pulled a U-turn, and sped out of there. No cars or lights behind me.

I decided to stay off the highway, sticking to side streets the whole way home. Thoughts flooded my head. How did what happen reconcile with what I had planned for getting off Scot-free? Could it have still been a crime of passion? Or did it even need to be? With the thumping he gave me, I could claim self-defense. I thought the only problem with that might be my use of a weapon, but if a person fears for their life, could they be blamed for doing whatever was necessary to survive? I began outlining my story.

I followed him home from Melanie's to confront him. I walked up his driveway, told him I wanted to talk, that he needed to stay away from my girlfriend. He was rude and said something inciting like "I'll fuck that bitch whenever I want," to which I replied with a warning and a shove. He shoved me back and said something even worse about Melanie … perhaps something about oral sex … yes, something about swallowing. I took a swing, he blocked it with his masterful martial arts skill, then proceeded to beat me to a point where I thought I was going to be killed. Everything the baton did to his body happened after that point, not before.

I felt good about my story. I would act shocked and distraught to learn that he actually died from his injuries when all I did was hit him a few times to get away. I had to get home and get cleaned up.

As I entered my house, a new thought struck me. Should *I* call the police? Tell them how I was assaulted? Hmm … it would play well with my story—go a long way. But what if his death was never even traced back to me at all? I could get away with murder without talking to a single cop or seeing the inside of a courtroom!

I went to the downstairs bath and looked at myself in the mirror. I looked like I'd been in a car accident. Would that be my story to friends? What about Melanie? Was she even interested in me anymore? What was the point of killing him if not, besides pure jealous rage and revenge? It didn't matter, I decided. I was happier with him dead, and that was what counted. If I could still have Melanie, well then everything would be right in the world. Justice indeed.

I showered, put my clothes in the wash, fed the animals, and tended to my wounds: a long cut just above my hairline, abrasions with tiny fragments beneath the skin of my hands, neck, and cheek, along with a couple of potentially dislocated ribs. Deep breaths were agonizing. Once cleaned up, I went back downstairs and ate some grapes, cheese, and crackers. I was famished.

When the doorbell rang, and four loud raps struck the front door, it felt like a hundred hairy spiders had run up from the small of my back, to my neck, and into the hair at the back of my head. Walking out of the kitchen I could already see the red and blue lights sweeping across my front window. I took a deep breath, prepared my face, and opened the door.

"Evening, officer," I said solemnly.

"Joseph Cling?" He said. His nameplate read HOLLIS. He had a partner right behind him with a hand resting lightly on his holster. Two more uniformed officers stood on the walkway, studying me. One patrol car blocked my driveway, the other was double parked beside the first, as if to block a bulldozer from escaping my driveway.

"That's me. I was honestly just getting myself together before calling you guys."

"Is that right?" Officer Hollis said. "Well, do me a favor, Mr. Cling, and don't say anything else until I've read you your rights." He pulled out his handcuffs and I held my arms out for him to take them. "Joseph Cling, you are under arrest for assault with a deadly weapon ..."

(That meant the doctor wasn't dead)

12. Split

Word apparently spreads quickly when a violent crime occurs in Frederick, and nobody that knew Joseph could believe that he would beat someone half to death. An attorney named Alyssa Browine showed up first, referred to me by my coworker, Scott. She seemed competent, a fast talker that didn't even want me speaking with my parents until she and I had time to sit down privately.

We spoke alone in my "cell", me recounting my tale as rehearsed, as she dispassionately told me what I was in for. My cell at the Sherriff's office looked more like an undecorated meeting room with a bed against one wall. We sat at opposite ends of a white plastic table. Occasionally, someone would appear in my door's large rectangular window—embedded in one side, stretching nearly from top to bottom—and either peer in or flash quickly by. The deputies interacting with me were cordial, almost friendly, but always with a wary eye on me, as if they couldn't quite figure me out. I suppose that made sense, given my career and calm, regretful demeanor.

I learned from Ms. Browine that Dr. Kalestian had suffered numerous, severe contusions, a shattered fibula, several cracked ribs, broken zygoma (cheekbone), and dislocated jaw. No skull fracture. As she listed, I poked cautiously at my lump-ridden head and face. It felt like I was wearing a mask, and I could only imagine how terrible I looked. Apparently, not as bad as the doctor. I guessed that my final swing to his head struck the cheek as he turned to look up at me. I essentially broke his face, which while altogether satisfying to hear, left me in a difficult legal position. My crime could easily land me twenty-five years in prison, but even if that time were reduced or somehow commuted, the poor doctor would be permanently deformed. This meant he could come after me in civil court for more money than I could make in a lifetime.

"How does that all change if he should die?" I asked her as she played with her scarf and scrawled in her notepad. She gave me a curious look in return and then returned to her notes.

She said, "There's no danger of that happening, Mr. Cling. He sustained no life-threatening injuries."

"Ah," I said. "Phew."

She looked up from her notepad again and studied my face. She chewed on the inside of her cheek while tapping her pen against her chin. "We need photos of your injuries before they begin to fade. Let me see your body."

Her phrasing caught me off guard, but I stood and lifted my shirt, spun in a slow circle while she hummed "mm-h-m-m" with varying pitches. She stood up and had me stand near the white brick wall as she took a few photos of my swollen face with a small camera.

"The bruises on your face and body should be at their worst tomorrow or Monday, though the swelling looks pretty good right now. I'll send an assistant to catch some more snaps. We need to be able to demonstrate just how badly that guy beat you." She leaned forward and spoke in a hushed voice. "To tell you the truth, the cops here seem to think you were completely within your rights to defend yourself. If you hadn't been on his property, you probably wouldn't even be here right now."

In other words, I should have confronted him in front of Melanie's. Hindsight … Then again, if I hadn't been at his house, with a porch light turning on at a key moment, Dr. Kalestian's skull might have been properly caved in, as opposed to his cheekbone.

I had a bail hearing set for later that day, but more likely the following afternoon if a judge was unavailable. Said judge would examine a set of factors to determine the amount of my bail, or whether the option would even be presented. Ms. Alyssa Browine expected bail to be set at $100,000, whether or not anyone bought my self-defense story. Trying to include a bit of perspective, I appreciated the fact that this all happened in America, because officials and/or angry mobs in some of the other places I had lived might have already strung me up, cut off my head, or confined me within a highly unsanitary facility.

I anguished over the inevitability of Melanie finding out. She was the only reason I wasn't on a jet to Australia while Joseph's battered body lay face-down on the bank of the Potomac. I had hope that, by some miracle, things could somehow still work themselves out. My parents were certainly hopeful. They were let in as Ms. Browine exited.

I shared my tale once more, dancing around the subject of Melanie and whether she had actually cheated. Mom and Dad read between the lines and spared me from elaborating further on the specifics, but I had thrown Melanie under the bus with them and disregarded the future repercussions.

"Joey, sweetie," my mother said. "I don't want you to spend the rest of today and the night worrying about all this, you hear me? God doesn't let good people suffer unnecessarily." *Really?* I thought. "They're going to figure out this fella is lying and you'll be outta here in no time."

Dad nodded his agreement.

I winced and said, "It's probably not going to be that simple. I actually did go a little nuts and pushed the guy. I *started* it! I was on *his* property! And even though he attacked me, once I got the upper hand … I went too far. He could have been killed."

They stared at me, bewildered, trying to figure it all out. To them, it was like some complex puzzle that, if pieced together just right, would form an image of the good Joey they knew. Their faces displayed their desperation to find more pieces.

I dropped my face into my palms. "I just can't believe what I did …"

Soothing hands caressed my shoulders.

They stayed as long as the deputies would allow, talking about lawyer friends and stories they'd heard of good people getting off, and then they were asked to leave. Hugs and words of encouragement.

On her way out, Mom said, "I called James already, by the way. He said he would let ... *her* ... know right away."

Melanie? Oh, I'm sure he will. Through the window in my door, I watched them navigate the office area. Mom glanced back at me with concern before they disappeared behind a dividing wall. I plopped down onto my thin, spring-supported mattress and wondered when or if I would hear from Melanie.

* * *

I awoke to the sound of raps on my door. A deputy I didn't recognize was looking at me through the window, politely waiting for me to acknowledge him before simply barging in. Keys rattled, the door opened, and Melanie stepped in. I shot to my feet, but did not rush forward. Flashes of the doctor slapping her ass intermixed with us lying on a towel in the sand, and watching yachts float by on the Chesapeake.

I could see she had been crying, and her face spoke a number of messages: anger, confusion, anticipation, but all under the veil of a fragile, emotionless veneer. She was here to hear my story firsthand—make her judgment after that. She had never been an irrational, fly-off-the-handle sort, and now I was seeing her in the worst situation yet. But still, she was keeping it together.

The deputy closed and locked the door. From the moment she'd arrived, her eyes remained fixed on mine. She slid one of the plastic chairs alongside the table so there would be nothing between us.

"Sit down, please," she said. I sat back down on the bed, and she sat in the chair. "Go ahead." She folded her hands in her lap and looked at me expectantly.

"You ..." I hesitated. "You want me to—?"

She gave me a curt nod, yes. I took a deep breath and told her everything, starting with her growing distance over the past week. I lied and said I had decided to pop over to check on her, happening to arrive just as Dr. Kalestian was walking up her steps. She tried to keep her voice impassive, but I could see her chest rise and pause as she stifled responses. I told her how I was devastated, that her aloofness suddenly made sense. I had remained in the car, sitting in horror as every minute passed without her apartment door reopening. I told her how, when it finally did open, that on a whim I decided to follow this man, find out who he was. And then I shared my practiced tale of defending myself against a superior attacker. I told her how I would never hurt anyone— had never before that night hurt someone.

I was quiet awaiting her response. She stared at me, pained, contemplating. And then she began.

"First, I want to tell you that the man you almost killed was my boss. He's a doctor. And nothing was going on. Second, my 'pulling away from you' had nothing to do with you and me, and everything to do with you making … with *seeing* my mother's brother. That said, rational human adults do not beat people bloody, no matter what they think was going on. It's irrelevant what my relationship with him is. You have apparently destroyed Andrew's face … I haven't gone to see him, I came here first to hear what you had to say … his wife … I can only imagine what she's going through right now. His kids … he's someone's *daddy*." She stopped and looked at the floor for a moment, wringing her hands, then faced me square on. "You are *not* who I thought you were. No matter the reasons … the person I thought I knew simply would not have done *any* of what you did. Stalking outside my—"

"I wasn't stalking—"

"*Stalking* me outside my apartment, following somebody to their house … I mean, why would you even have a weapon on you unless you were planning on doing something? I'm not stupid, okay? I know exactly what you thought you were going to do!" She shifted to the edge of her seat to get up, her chest heaving as she calculated her final words. "I should have known it was too perfect. Damaged goods don't suddenly repair themselves anew. Your brother was right."

That last sentence threw me so hard that I had no words in response as she stood and walked to the door. What had James told her? Had he been trying to poison her against me all this time? Of course he had. But it didn't matter at that moment. I had to say something! It may have been over between us, but either my love for her or my ego couldn't leave it like that.

I stood up and said, "I love you more than anything in the world, including myself. I've never felt this way about anyone." The deputy unlocked the door and Melanie glanced back at me. Her eyes were already pooling. "I'm filled with shame, have no excuses, and will love you forever, whether I see you again or not." And I meant it.

The door was locked and I watched as she strode through the station without a backward glance. There was a finality to that walk that struck me much harder than her words. I curled up on that bed and cried. I cried real tears for the first time in my life.

In years past, I chided and mocked weak minds that succumb to suicidal thoughts, even as I staged scenes of the act to cover my tracks. Despair, for me no longer a word inextricably associated with histrionics, weighed upon my body like a collapsed mine. Life seeped from every orifice, every pore, as the weight grew ever heavier. I had no interest in leaving this body to go start afresh, because in reality, there was no escaping *myself*. It was with this realization that I wondered if it were even possible for me to die, if I so chose. The dark shadow of an answer loomed, and it was *No. This is what it is to be a demon.* This was how I would become the archetypal malevolent entity—a part of the process, an inevitability, a rite of passage. This was why destiny brought me back to Leesburg, guided me to the Demotte house, to Melanie. It was my time.

I pressed my hands tighter against my ears, as if to mute my own disconsolate inner voice. And soon, it had worked, as I heard only a deep, muffled voice. And then something pushed my elbow—something real. I opened my arms and my eyes and saw a blurry silhouette surrounded by glaring fluorescent light. It was Joseph, standing over me. My face looked understandably somber, but almost forgiving. And then I noticed my choice of clothes: a cheap wrinkled polo shirt with a technology company logo, old, weathered khakis, and a huge-faced watch. It was James, and he was probably outraged by what I had done with his brother's body.

"Let's go," he said. I saw his eyes shift from lump to lump on my face. I saw his Adam's apple rise and fall. It looked as though he was going to help me up, but thought better of it, not wanting to touch me. He stepped back.

"Where are we going?" I asked as I stood.

"I posted your bail. Come on." He sounded almost … nice. It was disarming.

I followed him out the door, signed paperwork at the front desk, and had a tracking device secured to my ankle—a condition of my bail. He walked around to the driver's side of his SUV and pointed me to the passenger door.

"Go ahead, get in," he said.

I gave him a dubious look. "Really? And you take me where? To the town line … tell me to run off and never come back?"

He paused in the open door. "No. I think we'll go to Joseph's house."

I hesitated. James would never hurt his brother's body, but who knew what kind of craziness he had going through his head. I mean, seriously, what sort of lunatic believes in demons? He shut his door and started the engine. I got in.

We drove in silence to my house. My white sedan was gone. It must have been towed, either for evidence or because my superiors were confiscating it as part of my termination, I guessed.

Inside, James guided me to the TV room where we sat at opposite ends of my couch. Jaxy ran in from the open side door and greeted me before giving James the sniff treatment.

"You want anything to drink?" He asked, as if the host of our little get-together.

"I'm fine, thanks."

He stretched his neck and rolled his shoulders.

"We're going to have a real conversation, all right?" he said. I nodded. "I'm going to be honest and forthright. You … you aren't what you think you are." I raised my eyebrows, but didn't speak. "You've been on my mind—obviously—since we first met, and it was only in the past day or two that some things began to click for me …

like a revelation! The revelation is this … you don't even know what you are! You've been going around with this … *impression* of yourself based off … I don't know, based off nothing! Movies, maybe … a few books."

Irritation was quickly pushing away my sorrow. I didn't think he realized how patronizing he sounded. My face must have shown some sign of my reaction, because he put a hand out and shook a finger.

"No, no, don't get the wrong idea," he said, smiling a little. "This is a *good* thing. It's okay, really. Hear me out. You'll get what I'm saying, and you'll know that it's right."

"Maybe I do need a drink," I said.

He ignored me. "Beings like you have existed for thousands of years, perhaps hundreds of thousands. You are the living proof of the human soul's existence." He paused on that, let it sink in. I waited for him to go on while thinking about Joseph's painkiller smorgasbord. "We live in an age of diehard atheists. A culture of cynics and skeptics, exacerbated by and emboldened in response to a hardline church. But before all … *that* … the world's wisest people—scholars, philosophers—spent their days pondering the nature of the soul and of *daimons*." He gave me a little nod. "You with me?"

"Sure."

He went on, "In ancient Egypt, they believed in two separate spirits, the *Ka* and the *Ba*, which together made up the human being … that is, everything but the body. *Ka* was essentially the life-force that transcended the physical body, even after death. But beyond that, it was like this pool of spiritual energy that also housed the essences of one's ancestors." He sounded like a cable TV documentary.

"I get it," I said, scratching Jaxy's head. "Are you saying I'm an unknowing member of this universal '*Ka*' conglomerate?"

"No, I'm not. Let me finish. *Ba* is what they considered a person's unique *identity* or character. *Ba* was the *soul* part of the equation. After death, *Ka* and *Ba* remerged for the afterlife. This is just one example— how the Egyptians saw it. Now, a couple thousand years later, a Greek philosopher named Empedocles professed his belief in the immortal soul—the daimon. Not only that, he proclaimed that he himself was a daimon—that he lived this daimonic life. In one of his many writings, he said 'I too am now one of these, an exile from the gods and a wanderer, trusting in mad strife.'"

He had gotten my attention and knew it.

"That particular line speak to you at all?" He asked with a wry smile. I gestured for him to go on. "A contemporary of Empedocles, Heraclitis, became famous for his motto, *Ethos anthropos daimon*. It means 'character is fate' or 'your character *is* your daimon'. The whole concept of a devil, or some wily, treacherous demons running around possessing people appeared a thousand-plus years later, concocted based upon mistranslations of *angelos* and *daimones*, which at one point were used interchangeably—angel and demon! They meant the same thing before being translated: messenger of God. It's fascinating when you start to put these things together, all in order, over thousands of years. From this writer to that mythology to a pope or two, and here we are with beautiful winged angels and horned, red-skinned, tail-wagging demons."

"I never believed in any of that nonsense," I said. *I told you those characters were all bullshit, didn't I?*

"Well, good," he said. "I mean, it's all out there ... hundreds of books that paint this original picture of the separate soul. Books you could have been reading and—"

"Don't fucking start with that, James," I interrupted. "You were doing fine."

"Sorry. Perhaps you can see my frustration ... Moving on. In ancient times, the average person did not question the accepted belief that an entity came to them at birth and left at death. An entity that can fly, occupies the human body, giving it consciousness, and later transcends the death of the body. Sounds like angel, demon, and human soul all rolled into one, doesn't it?" He took a breath. "Now, where do *you* fit into all this? You are all of these things, or, if you like, simply a soul ... disjoined from a body after death, but for some reason failed to go ... wherever you're supposed to go!"

"Where was I supposed to go?"

"I don't know ... heaven? Tons written on that subject, too, of course, but who knows? Personally, I like the idea of the Ba. You can find it in most cultures: chi, mana, The Force in *Star Wars*. An energy which exists in all living things, connected to us with invisible tendrils, be it plant, animal."

"I've seen it," I said. "Waves that emanate from everybody. I don't know about plants though ..." I looked at Jaxy to see if she had waves, but I couldn't tell.

James nodded knowingly, unsurprised. "Yup, I think humans have a higher concentration of that energy. Anyway, the reason I'm telling you all this, if you haven't figured it out already, is because I want you to know that you were a soul like any other person on the planet. And however you got 'loose', I guess, was some kind of anomaly. That said, you exist, and you have an inherent desire to be back in a body, and the *means* to be in whomever you wish. This is a huge responsibility, and one you haven't appreciated thus far."

"That's *your* opinion," I said. I had nothing better.

"You jump into a grown man's life, picking up where he left off, and don't think that's irresponsible? You could be using this ability to relieve the parents of a child born without mental faculties! Or to 'cure' an injured person in a vegetative state for the benefit of their friends and family. You get a body to live in for a lifetime, a family that will love you, and vice-versa. Think about how many times you've heard about someone waking up from a decades-long coma? It's rare, but it happens, and who knows the real forces behind those events ..."

He had interesting points, but the sanctimonious tone was getting on my already singed nerves. I stood up and went to the kitchen to put on some coffee. James followed me.

"I hope you're not taking all this the wrong way," he said.

"I think I'm taking it correctly," I said. "Use your power for good instead of evil."

"You sound pretty blasé about it. I hope you know how hard it is for me to talk to you—looking at my brother's eyes, knowing he's cramped away in a dark chest, asleep, and I'm having a normal conversation with the soul using his body."

"This isn't a normal conversation," I said. "And I told you before, he's not in here. He's been gone since the moment I arrived. That's just how it works."

He closed his eyes, squeezed them tight, shook his head. "That's not correct," he said. "Entities like you can come and go without doing damage. It's probably hard to hear this, knowing the ... God knows how many people you've ... *erased* ... but it just means you're doing it wrong. You're not leaving properly... gracefully. If you did it right, the person would wake up puzzled, with only slightly tarnished memories from before you shoved them aside. Like waking from a coma. It looks the same."

I poured the grounds into my coffee maker, set it to run, and turned to face him. "And how exactly would you know this?" I said. "Are you going to try to tell me this is all in a book at a college library?"

He looked away and shook his head, "No, I'm not trying to tell you that." He sighed. "I know because ... we're the *same* ... you and I."

13. Purity

"**Y**ou're a fucking liar," I said.

James shrugged and sat in silence as I replayed our every prior interaction in my mind. I sat at the edge of the couch in a daze, inserting this possibility into my memories. His face when we spoke outside our parents' house. Testing me with the secret language only he and his brother knew. He had been confident from day one, never a shred of doubt that I wasn't Joseph. And he was little Morgan's buddy on the path that day, my first day. That boy's expression was not afraid, not even perplexed, but surprised, and then suspicious. He knew precisely what had happened, even then. It was true. He was the same thing as me.

"You *are* a fucking liar ..." I said, "... either way! Wait ... let me get this straight ... You're not James!" I stood up and pointed. "You're telling me *I* have to leave, that *I'm* evil—all that bullshit! You said I changed your life ... you studied for years from all the trauma—"

He simply nodded—not at all apologetic, but certainly with an air of "you got me." I began to pace, calling up all of his previous vilifying words.

"It's true," he said. "I shifted some timing around in what I shared with you. I've studied our kind for decades, something you should have been doing, but apparently thought it a low priority. But none of that matters. Don't get lost in those details, because it doesn't really change anything. I *am* James. My parents have never known anyone else."

"So you're going to tell me that James was born in a vegetative state and you charitably climbed in there to save his parents from suffering? I can't believe I actually thought about that pure, good, and evil bullshit. You just wanted me gone!" But just as I said it, a memory popped in my head. At the anniversary party, speaking with our father. Dad had said that he and Mom had worried about losing James to some medical condition when he was just a baby. That must have been when the real James was replaced by *this* James.

James had his hands up in a *settle down* gesture, "Hold on, hold on, you're running too far with this. Let me go on and explain things, and then we'll get to the real point of me telling you all this. I'm going to teach you how you actually work. While I am, by my very nature, a liar, I haven't been lying to you … just omitting an obvious *detail* …" He gestured to himself. "…and changing up some critical timing. Now, please, have a seat and hear me out. You probably won't have this opportunity again." I exhaled and sat down. "I've only met one other daimon in my life, spotted two others I was certain of, though never actually conversed. I'm fairly confident that we are an extremely rare breed.

"Now, let me answer your first few questions," he said as he sat back down on the couch. "How long have I existed? Nineteen thirty-three. That's when I appeared. Orange County in Southern California. A pick-up truck was parked on a country road, groves of trees on either side. A man in his fifties was hunched over something in the ditch. I flew close and looked and saw a body, facedown, twisted. It looked like a teenager. The man poked the boy with his foot, but the boy didn't move. I looked at the front of the truck and saw where the impact had happened, and I could see one of the boy's shoes a short distance down the road. I didn't fully understand who I was, where I was, what had happened, or care for that matter, because all I wanted to do was get inside that man's body. And so I did, and it felt good, and I started walking. An hour or so later I was picked up by police and interrogated about the boy I had run down. I told the truth, that I didn't remember. But they didn't believe me. I had no injuries on my body, but was acting like I had amnesia. I couldn't remember my own name, my wife, where I lived, any of it. But it was true, as you know."

"You were the dead kid on the road," I said.

"Yes, and I later found out all sorts of details about my previous life. They are these still images in my mind, like looking through a photo album."

"I don't remember anything from before the courthouse and Morgan," I said. "Nothing. Only 'Frederick.'"

"You remember the town?" He said, shocked.

"No, just the name. It's what I call myself."

He frowned, intrigued. "Hm … that's interesting. I call myself Samuel. I don't feel any real connection to the name, but it was *his* name … the boy."

"So did you end up in prison for killing yourself? Killing Samuel?" I asked.

"No—well, not *me*. I had left well before the trial. I flew free for a couple days and watched the police interrogating the old man's vacant body. They thought it was his new act, after the amnesia didn't convince them."

"So you had erased him."

"Yes, but he was my first. I didn't know what I was doing. It happened again with a policeman I took, but then I figured it out after him. It was *important* to me, see, to not destroy these people's minds." He gave me a reproachful glare.

I wanted to say, "Hey, screw you, I didn't know," but he was right. I never did try. But how would I know? To that he would have said "If it was *important* to you, you would have kept trying," so I wasn't going to set him up for a retort. I wanted to know what he knew.

"So, if I wanted to … I'm not saying I do, but if I did … how is it done?" I asked. "Leaving … *properly*."

He nodded, clearly pleased that I asked. He shifted in his seat, and spoke more animatedly than before. "Good, yes. Now here's the thing, when you get inside somebody, their soul is still in there with you, just buried deep. You have to think of it in those terms, that you're this guest inside their body, always keeping yourself slightly separated. And then when you go, you do it slowly. You should feel sections disconnecting, like Velcro almost, the whole time being careful that you're not pulling anything with you. When all the tendrils are free, you've disconnected and control of the brain returns to them. You don't even have to practice it, once you've done it right one time. I'm just … I'm a little nervous about him being your first …"

A presumptuous statement on his part, but certainly well-timed. There really wasn't much keeping me here. The key question, then, was who did I care about more: myself or Melanie? If it was me, I'd leave and take my beloved body with me and start anew as I had planned before. But if it was Melanie, I would try to leave her the old Joseph—one without the memory of the past few months, and if prison was somehow avoided—a big *if*—perhaps they would have a chance of making a life together. James would certainly champion that cause, reversing anything he had said to her before …

"Hey," I said. "What did you tell Melanie about me? When you were trying to break us up."

"Trying to … What are you talking about?"

"She came to see me at the police station," I said. "Told me that you were right … something about me being damaged goods. You instigated this whole fucking thing, didn't you?"

He shrugged, "Before calling her today, I hadn't spoken to her for months."

"She said 'your brother was right.' That's exactly what she said."

James thought for a moment then his face lit up. "Oh! Well... that's… She's talking about an *old* old conversation. Before you even came around. When I was trying to fix them up. I told her about Joseph's fiancée that passed away, how he was permanently damaged by it, but that I thought he could still have a mostly-normal relationship. Thing was, I care deeply for Melanie as well, and I didn't want to sacrifice her happiness for my brother's. I warned her that in his broken state, things might not end up working out. She's an amazing person, you know. There aren't many like her."

"Yes, I know," I said, and realized that now I had tarnished some of that luster of hers. Looking back, she would think of whatever Uncle

Dom had done to her, and now that psycho, Joey Cling. I had thrown a sheet over her lamp, and I could think of only one possible way to remove it.

James seemed confident that Joseph was still in here with me.

"So tell me," I said. "What if Joseph was erased when I entered? I've never felt anything close to what you described—this other person pushed in the back—not with this body, or any other before it."

"He's in there," James said with a gentle smile. "Trust me. It's possible to bounce a person out, but that requires skill and practice far beyond the graceful exit. If you haven't left the body yet, he's there. It wouldn't happen accidentally. It can't."

I inhaled a deep breath, suddenly feeling very positive. If Joseph was in here with me, that changed everything. James insisted that Joseph would remember everything from before I took over. The only problem was that I couldn't reset Melanie's memory back to that time. Nor could I undo Dr. Kalestian, but James told me he would be able to help with that. He certainly didn't want his brother to wake up and find himself in jail for twenty-five years for a crime he couldn't remember committing. I didn't know what influence he had, but he seemed confident that he could fix it. I was curious if his planned "fix" was of the human sort or via some sort of *daimonic* skill. I knew there was more to us than what he had shared. Perhaps he would teach me more if I continued to cooperate.

After James had left, I sat in a sort of shock at the revelation. *James is like me. There are more like me. I don't have to wipe minds. James is a fucking demon! What are the odds of that? What is it about the Cling brothers that draws in "lost souls?" It can't be some crazy coincidence that twin brothers both ended up possessed.* My mind was thoroughly blown.

I couldn't organize the chaos in my head into anything coherent, so I went upstairs and stripped down to shower. I stopped in front of the body-length mirror. Despite the lumps and bruises, I still loved this body. It's difficult to describe to someone who has always had the same flesh and bones, but imagine that all of your clothes were too tight, too loose, or pinched at the crotch, gave you a constant wedgie, or itched. And then someone bought you a set of clothes that fit so perfectly that you forget you're even wearing them. That was Joseph for me. I didn't even think of him as a body I was in. I was simply him, and he was me.

I stepped into the shower. It hurt to shampoo my head, and my face was unbearably sensitive, like a giant testicle smashed by a heavy boot. Once clean, I got out, dressed, and fed Jaxy. That's when I realized that Kiki was gone. I checked the laundry room and, indeed, the litter box had been taken. Melanie must have let herself in while I was in jail. Upstairs, I found her clothes still hanging. Her toothbrush still stood beside mine in the holder. Her other toiletries filled the second medicine cabinet. I supposed the cat was the only thing at risk of perishing due to neglect. I knew she must have considered taking Jaxy, too. Maybe she assumed someone would come take care of her.

I grabbed a can of soda from the fridge and walked out to the backyard. I was going to go—that much was certain. I would leave Joseph's body behind and let him deal with the aftermath of my stay. James and Mandy had influence over Melanie, and if she was forgiving enough, they could bring her around back to Joseph. I would be clean, and it would be in their hands. On James's sliding scale of evil and purity I would shoot straight to pure, not even pausing at *good* to take a breather!

And then James's fucking voice echoed in my head, my uninvited new conscience, "But really for *them*? *Really?* In the end, who is the act actually for?"

While Jaxy walked the perimeter of the backyard, sniffing roses and jasmine for minute changes since her last patrol, I looked at my hands. They, too, were a bit beat up—tiny bits of gravel from the doctor's driveway still nestled beneath my skin. But my nails were clean. I thought about where these hands had been on Melanie's body. I thought about giving them back to someone else, and him getting to do those same things, only not as well as I could. Was it for Melanie that I had decided to go? Was it for Joseph to give him back his life? James, to return to him his beloved brother? Or was it for me to escape like I always had when things got sticky? When had I ever experienced a real consequence? Had I ever sacrificed? I wondered what would be more "pure", by James's philosopher's definition. To stay and accept the consequences of my behavior, and afterwards possibly rebuild a normal life, or to drop those consequences in the laps of others, while sacrificing the life and body I so loved? I knew what James would say. That much was obvious, but could he truly be my voice of reason while blinded by bias and dismissing his blatant hypocrisy?

And then a better question—a question I rather liked—occurred to me: Do I really care about any of this? Since when am I a "good person?" These were James's standards for living, and whatever he wanted to call our kind, I am who I am. Screw him.

.

14. Clarity

I wasn't fired from the Postal Inspection Service ... yet. Thanks to a spotless record and maybe a bit of fear on the part of my boss—fear of being ratted out about the anticipatory search warrant shenanigans—I was on unpaid suspension pending my trial. I also had a great relationship with everyone in my department. I have no illusions that this savings account of goodwill had anything to do with me. No, I had Joseph to thank for that. Though to my credit, everyone seemed to buy my self-defense story without reservation.

I spent my free time reading, walking my dog, and avoiding people. Mom and Dad called daily, but understood each time I told them I wasn't ready to talk. Melanie hadn't contacted me, not even to arrange pick-up her clothes and bathroom sundries. Strangely, seeing a box of tampons every time I opened the cabinet for a Q-tip offered an unexpected dose of calm, as if the current state of things was temporary.

One day I began cleaning my house. There had been a foul smell in the kitchen—some rotting thing buried deep beneath innocuous paper trash. I took it outside and dumped in the bin, and came back inside. The scent lingered, of course, as it needed time to air out, but I was suddenly inspecting every surface and floor. I found dust and crumbs and indeterminate sticky spots. Dog and cat hair clung to every patch of carpet or furniture. The house was disgusting. When had I become a slob?

I cleaned from top to bottom, dusting first, vacuuming last. I reorganized the upstairs office. I washed linens. I disinfected the bathrooms.

I took a short break to catch my breath and drink some water, feeling accomplished and positive. But in the back of my head, there was a room I had ignored since moving in. The extra room upstairs at the opposite end of the hall from my bedroom. It had been Joseph's one "fuck it" room, full of boxes, an exercise bike, treadmill, old tube-style television, grungy recliner, and who-knew-what-else. I had kept the door closed at all times and hoped one day some burglars would break in and steal everything from only that room.

I gulped down a second glass of water and decided I would tackle the garbage room.

Joseph had numerous boxes of old files: paid bills, papers from school, receipts. Five boxes dropped deep into the recycle bin with a pleasant rustle.

Joseph had an equal number of boxes full of VHS tapes. He had apparently been a fan of eighties and nineties comedy films. Three boxes dropped into the garbage bin with a pleasant rattle. But two of the tape boxes contained what appeared to be home videos. The majority were the small, 8mm sort, but there were also many full-sized VHS tapes. I perused the labels: FASL 9/2/93, FASL 9/6/94 CHAMPS!, and more like this.

A box marked "Fragile" was a treasure trove of FASL-contemporary electronics, one of which was a VCR. I brought it downstairs and hooked it up to the big plasma TV. It worked perfectly, and I had my first view of a younger Joseph. FASL was an adult soccer league, and I knew soccer (well, *football,* everywhere else I had lived) enough to see that Joseph was good. He was quick and agile, aggressive, but not a dick. I could hear James's, or perhaps Dad's voice behind the camera, commentating here and there.

"Ooh, nice!" and "Foul! That was such a foul! Come on, ref!"

Many of the tapes were labeled with only the year. A tape from 1996 was full of unrelated videos, each an eye-opening window into Joseph. Ten minutes of clips from a house party revealed a relaxed, deeply philosophical Joey nestled in an over-sized couch in basketball shorts and a tank top.

"Say it again," the female voice behind the camera says.

Joey smiles shyly and shakes his head. "Not if it's going to be documented!"

A chorus of party guests insist.

Joey rolls his eyes, slaps his knees, and grabs the camera, holding it only a few inches from his mouth. "Fine!" His face is thin and long, his good jaw still developing. His still-thick hair is slicked back with gel.

Joey clears his throat, looks straight into the lens as if a tiny little person were trapped behind it.

"Three sides!" He says. "There are three sides, not two! Divinity classes are going to give you a totally biased two; atheists, guaranteed one side. Some of the better, less-invested professors may give you information—critical thought stuff—let you crunch it yourself, but they're always going to say you need to pick which side speaks to you more. To those jokers, 'which side' means two sides!"

It may have been my limited perspective, but I felt like he was responding to James—perhaps something James had been preaching since he had a passion for these subjects. I was also fascinated by his speech pattern. He didn't speak the same way that he had with Melanie that night. I wondered if that was what James had been referencing when asking why I was talking "that way." But then I was reminded that people speak differently to different people. At work, on the phone, with a date. It's not that they put on a façade for each audience, but certainly learn over time to adopt an appropriate tone for differing situations. I had only observed Joseph in one.

"But let me tell you about the third side, all right?" Joseph said in a silly, condescending sort of tone. Unseen others laughed. "Secular ethics are not a new thing. Yes, humanist philosophy has had this resurgence, and whether a person draws their moral guidance from religion or the still-pertinent teachings of Confucius or Buddha, there can be people, believe it or not, who draw from both, or *neither*! And they don't end up rampaging through the streets raping dogs, blowing shit up, and eating people ..."

His audience laughed hysterically, and he laughed at himself, too— seemingly aware of the inherently comical nature of such a passionate sermon. But he went on for another five minutes, rambling yet coherent, and actually got me thinking about much of his observations and the concept of a third side of morality, neither starkly religious nor anti-God. A more present, heady sort of Agnostic, I suppose. But this line of thought left my head instantly when the video abruptly flipped to a beach at night.

The tinny sound of crashing waves filled the background as a small campfire flickered in the middle of a circle of people, seated on logs and rocks. The camera clacked and bounced around until it settled on a shot of someone's considerable cleavage. Indistinguishable chatter for a beat, then the lens tilted up to a face. It was James's wife, Mandy, in her late twenties. She brought the camera close to her lips and whispered "They're doing it right now." The video blurred as she spun it around and stabilized on James and Joseph, identical, facing each other and talking. She zoomed slowly in and the microphone seemed to zoom as well, focusing on the brothers.

I couldn't tell which one was which. The one on the left was speaking gibberish. "Ish da-wa tee tish ha becahsh siz-per senshtif."

It was their secret language. The one on the right said, "If shoo-dough tish ha new, shooll pa-fer int laysha." The discovery of this VHS codex was a couple months late to have made a difference with James, but I wondered if I could decipher the language from this video.

The other replied, "Er, intcer maysh this wharf."

"Er, intcer maysh this besher."

That, I caught! "Or, it could make this better." Which meant the line before that was "Or, it could make this worse." They were exchanging *sh* for certain letters. Changing a few vowel sounds around. Of course it wouldn't be some complex dialect. They made it up when they were kids. I rewound and watched it again, then let the video play out.

Over the course of the next two weeks, I spent hours with the old Joseph—work I should have done in the very beginning, had I not been so distracted by Melanie. I realized that I hadn't known Joseph at all. And how would I? From a few hours observation on a date and from his email and text history? Lord, I was an idiot. A somewhat less welcome result of getting to know Joseph was that I actually liked the guy. I understood why his entrance to the Cling anniversary party had me feeling like a celebrity. He was just a genuinely likable person. Fucker.

There were also a few calls from James over those couple weeks. I ignored them. I was certain he had begun to suspect that I was biding my time, waiting to see how the trial and everything panned out. But that wasn't *entirely* where I stood. Surprisingly, I sat equally on two distinct sides of a fence, both with their own voice in my ear. One side sounded very much like James. But the other, more appealing voice, presented apropos questions such as "How do you know you can even leave that body with Joseph intact?" Good point, voice, I don't. "Did Melanie even *like* the old Joseph?" I have my doubts, voice.

But some things one hears cannot be unheard, and James's sliding scale was ever-present in these fantasy conversations. Damn, if the voice I liked better didn't seem to tread neck-deep in the *Self* side of the pool. And as much as I tried, I couldn't seem to embrace my supposedly evil former outlook. One day, I even found myself immersed in a fully-conscious bout of sympathy. It was something from Melanie's point of view—I don't know—I don't remember what it was, but it matters not. I didn't think that was even possible for me. And then I got *really* angry. Because it dawned on me that not only was this current life in shambles, but that for the rest of my existence, I would forever drag behind me this weight of self-doubt and concepts of evil and good and purity. It felt very human and frustrating.

There was no point in arguing with myself any longer. I would leave Joseph's body—just to see, mind you! I wasn't done yet! But I needed to *know*. I needed to see him come to: foggy, confused. And in that moment, seeing him, I felt that I would *know*. Perhaps I would jump right back in, or I would take that as my cue to take my invisible bow. Or maybe, just maybe, he wouldn't wake up at all ...

Two weeks and a few days after I smashed in the face of her former boss, I decided I would first go to Melanie's house. Say my goodbyes ... you know ... *in case*. And maybe there would be a glint in her eye, still-pink scars she might mistake for overlooked feelings she didn't know remained, some leftover scraps of the love she once felt for me. If I could see that—have that to take with me—I may feel less anguish at the thought of a lifetime without her. I hoped it would not be the opposites. A) No glint whatsoever, or B) Glint, but only makes me feel worse.

Her car was in the lot so I knew she was home. I hesitated at the door, sweating, before I knocked.

I heard the bolt retract, a pause, and then the door crept open. Her lips were pressed together and her chin quivered ever-so-slightly. I was stunned by how good she looked. I had expected her to be a mess— tattered sweatpants, a greying white t-shirt, hair a frizzed nest, and dark bags under her eyes. Instead, she was in a pair of dark jeans, a tight long-sleeved top (her arms crossed beneath her lovely breasts), a thin silver necklace, and her hair was its usual well-managed poof of beauty. Then I remembered the day. It was a Wednesday and she would have been home from work for less than an hour. Her life had gone on. Of course it had.

"Mel," I said quietly.

She shook her head, glassy eyes seeming to search my own. I couldn't tell if her face was saying "What the fuck are you doing here, reopening my healing wounds?" or if it divulged that she had in fact powerfully missed me.

"Seventeen," she finally said, and a tear slid from one eye, rushed down her cheek, and prepared to drop from her jaw. "Seventeen days. Nothing. Not a word."

I blinked, baffled, tried to speak but only managed a very *self*-leaning "I ... I ..."

She sprang forward at me, slamming into my chest, her arms wrapping tightly around my back, and I heard her muffled sobs, felt her tears saturate my polo shirt, and hugged her back, smelled her hair, her perfume, kissed her head. It felt a bit fatherly for a brief moment, and I even caught her inhaling my deodorant as she had with her father the first time I saw her in person.

She pulled her head away from my chest and looked up; the mess I had originally expected to see now stared up at me.

"How …" she said, shaking her head. "How could you just turn it all off?"

"Turn …" I blathered. "Turn what … I didn't turn anything off! You thought I turned off?" I held her cheeks in front of me. Her hands remained firmly clasped at the small of my back.

"Why would you just disappear though? We were supposed to get together, work it out, figure everything out *together*. Every day that passed—"

A car door closed in the parking lot behind me and the alarm chirped as its owner locked it. The sound reminded us both where we were and she quickly let go of my waist, grabbed my wrist, and pulled me inside. The TV was on a *Funniest Videos* show, the sound muted.

She sat me down on the couch, straddled me, and sat back on my knees. My mind and emotions were racing at light-speed. She grabbed a tissue from the end table and I noticed several balled up around the box and on the carpet below. She dabbed around her eyes and noisily blew her nose. I had to hold back both a smile and tears because it was tremendously adorable, and because I was actually sitting there, on her couch, our faces a foot away from each other.

"What was I saying?" She said.

"Every day that passed."

My hands sat on her hips. My thumbs caressed the tiny strip of exposed skin above her jeans.

"Yes! Every day that passed was like a new level of torture, like you were punishing me for being upset. Why wouldn't you call? I know James got you out. Why didn't you try?"

"I didn't think—"

"Am I not important enough to fight for?"

"No, I didn't think there was anything I could say … I don't even know what to say now!"

She struck my chest with both fists. "Say you fucking love me! Say I'm worth it! Tell me … tell me you're not some crazy person! Tell me you love me. But don't fucking lie to me."

"I love you so much, Melanie. I … I thought I'd lost you. I really did. I thought you were done and there was just nothing I could say or do to fix it."

"I thought you didn't believe me about Andrew," she said. "I thought you were done with me because you thought I had cheated on you. That you could just throw me away like trash. That you think I'm trash."

"No, oh God, no …" I pulled her to me and she burst into tears again. "Never, never."

I felt my own throat seizing up. Swallowing hurt. My eyes stung. It was the most powerful release of emotions I had ever experienced. One on top of another on top of another. Joy at the revelations, that she hadn't cheated on me, feeling the outpouring of pain and suffering she'd gone through—feeling it as if it were my own, knowing that it was my fault, my actions, my inactions that had directly caused it all. And all of that—all of that draining, exhausting anguish—in the person I wanted to protect more than anyone else. The only person I cared about keeping happy. It makes me cry to think back to that moment, the height of every emotion I'd ever felt, and everything bursting like an overfilled balloon.

She cleaned her face with another tissue, looked up at me, and out came a blubbery cry laugh. I suppose she hadn't expected to see me a mess as well. She grabbed a fresh tissue and cleaned my face with a sympathetic little smile-frown, like a mother soothing a wounded child.

We hugged and rocked and eased each other's tender souls. She kissed my lips, ever so gently, and it was over too fast, my lips following hers as she pulled back and looked at me. She sighed and rubbed my chest.

"You do love me," she said.

"I do. Absolutely."

"Okay then," she said, and climbed off of me, crawling away on the couch. She faced me and crossed her legs, her gray-painted toes sticking out from under her knees. "Now talk to me."

I inhaled deep, faced her, and repeated for her my story about the doctor. This time, however, I felt a crushing guilt with each detail omitted, every fabrication spewed. It felt so wrong as I spoke that I doubted my own ability to make it sound convincing. But she nodded as I spoke, closed her eyes and shook her head as I recounted his every kick and degrading name he had used to disparage her. He was quite the villain, by my recollection of events. All the while I fought the urge to grimace as, beyond her, teenagers on the silent TV attempted ill-advised skateboard tricks, invariably ending up with tailbone or groin injuries.

"Well," she began. "Since we're being honest here, I have to say it all." I nodded affirmative. "He and I … *did* have a thing at one point." She studied my face for a reaction. I was wistful, yet accepting. "It was horrible, awkward, wrong …" she went on. "But I ended it right after our night at the waterfall."

I feigned shock at the overlap.

"So you … you were still … while we were together?"

"Yes I was," she said plainly. "When you and I were just dating. *You* made that clear at the very beginning that this was a 'see where it goes' type of thing and that you would keep seeing other people. But," she held up a finger, "things got *real* between us, and it was turning into an actual relationship, and then it did—it turned—like overnight! We didn't talk about it, you and me. We didn't have to, right? It was like we both knew that something had changed and *wow*, everything was so great! Just perfect and unexpected and wonderful."

"So you didn't see him at *all* between the waterfall and dinner at my house a week later?"

"We went to dinner once," she said. "He was still pushing and I needed it to be clear. He was still my boss at that point. He tried to parlay the dinner into a visit to my apartment, but I refused."

"Sounds like an asshole."

"Yeah ... but anyway, I don't want to talk about him anymore."

"What did you think of me before the dinner at my house?" I asked.

She shrugged and peered up at the ceiling. "I don't know ... I liked you, I guess. I really did, but I always thought you were so ... *broken* that we weren't going to go anywhere. She ... I don't want to bring that up. Nevermind."

"No," I said. "It's all right, go ahead."

"*She* was obviously always with you. But she seemed to leave after the waterfall night, and you were suddenly this free person. The same, but unrestrained. Nothing looming, I guess." She looked at me apologetically. "I'm sorry. I shouldn't have said anything about that."

"No, honestly, it's okay. I want us to talk about everything. Nothing's off the table. Agreed?"

She nodded and smiled, relieved.

"So what else did you like about me after the waterfall night?"

She glared with a little smirk, "When exactly did this become the stroke Joey's ego chat?"

"Sorry. Let's get back to it."

"Hang on," she said, wiping makeup from beneath her eyes. "Let me clean up." She got up and disappeared down the hall.

I couldn't believe how well things were going. I wanted to jump up and dance or swing from monkey bars, or bounce on a trampoline. Never would I have imagined this would be the outcome of my dreaded final visit to Melanie's. Final visit. What now? What was I doing? I know what I was doing! I was following my heart and setting things right for the two of us, but what about *self* and *others* and Joseph stowed away in the corner of his own brain? I didn't want to care, and in that moment, I refused to care. I would have this evening, free from guilt, unburdened by the realities of the future, whatever they may be. This night was for both of us, Melanie and Frederick, the man she loved. Outside her balcony, the cloud-smattered sky was growing dark.

"Sorry about that," she said as she breezed past. Her scent was renewed in my nose from her absence. Or did she maybe walk through a fresh cloud of perfume, spritzed before her in the bathroom? "You were saying?"

"I wanted to ask you why you shut off in the first place. When you went silent a few weeks ago."

Uh oh, her face and shoulders said that was the wrong subject to bring up. She scratched the back of her head and clenched her jaw, swallowed. There was a little something else in that expression, too. A hint of disappointment, perhaps, that I didn't already know. Of course I assumed it started with Uncle Dom, but didn't think that would have caused such a prolonged separation and ignoring of texts and calls. She had closed me out, and yet "Andrew" had been allowed to come over.

"Well," she said, but did not continue. She scanned around the room, grabbed the square throw pillow off the recliner and hugged it in her lap. "First, I want you to know that how I felt then was not how I feel now. But I'm going to tell you all this from my point of view from then."

I nodded. "Sure, I understand."

"You and I had a conversation in the very beginning about our demons. You remember? On the patio at the Longhouse."

"Of course." Of course I had no idea what she was talking about. Before my time.

"You told me about the drunk driver. Told me how you had never finished unpacking the house you two had bought together. I told you that I had a bad experience with an uncle. I didn't go into detail, but you got the message, right?"

"Sure, yeah."

Then why the fuck did you insist on me going to see him? She must have thought. I almost defended myself by saying I didn't know he was *that* uncle, but that could have very easily been disproven, depending upon other conversations I didn't know about.

"So then maybe you could understand me being a little taken aback when you suggested we go see him. Like it was nothing. That it would be good for me, you said." I began to feel like a piece of shit again, no longer nodding. My face surely told her that I got the message loud and clear, but she went on. "Dominic is fifteen years older than me.

He changed my diapers when I was a baby. He was there at every party, Christmas, birthday, art show. When I was fourteen, our relationship got a little weird. I flirted with him … it sounds weird, but it happens sometimes with young girls around that age. I wanted him to desire me, but not in any sort of *real* way. He was my uncle, for fuck's sake. But he ate it up, and by the time I was fifteen, if other people weren't around, he would slap my ass in passing or quickly grope a tit. I was already big at that age."

She sucked in a deep breath, glanced at the busy, muted TV with annoyance, and grabbed the remote to turn it off. Suddenly, the room was almost completely dark. I switched on the lamp behind me, the room now bathed in a soft yellow. Her face was always beautiful to me, but especially so in this light. I tried to focus on that—the pleasure of her in front of me at all—lest I think about Uncle Dom and how easy it would have been to suffocate him with a pillow.

"I'd love to say that I was disgusted by his inappropriate behavior, but I was stupid. Really, really stupid. He made me feel sexy and desirable, but in a different way than boys at school. Because he had always been around, and because he progressed slowly, it didn't seem as *wrong* as it should have. I knew it was wrong enough that I was sure to keep others from knowing, but there was also something strangely exciting about having this secret. At seventeen, after a party at his house, I was helping clean up and he told my parents he would give me a ride home. When everyone was gone, he took my virginity."

I couldn't be silent any longer. "Fucker! Fuck! I didn't know, Mel, I swear I didn't know it went that far …"

She put her hand on my knee to shush me. "It happened again a couple days later. He had me ditch school to meet me at my house. He wanted to do it in my room this time. I didn't think of it as creepy at all. I wanted it too. I told you, I was really fucking stupid." She was crying now, but didn't want to be touched. "At some point after that he had gotten a job in Baltimore and moved to the city. He'd come back a few times a year to have sex with me, all the way until I was twenty-one, when I tried to cut it off. I had a boyfriend—not a great guy, but basically cool. When I told Dom no more, he threatened to tell my mother about us. Things changed after that … he felt he had the power to do whatever he wanted to me, whenever he wanted, knowing he had the control. That had been his plan all along, to setup this arrangement with someone with even more at stake than him, or at least that they'd see it that way. And I did. No one could know. Ever.

"I started working at Johns Hopkins after college, met Mandy that year, then James. I got to be really good friends with Mandy. One night I was hanging out with her and got a call from Dominic saying he would be in town to see me the next week. I got more and more drunk, started crying right there in front of her, and she got it out of me. Confessed the whole thing. One evening, three weeks later, Dom was found in his car in front of his house. He'd never left for work. He was just sitting there, comatose."

James.

"So you ask why I needed some time? We're being honest here, so I'll just say it, Joey. It was more than a little heartbreaking. You had gotten past your fiancée's death, and now you were ready for me to conquer my own past. *You* were ready, so of course I should be." I tried to protest, but there wasn't a chance. "'Let's get you in front of your uncle and work this thing out. It'll be good for you, sweetie.' That's what you were telling me."

"It's really not—" I attempted.

"That's what I heard, and I just needed some time alone to recover from that horrible horrible fucking day. At the end of the week, Andrew called and said he wanted to see me … 'just to talk …' I told him no, but he showed up anyway. He tried to seduce me—predictably—and I wasn't having it. I told him fifty times that it would never ever happen again. Finally, after I don't know how long, he shouts 'Okay!' and stomps out. There was this hint of 'if that's the way you want it …' as if he was going to do something to screw with my job, but he's in a completely different department now, so I knew he couldn't do anything. I was just relieved because it seemed like he had finally gotten the message and would leave me the fuck alone." She paused and gave me a condemnatory look. "But someone else thought he needed a stronger message."

We sat quietly in the dimly lit room for a few minutes.

Finally, she broke the silence. "I know there's some psychological reason why I started with him in the first place. Something left over from my uncle. This subconscious desire for the illicit, a willingness to let a strong personality dominate me and push me into doing things I know I shouldn't. It sickens me to make that parallel, but there it is. But you were never that. You were this pure thing, someone kind and cautious and sensitive. Maybe that's one part I liked better before things got real with us. The way you were so tentative about everything. And then I let you push me into visiting him, and suddenly you crossed over this line into the realm of people who make me do things I don't want to."

"I'll never do that again. Never."

She nodded. She knew I wouldn't. She saw that I understood, and interpreted my thoughtlessness about her uncle as just that. She was forgiving me for all of it. Forgiving so we could go on and be happy and have this perfect life together.

She slid close to me, leaned across my body to grab a new tissue. I put my arms around her and hugged her tight. She put her face in my neck and I kissed her ear. Soon, she was sideways on my lap and we were kissing with increasing passion. Our lips and tongues tangled, reintroducing themselves to each other. She pulled off my shirt, scratching my back with her nails on the way up. My shirt landed somewhere across the room. I slid hers up over her head, yanked her bra down under her breasts and sucked a nipple deep into my mouth. She seized up a little, clawed my neck, ground herself into my lap.

This was building to something beyond anything we had previously experienced. Violent, impassioned, the release of a thousand emotions, the rejoining of two people crazy in love with each other. She stood up, I followed, picked her up. Her legs wrapped around me, I took her into the bedroom, dropped her gently on the down comforter, and practically ripped her jeans off. I dropped my own jeans and she immediately lunged forward, wanting to put her mouth on me but I pushed her back to climb directly on top of her. She wasn't having it. She pushed me back harder, clutched the sides of my head and pulled my face between her thighs.

I reached up to grab a breast, but she slapped my hand away and held my head tighter. She was beyond any outside influence. She was going to own me and own this moment and her body and she did. She was in charge. When *she* was ready, she let me go, turned me over, and climbed on top. She held my wrists against the bed and did not bounce, but instead *writhed*.

That night was and forever will be ours. I had never made love like that before, and have not again since. I imagine she would say the same. But that was only half of it—the sex, that is—because there was something at work between us that transcended the physical. If you've experienced anything like it, you might understand the sensation, though without the visuals that I was able to observe. Her waves had brightened, expanded and stretched out from her, interlocking with my own. Our souls essentially made love along with us like a pair of tied-up jellyfish.

I hope you *have* felt that. Every person should have a transcendent experience at least once in their life.

* * *

The next morning, before sunrise, I awoke to jolts of agonizing abdominal pain. In a stupor, I thought I must have pulled something during our escapades, but then realized that I simply had to urinate. Bending carefully to climb out of bed, I thought my bladder would burst from the sheer pressure. I walked hunched to the toilet, waited for the pipes to activate, and the pain eased away ever so slowly.

Reentering the bedroom, I saw the outline of slumbering Melanie in the glow of her nightstand clock. She was silent and still. I guessed she was enjoying her first restful sleep in some time. She may have been dreaming beautiful dreams. And this is when I surprised myself.

I made up my mind to leave, to see if I could perform a "graceful exit." Determine if Joseph indeed lay resting in a cave. Most unexpected of all, this decision came after *that* night. Normally, it would have validated and reaffirmed every justification to remain. But as I walked down the stairs to the parking lot, the outside air a light charcoal, thin fog hovering a few feet above ground, I wore a smile. The murkiness outside offered no appropriate literary symbolism to coincide with my newfound outlook. My mind was clear, and I felt refreshingly optimistic about whatever lay ahead for me. And I hadn't a clue what lay ahead.

For once, I truly hoped that Joseph would be there: groggy and stupid and undeserving of my clemency. I would observe for a time, but not too long. I didn't want to see him with Melanie. I didn't want to see her ever again, because I didn't know if I would be able to take a walk down those stairs again. No, I would see him find his way home, or perhaps just make a call to James to tell him he didn't know how he had gotten where he was. And that he was wearing very comfortable, clearly expensive, Italian underwear he couldn't remember buying. And then I would go and never look back.

I sat in my SUV and considered where I wanted to try it. Where would be best for me, emotionally, and where would be best for Joseph, logistically. I knew that treading water in the middle of the Potomac would be impractical, or deep in the woods. The sun would rise soon, so perhaps a hilltop with a decent eastward view. Now that would be an unbeatable metaphor.

Melanie and I had gotten up early to watch the sunrise several weeks prior. We had driven to Catoctin Mountain Park, where the President's private retreat, Camp David, is located. We had hiked into the public portion, a short, yet rigorous walk of perhaps two miles, and climbed to the top of "Chimney Rock." It remained a cherished memory, and so that was where I would return Joseph to Joseph.

I stopped at a convenience store, bought a bottle of water, and headed north to Thurmont. Fittingly, the park was mere minutes from Cunningham Falls and the decrepit armory where I entered Joseph's body, sleeping beside Melanie for the first time. I left the Rover in the vacant parking lot and hiked in, the eastern sky slowly brightening and the frigid air slowly warming. The hike was peaceful. I appreciated the quiet and solitude. By the time I reached the summit, a large, craggy area just above the tree tops, deep blue gradients above had shifted to turquoise. I hopped across a narrow gap, climbed atop a large flat rock, and sat down to wait for the sun to make its appearance.

Minutes passed. A mourning dove landed on the namesake Chimney Rock a few yards in front of me and howled its distinctive call, *woo-OO-ooh*. I grabbed a rock and chucked it at the bird. It flew away. Mourning doves are basically tan pigeons and I don't know if I ever mentioned it, but I hate fucking pigeons. They're like dirty little flying bad omens, if I believed in bullshit.

Wringing my hands, tiny doubts crept in. I saw the sun would poke up any minute beyond the distant mountaintops. I closed my eyes and slowed my breathing, began working in my mind. James had said how to think of it. Remind myself I'm in a body, like a room. Make myself aware of this other presence—even if I don't feel him right away—*believe* he's in there, *know* he's there, sitting in a dark corner. More fears. It *was* going to work. *That* was my biggest fear.

Wait for the sun, I told myself. When the light hit my eyelids, burning red, then I would proceed. It was going to fucking work. Why was I doing it? This wasn't *me*, doing this. It was the opposite of me.

I felt the heat on my head first, and my eyelids didn't instantly light up, but rather brightened as if by a dimmer switch. This was it, no more doubts. After all, if it did work, and I changed my mind, I could simply jump back in, right? There was nothing to keep me from doing just that.

Go.

I exhaled and leaned forward. Not my body, but *me*. I leaned out, slowly, carefully. I kept my focus on the sensations in my ... ends, I guess I'd call them. James called them tendrils, but that evokes some sort of creepy alien. I continued forward, and didn't feel anything snapping or popping behind me, just stretching out. Half-in and half-out, they grew taut and it felt like something would surely break if I kept going. The body wouldn't let go of me. I had never felt this before, though admittedly had never tried to leave so slowly. Normally I would simply go. Over in a second, bam!

And then I felt the first release, like Velcro, just as James had described it. There was another, then another, and I pulled harder. I was leaving things behind me. It was working. My fear left me as I tugged gently at the last few stubborn wisps. I had done it! I was free, floating, naked! It didn't feel good, mind you. It felt like going from fully sated after a good meal to starving like you haven't eaten in three days. I was empty and loose. In fact, I would say I felt worse physically than any other previous exit. But mentally, I felt triumphant and *pure*. There was no question that the act I'd just performed was entirely for others, and in no way for myself.

I watched my body ... Joseph's body ... remain seated as I had left it. Nothing happened, but then after a moment, it slowly began to lean ... tilting to the right, ever faster ... *thunk!* Ouch! The shoulder and head struck rock and lay still in an awkward sort of position, legs still mostly crossed together, hands in lap, neck crooked. I thought for sure the impact would wake Joseph and he would sit up and say aloud "Where the fuck am I?" That's what *I* would have said, anyway. But he said nothing. He did nothing.

I waited ten minutes, twenty, an hour. I silently shouted for him to wake up. I tried to give him little shocks (that had in the past worked to shoo away cats), but getting too close would send waves out, grabbing hold of me, tugging, so I stayed back and waited. Another twenty minutes passed and I heard voices coming up the rocks. Other hikers, come to see the view on a beautiful morning. I couldn't just leave him like that. Honestly! I'm not making excuses! I couldn't leave him at the top of these rocks, five feet from a deadly drop-off, looking like a strong gust of wind knocked him over. I had to go back in. He simply wasn't in there. My initial belief had been right: he'd been gone since the second I got there. My reaction to this realization was unexpected. I was angry. I'd been somehow cheated. It wasn't the least bit rational, I know.

And so I did it, I went back in. I sucked a deep breath into my lungs, as if after surfacing from deep water.

"Oh, hey there," a sporty young woman said as I sat up. "You, uh, sleep out here?"

I laughed a little. "Ah, no. Just came out early to see the sunrise."

The young man with her gave me a dirty look and didn't say anything. I think he had hoped to be up here with her alone.

"Oh, musta been beautiful!" she said.

"Yeah, it was nice." I stood up and brushed off my clothes. "Take care."

"Oh, you're leavin'? You don't have to go, we're just—"

"Tanya," the kid said.

"It's all right, really," I said. "I was just about to go." I made eye contact with the boy, looking for some amount of silent thanks, but he gave me a snotty smirk and popped his eyebrows down the rocks in a "Just get the hell out of here, asshole" gesture. I hopped back across the crevasse and looked at him.

"Yeah?" he said to me, but he was really saying, *"What the fuck, bro? Go!"*

And suddenly, all of my anger and frustration and uncertainty consolidated into a tightly focused beam focused squarely on this fucking punk. I felt an overwhelming urge to wipe him. Just stop his worthless existence right there, his empty shell falling thirty feet off the cliff, bones crunching together inside that fleshsack like a bag of potato chips underfoot. And now I knew that I could leave my body and come back to it without any problems. Just as James had when he put Uncle Dom out of commission. Such a simple act, really. This little fuck didn't deserve his life. *Joseph* deserved his life. This piece of shit was a spoiled, entitled prick that was probably just burning to screw this young lady in an exotic semi-public locale.

No. Fuck that.

15. Asperity

"**D**ude, we gotta do that sometime," the girl said to her companion. "If we'd just left like a half hour earlier we coulda totally seen it."

He ignored her, still gawking at me, and put his hands up. "What, dude?"

I took a deep breath, tried to think of a clever threat, a deeply disconcerting mindfuck to leave him with, but the girl hugged him around the waist and put her chin on his shoulder. She was oblivious.

"Have a nice day," I said. "Watch the cliff."

They glanced behind them to the gap.

"Thanks!" she said as I turned and left.

I heard him grumbling, but continued down the rocks. I felt stupid as the old adage "He's not worth it" streamed through my thoughts. Yes, it was clichéd, but it was also untrue. He would have been very worth it. Fucker. But it wouldn't have just been him. Even if he was only a friend, she would have been forever traumatized, and he wasn't worth *that*. And I had things to do.

I turned on my phone and saw that I had no signal. It remained that way until halfway down the trail to the parking lot when service resumed and a message popped up from Melanie.

> Hey, kind of weird leaving without saying anything or even note. Are we good or no?

I didn't reply, instead sending James a text message.

> Need to talk. Now. Where?

Less than a minute later, he replied.

Jojo?

No. Still here. Where to meet?

Baker? Same spot?

I agreed, told him when I'd be there, and hiked the rest of the way back.

* * *

"You erased Melanie's uncle," I said.

James lowered his head, almost shamefully.

"I'm sure the history there provided you with ample justification," I went on. "Bet you feel entirely righteous on that one, huh? Proud of yourself?"

He shook his head, leaned back on the bench. I remained standing, arms crossed.

"It's an extremely violent act," he said quietly, "akin to strangling, or stabbing a person to death. No, I am not proud in the slightest. I took away a fully-conscious person's life. Yes, I helped another to have her life back ... but no, not proud."

"Bullshit," I said. "You felt like a fucking hero."

He glared at me, the veil of shame gone from his face. He looked around, verifying no one was around. "He was a piece of shit. He didn't deserve to live. And who knows how many other women or girls I saved from him? So no, I don't feel like a hero. But what I did was right. That's really none of your business though. Why are you still here?"

I put my hands in my pockets and looked around, considered whether to tell him that I had tried to leave, that Joseph was indeed gone forever. I didn't see what I would get out of it. On the drive there, I recalled the pure bliss of the night before and imagined a life with Melanie. Dinners, children, trips, talks, adventures, nights in bed, mornings in bed. Without the real Joseph to give back to her, the idea of leaving her forever felt decidedly less altruistic. If I left, I would be leaving either a shell or a dead body behind me. That was what Melanie would have with her for the rest of her life. How exactly would that be the selfless choice for me to make?

"Just doing my rounds," I said. "Wrapping up loose ends. I want to see Mom and Dad."

He shook his head. "Why? You have no connection to any of these people. Don't misunderstand their affection for Joseph as affection for you. You're not going over there."

"Still want to see them. Sorry you don't like it, but I'm not asking your permission."

I walked away. James called behind me. "Don't get lost in the fantasy, Frederick! No one actually cares about *you!* You have to *build* relationships, not inherit them!"

I kept walking. He was wrong—at least about Melanie. I knew that much for sure.

I stopped for gas, went home for a shower, and put on fresh clothes. I called my parents and Mom answered. She said I could come over whenever I wanted, and that they had been waiting to talk to me anyway. I was there in fifteen minutes, wondering along the way what, if anything, James had said to them. I couldn't imagine he would try to poison his parents against me. He still expected me to leave. But if I decided to stay forever, and that was clear to him, who knew what he might say or do to destroy my life?

* * *

I shut my door and heard Mom call from the backyard, "We're in back! Come around, darling!"

I walked around the flagstone path, past the shaded side of the house where James had first realized I wasn't the Joseph he loved. I rounded the last corner to the backyard, the bright sun hitting my face. I put a shading hand up as I walked and saw them seated at the table near the pool. But as I approached, I saw that the man and woman awaiting me were not my mother and father. It was my mother's best friend, Annette, and James.

Annette stood, head tilted lovingly to the side, arms outstretched for a hug.

"Darling," she said.

James remained seated, leaning back in the chair with his hands clasped over his belly. He wore a smug smile.

"So good to see you," I said as she squeezed. I faked a peaceful smile to James, but his satisfied expression remained.

"Annette called me as soon as she heard you were coming over," he said. "She's only in town for a couple days."

"Sure, great," I said as I pulled out a chair to sit. "Where are Mom and Dad?"

"Early tee time," Annette said. "They assumed you wouldn't be here 'til around lunch."

"Ah," I said as I sat.

"But that's okay, dear," Annette said. "I know all about your troubles and Jamey and I thought it'd be a good chance for us to talk without them. You know how Lani tries to keep everything on the positive ... but no one would ever get to be *real* if you can't bring up the bad with the good, right?" Her jangly bracelets and large rings sparkled in the sunlight as she gulped her tall mimosa.

"We want to talk real," James said.

I realized my knee was shaking so I stopped it. "Absolutely!" I said. "Real it is. Who's first, Jamey? Me or you?"

He chuckled silently. "I think the wisest of us should say her piece, what do you think, 'Nette?"

"Suck it, Jamey," she said with a wink. "Wise is just pussy for *old*, and I don't speak pussy."

I laughed as genuinely as I could muster, definitely not pleased with this ambush, regardless of the intended message.

"You know I love you, darling." A foreboding preamble. "But Lan and Stephen ain't gonna say what needs to be said. And as happy as you seemed to be in the beginning with her ... well, we all want the old Joey back." I glanced at James, rolling his thumbs in little circles over his belly, nodding. "She's just not good for you, hon. It's hard to hear, I'm sure, and they woulda danced around it with you, but they tell me straight-up: 'That girl's the worst thing that's happened to him since …' Well, since the last bad thing that happened to you, sugar."

She leaned forward and stroked my knee.

"And why would they feel that way?" I asked her, but I was looking at James.

"Well, it's pretty obvious, I think." Annette said. "You ain't yourself! You're a goddamn mess, hurtin' folks like you did. You know … just real *out-of-character* type stuff, doll."

I felt like everything she was saying was fed directly to her by James, but I was not deluded enough to believe that was the only possibility. There were legitimate reasons for my parents to feel that way, but to blame it on Melanie? I guessed that was James's doing. He wanted to lower the appeal of staying. He wanted me to know that my relationships with others I cared about would be strained, especially if I continued a relationship with Melanie—a guarantee if I were to remain.

"Before you got here …" James said as he leaned onto the table. "… Annette and me were discussing how people can change so drastically … so suddenly …"

I interrupted, "Well, as much as I love a good intervention—"

James continued, "And she just *loves* to remind me of how much *I* changed when you and me were kids."

"Well," Annette said after another deep gulp of her drink. She turned to James. "To be honest, I like to say what a shit you were!"

James laughed heartily, maintaining eye contact with me.

"Lan and Stephen always wanna shut me up, but it's the God's truth and they know it. Before you two got scared shitless by the poison scare, Jamey was a fat hunka cement, holding the family under water, drownin'!"

"Haha, you always say that," James said merrily. "But I think I was just a little too clever for everyone's liking."

She turned back to him, aghast. I tried to figure out where he was trying to go with this; where he was veering her reminiscence. I knew it couldn't be a simple "we all change: sometimes for the better, sometimes for the worse." He wanted me to hear something he thought would give me pause.

"Clever, my ass!" she said, stabbing an accusing finger his way. "You were doggone *evil*. Didn't give two shits about anyone except maybe Joey, and even he had to suffer when the mood struck you." She turned back to me. "And a little pervert if ever there was one! Hiding in closets, under beds, peeping on the neighbors. I never told your parents about this, but one time I caught him yanking his little wiener on my bed, trying to leave a nasty present on my pillow! Slapped the shit out of him!"

"You slapped the shit out of me," he confirmed. "It's funny, but I don't remember any of that."

"Well, we all sure do. They had to move you two to only male teachers 'cause Jamey would hide under the teachers' desks to peep up their dresses!"

James laughed with her. I sat quietly, awaiting the point that was surely imminent.

"When was it that everything changed again?" he said, as if truly confused.

"Oh, I will never forget that day. It was like God himself had come down and banished the demon from your little body! It was just a week or two before that poor little girl from your school and all the others got sick. It hit you both so hard, but ... God bless her." Annette turned toward James again, fraught. "I truly feel that little girl lost her mind so you could have yours back. There, I said it!" She turned back to me. "You remember, don'tcha, hon? You got to have the brother you shoulda always had! Lan and Stephen won't admit to it now—probably blocked it all out—but we had us some heart to hearts in the thick of it, and I ain't afraid to say it, but a lot of the time ... well ... We all wished his Hirschsprung had taken him when he was a baby. No colon surgery ... Just let nature take its course like it shoulda." She paused and suddenly frowned, turning back to him. "But dear God, darlin', you know that ain't the case anymore!"

James put up his hands and shrugged his assent.

And then I got it. It hit me. Oh fuck, did it hit me. James had just won.

"I thank God for givin' all of us the strength to make it through that first decade," Annette continued. "And damn if didn't pay off. I just love you two so much ... gimme some." She waved for us to come and hug her, but I wasn't hugging anyone. James came around the table, leaned down, and hugged, rocking side to side with her.

"Love you so much, 'Nette," he said, muffled in her neck. "You know how sorry I am that I put everyone through that."

They noticed I'd gotten up when I was halfway to the side of the house.

"What the—Where you goin' darlin'?"

"Joseph, come on back," James called, but it was for her benefit.

I fumbled with my car door, unable to open it for some reason. I swore and yanked at it, punched the door and shouted at it. But I realized it was just locked and I used the fob to unlock it, climbed in, and slammed the door behind me. Then I couldn't seem to get the keys into the ignition. I was lost. I was shattered. He'd done it. He got me. He always had me. I jabbed the key repeatedly at the slot until it finally went in. The Land Rover revved to life. That's when James appeared in front of my car. His face was no longer smug, but he was certainly convicted, content, and perhaps a bit apologetic. I wanted to throw the gearshift into drive and run him over, crush him between the bumper and my parents' front wall, but I couldn't help but look at him differently. He was me, after all. I was James.

* * *

A dust cloud rose behind me as I sped down the driveway. Seconds from the road, a car turned in ahead of me and I slammed on the brakes and swerved. It was my parents, faces pale with fright. We ended up side-by-side, the front of my SUV a foot from their fence and tall hedge. They stared at me for a moment before Dad's window rolled down.

I wanted to speed away, but they were blocking the exit. I gestured for him to move forward but received only befuddled, concerned faces in return. Dad gestured for me to roll down my window. I opened it a crack.

"Please move," I shouted.

"What's going on, Joey?" Dad shouted.

"Honey, what's wrong?" Mom called from the passenger seat.

"I ... I just gotta go!" I yelled. "Please move!"

"Son, I am not moving one Christing inch until—"

"Move your fucking car, goddamn it!" I screamed. "Move it! Move the fucking car! Now!" I was frothing at the mouth, pounding my fists against my steering wheel. An instant migraine throbbed behind my eyes, pushing them outward—it wanted to pop them from my head entirely. "Fucking move!"

Terrified, Dad jolted their car forward, out of my way. I backed up, skidding, running over a low brick wall or jutting root, and then sped away, bouncing onto the road.

They were my parents. My real parents.

My phone vibrated in my pocket. I pulled it out as I swerved onto the highway. James, of course, calling to be sure we were clear now. I tossed the phone onto the passenger seat.

Joseph was my brother. The good one. I erased my own brother.

A new voicemail alert. "Get the picture?" I expected it said.

I erased my own brother and stole his girlfriend.

A new text message alert. I veered between the slow-moving vehicles on the highway, glanced at the screen alit beside me.

> I'm so sorry. It shouldn't have been that way. Please call me back. Don't do anything crazy.

He wasn't sorry; he was just worried about Joseph. I decided it was time for him to know he didn't need to worry anymore. I tapped the **CALL BACK** button and he picked up before I even heard a ring.

"Listen, I'm really sorry—" he said. There was already pleading in his voice.

"It doesn't matter," I interrupted. "I tried to leave him last night, like you said. It didn't work. If he wasn't gone before, he is now. *I'm really sorry.*"

A period of silence on the other end. I could hear breathing, so I knew he was still there. He tried to speak, but had a frog. He cleared his throat.

"Listen … You, ah …" He spoke with the pleasant, cheery tone of a good ol' buddy. "You meet me somewhere right now, yeah? I think … I think we need to be sure—"

"Trust me, he's gone. I waited an hour and nothing. I've done this enough times to know what it looks like."

Silence again. I put the phone on speaker and tossed it back to the seat. I was still passing cars at a dangerous speed, heading west on Highway 340 toward West Virginia. I had no destination in mind—it was just the first onramp I had come across that wouldn't lead me somewhere with *history*. Not south to Leesburg or D.C., not north to Thurmont and the parks, not east to Baltimore and the Chesapeake. I looked at the gas gauge and saw that I was over three quarters full. Someone honked at me as I darted in front of them.

"Are you still there?" James said. I'd forgotten about him. "Hello?"

"What?"

"What are you going to do now?" His voice was wistful.

"I don't know. What do you care?"

"I care because …" His tone became stern. "I care because it can't end this way. It can't be left open … for any of us. Forget about me. What about your mother and father? What about Melanie? They don't get to say goodbye? You just disappear?"

"Yup."

"We should get a funeral. At the very least, we should get that."

"You want me to kill myself," I said. "You want me to jump off a bridge? Have everyone wonder what they could have done differently to keep me from committing suicide? Have them all convinced it was their own fault? Yeah, that's fucking brilliant James. Excuse me … *Samuel.*"

"No … No, you're right. I don't want that."

"No. You don't," I said. "So shut up and leave me alone. It's done."

"I know it was wrong, what I did. But listen, it was decades ago. You've had a life ... you still have a life."

"You're a piece of fucking work, Samuel. An unbelievable hypocrite. It was at the courthouse, right? Not a noble takeover of a sick baby, but the fucking courthouse. That's where you did it, right? Pushed me out of my body? *I* was holding Morgan's hand, wasn't I?"

He cleared his throat and replied softly, "Yes."

"How long had you been watching me? How long did it take for you to make up your mind that I wasn't worthy of keeping that body you're in? *My* real fucking body?"

"Almost a week."

Traffic screeched to a halt in front of me. I laid on the horn.

"Great," I said. "So you gonna offer me my body back? Do what's right?"

"Er ... would you *want* it back? You want my wife and kids? I thought Mel ..."

That's why I was drawn to Joseph. Why he "fit" so well.

"No, no I don't." It was true—I didn't. "I don't know what... God, I fucking hate you."

"Listen," he said. "It has to be an accident. Drive off a cliff or something. It would be the best for everyone. And you just move on! You don't have to be reminded every time you look in the mirror ..."

"I'm touched how concerned you are for my welfare, Samuel. Truly fucking touched. Leave me the hell alone, now. I'm serious. Don't fucking call me or I swear I'll come back and bounce out Mandy and every one of your kids the way you did it to me. I am deadly serious."

His voice turned dark ... a voice different from any I'd heard before. I guessed it was his real voice. "You do that and I'll do Melanie. I won't hesitate for a second, you evil son of a bitch."

"Hell, I might just do that myself," I said. "If I can't have her, I don't think I can handle her being with anyone else."

He couldn't beat me in a contest of cruelty and he knew it. I passed an accident on the shoulder ahead—the focus of everyone in front of me, slamming on their brakes. I passed the wreckage and sped up.

"You don't deserve to be alive," he choked.

"Quite possibly. But don't think the truly twisted part of this story has escaped me, *brother*. Joseph is gone because of *you*. You made me. You kicked me out of your body—my body. I just jumped into the wrong twin when I came back. So whatever happens, you can always fall back on that knowledge. You know … if ever you need focus, or to determine where you sit on your sliding scale. You made the decision that you would be better at being me than I was—"

"And I was right," he said. "You heard what Annette said. They wished you were dead. *Everyone's* life got better after I booted you out. You came back and look what happened. Anyone's life get better besides your own?"

I wanted to say Melanie's had gotten better, but I wasn't so sure that was true anymore. I was through with him getting in my head, though. As much as he wanted to justify himself, and for as many people he could cite that preferred him to me as a child, the fact remained that *Joseph* was gone because of him and him only. There was no way around it. I accelerated, narrowly avoiding hitting a merging big rig.

"Kill yourself, Frederick!" he shouted. "You took so much! The least you can do is—"

I threw the phone out the window, watched through the side mirror as it disintegrated on the pavement. Idiotic drivers swerved as if it was a bomb.

I was done hearing James and done with this life.

16. The Gully Bridge

A quiet road, bordered on each side by swaying maples and oaks. Fallen leaves lined the sides like orange and brown snow banks. Ahead, there was only the road and the trees and the sliver of pale blue sky. All lines converged in the distance—geometry, or perhaps *perspective*, from an art class. There were no other cars behind me or passing from the opposite direction. I had exited the highway, taken a couple of random turns, and here I was.

I replayed the sequence of events in my head, though I still had no personal recollection. All this time, Samuel had wanted me to think he took James's body as an infant, and now it made sense. He didn't want me thinking about *his* role on that day in front of the courthouse. There *I* was, holding hands with Morgan Lampey. Samuel admitted he had been watching me for a week, studying me, judging my worthiness to live. He must have decided ahead of time that he wasn't going to try my body on for size. No, he had committed himself. He somehow pushed me out, thought he was killing me, sending me "wherever you're supposed to go." And that's when I was born and found myself atop a statue. Frantic pigeons fled.

It was *my* body's waves I saw in the group of children! Not Morgan's! It was calling me back. That feeling of being drawn in, just as I'd felt around Joseph's body before going in. Samuel had said I couldn't push him out if I wanted to. I wondered if he somehow deflected me into the girl.

Samuel had wanted me to believe that it was a random day in his life as James, when suddenly a "lost soul" took over his girlfriend. But he wasn't in my body more than a few minutes. How surprised he must have been when I showed up next to him.

"He's a doll now! Been a doll since before Junior High!"

How the fuck did I miss that?

"And she just *loves* to remind me how much *I* changed when you and me were kids."

I felt sicker and emptier every minute.

Despite the bright sky, I was driving in an endless black tunnel. I was the one curled up in a ball in the dark corner of the room in my head. My body was on autopilot. If the road had come to a T, or simply dead-ended, I probably would have driven straight on through whatever guardrail or tree trunk awaited me. But instead, the road began to curve subtly, and I curved with it, slowly right, then slowly left, then straight again.

And then I saw it. A small green sign that read CATOCTIN CREEK. And I saw the bridge beyond it. I slowed as I crossed and craned my neck up to see the deep gully and creek below. I couldn't tell how deep the water was, but the drop from the road was certainly significant. On the other side of the bridge, a wide space stretched from the guardrail to the nearest tree—more than enough for a vehicle to fit. I sped up and continued down the road another two miles before stopping and turning around.

I waited a moment, stopped in the middle of the shoulderless road, and feebly wondered if this would be it for both Joseph and me. If I … *my soul* … was fooled into thinking this was my body, could I perhaps die with it? And go … "wherever it is people go," as James—no, Samuel—had put it. I didn't know if I cared either way. I just needed something to end. I needed punctuation.

I pressed the gas pedal to the floor.

By the time the bridge reentered view, the Rover's speedometer needle had kissed the pin beside 120, maxed out. I inched left across the double yellow line to the other side of the road, then steered toward the gap on the right side of bridge. As it rapidly neared, it felt as though I was still accelerating, moving faster than I had realized. The guardrail and tree trunk passed in a blink and I found myself airborne, the engine revving up to a screaming whine, my foot still holding it firmly to the floor. I closed my eyes, gripped the steering wheel, and waited for impact.

The dropping sensation was sickening, but lasted only an instant before the world exploded and twisted and jolted around me. I heard and felt too many things at once to process any of it. Noise and pain. Wet and warm. Everything was dark, and then all at once it was blinding and all pain left me. Albeit much slower, I thought it must feel that way to be a dying patient, imprisoned by one's failing body, wishing only to be released. I imagine that people's desire for heaven becomes less important at the bitter end, and that if there is no such place to which a person travels, heaven instead manifests itself as the absence of suffering. What happens beyond that is no longer relevant. It is peace, whether the soul lives on, disappears, or fuses with some cosmic *Ka* or *chi*.

I felt peace. I felt calm.

But I hadn't disappeared, or gone much of anywhere, in fact. I sat on the muddy bank of a shallow creek, appreciative of the serenity of the scene. Birds tweeted and squawked, unseen within the crowns of the trees above. River rocks clattered at water level, which, it turned out, was less than a foot at its deepest. The Land Rover had rolled at least twice before smashing into the far side of the gully, then rolled back onto the driver side where it now sat, clanking and hissing in the cold shallow water.

I went to it, hopped on top and peered through the opening where the passenger window used to be. My body looked like it had been down a garbage disposer. Glass was strewn everywhere. Strangely, a floor mat lay resting on my thigh. My blood and glovebox contents had been distributed all over the wreckage, deflated airbag, dashboard, and upholstery.

While Joseph had died, I had not. It was the same as any other instance where I remained inside during the body's death. My euphoria had come only from the act. The finality of it. Had I continued to cling to that life, I would have remained entrenched, forever punished by my behavior and deeds, old and recent. The option to change my mind was gone. The future was once again simple—a matter of semi-detached choices, unbound from the baggage-laden trappings of my human existence and history.

I heard a car coming and looked up. A shiny black sedan cruised by without a tap of the brakes. The SUV was clearly visible from the bridge, but someone would have to intentionally look to see it. A few minutes later, the distinct sound of a big rig approached. It roared across the bridge, small particles shaking loose from the supporting structure, falling down to the creek. Engine brakes came to life with their signature blat-blat-blat sound as the wheels continued to squeal well after crossing the bridge and disappearing. The truck shifted into reverse and reappeared a moment later.

The driver got out, cell phone attached to his ear, ran to the end of the bridge, and slid clumsily down the dirt slope. He splashed across the shallow creek, shouting his location to someone on the other end of the line.

"'Bout two miles from Jefferson Pike near three forty. Thing's still steaming, lady! I think it musta just happened!"

He reached the Land Rover, and hunched over to try to see in the crushed windshield. He tapped the roof of the vehicle, apparently checking to see if it was hot, stuffed his phone into his back pocket, then grabbed hold of the top and lifted himself up to where I sat.

"Almighty ..." he breathed.

He didn't bother saying "Mister?" or anything like that. It was pretty clear that the corpse inside hadn't made it.

My body now in the able hands of others, I left.

* * *

Melanie hadn't heard. She had begun a new painting by her sliding glass door. I sat on the back of the couch and watched as music streamed from her computer speakers. An acoustic song came on and she quietly sang along, her voice harmonizing perfectly with his.

"You said always and forever, now I believe you baby …" They crooned together, lyrics I would sing to her given the opportunity, or the slightest hint of vocal talent.

The painting began to take form. While I had hoped for a portrait of Joseph, it turned out to be an oil version of one of her waterfall photographs—the original picture taped to the easel. I tried not to read too much into it, but that is essentially what I do at all times and in all situations. It could mean that the night she spent with the old Joseph meant the most to her, or that the time we spent together thereafter had, in hindsight, highlighted that night as the beginning.

It reminded me of the day—a month after the waterfall—she got the news that her submission to the tourism board had won the top prize, and that it would be used in all of their new marketing materials for the park. She was elated and wanted to celebrate. I told her I knew she would win because "… not that many people submit entries." She was, of course, deflated by this statement. This was, of course, all to protect my ego, and all at her cost.

See, I left that part out when I fast-forwarded in the middle of the story. But hey, I can be a jerk when hurt like anyone else. In the aforementioned case, I didn't like the sudden visit from Old Joseph, the recipient of her gratitude. I apologized later that night, made up some bullshit story about being distracted about work. She felt better, but I had stolen the moment. See, this sort of thing occurs when one prioritizes their own needs ahead of others. According to James/Samuel, this behavior is the root of all evil. But I'll be damned if James/Samuel hasn't tilted toward that side of the scale himself. I doubt there are many who could honestly say they haven't. So I suppose the trick is to aim for *purity*, be conscious of *evil*, and maybe you'll end up floating around *good* with the best of us.

This sounded like a good moral with which to end my story. I did say that it would begin with my introduction to a man named Joseph Cling, and end with the death of said man. I could leave it there. We have all learned something, haven't we? No? Well, all right …

I guess there is a *little* more to the story. But if you're happy with what you've read—or, more importantly, I suppose—if you're happy with *me* at this point, perhaps just close the book or set down the e-reader. Leave well enough alone, shall we? Still no?

* * *

I wanted to spend one last night with my Melanie. I watched as she painted, fixed herself a snack of fruit, nuts, and a smoothie, and checked her phone. I listened to her leave voicemail messages on my phone.

"Checking in again …"

"Trying not to take your silence wrong …"

"I love you. Will wait for you."

She sent a couple text messages to James and Mandy.

To James: "Hear from Joey at all?"

To Mandy: "Call me when you can. Need to talk."

As night fell, Melanie grew increasingly unsettled. She went out the front door onto the porch, scanning the parking lot and watching the street. She did this at least once an hour until finally going to bed.

Unlike the first time I spent an evening on her pillow, Melanie lay on one side of the bed—her side, when we were together. She kept her eyes open and startled every time a loud car passed outside. At one point, she heard footsteps climbing the stairs outside. She sat up on an elbow and listened, waiting for a knock at the door, or for me to simply let myself in.

While all of this would have previously been joyous acts for me to observe, I enjoyed not one bit of it, knowing full well that no one was coming, that I would never return another text or call, and worse: that at some point she would receive a devastating call from someone. And as much as her anguish grew through the night, I wanted it to last as long as possible. No calls tonight, please. Let her sleep.

She sent a final text message to my phone before succumbing.

"Going to sleep now, but still call me whenever you get this. Please. I love you so much."

Well, they at least waited until sunrise. At around 6:45 in the morning, Melanie's phone rang. It was Mandy. I felt compelled to watch, but I fought it. It wasn't as difficult as you may think, the decision to leave once and for all. The idea of seeing her in pain and unable to do anything about it, it was too much. I slid off the bed and went to the living room.

I heard her mumbling at first, confused, repeating words like "how" and "where" and then, instead of the scream I expected, she became even more garbled. I moved to the doorway and looked into the bedroom. She was facing away from me, sitting on the edge of her side of the bed. One hand was over her mouth, the other pressed the phone against her ear as she shook her head, no. Just as I expected, I couldn't watch. I had spent my last night with her and there was nothing more I could do for her. I would finally go this time.

I wished I had written her something, but then it wouldn't really have been taken as an accident, would it?

As I went to the front door I was suddenly bombarded with terrible thoughts. She would of course take care of Jaxy, but what about the rest of my house? What sort of incriminating things would she find? What had I left on my computer screen, the one without password protection? Nothing came directly to mind. It wasn't as though she hadn't been living there with me most of the time. My phone was speckled across a Maryland highway, so I didn't have to worry about her seeing my text history with James. What about e-mail …

Suddenly, a foot passed through me, and up the hall. Keys jingled off the key rack, and Melanie hurriedly opened then slammed the front door behind her. I heard her descend the stairs and wondered what I should do. Did I want to see her see me? Did I want to see my parents, James, others? I did wonder what sort of show James would put on, but then recognized that some amount of mourning would be warranted from him, and surely genuine.

I made a snap decision and rushed through the door, glided down the stairs, and leapt into Melanie's car just as she was pulling away. She was hyperventilating, juggling her glasses and the steering wheel as she wiped her eyes on her sleeves to clear her vision. We took corners at unsafe speeds, and bottomed out flying across a drainage dip.

I could tell she didn't believe it was true. She had to see my body for herself. Only then would it all be real. Her demeanor as she drove was not one of bereavement, but of grave concern, as a mother rushing to the hospital upon hearing their child broke a leg at a soccer game.

Her phone buzzed and toned and she glanced at it after veering onto the highway. She quickly tossed it back into her cup holder, facedown, before I could read what it said. Whatever it was, it didn't change anything. She was driving how I had the day before. I instantly began to panic, fearing she would get herself into a horrendous accident on her way to see my corpse.

"Jesus, Joey," she said, then blurted, "What the fuck?" She mashed on her horn and screamed, "Move! Yes, you, idiot! Move!" She honked again and slammed on the gas, pulling onto the shoulder to pass the congestion. "I'm coming, Joey ... I'm coming ..."

I regretted going with her. I didn't need to see any of this.

She took the exit to Frederick Medical Center, where she worked, rounding two corners before pulling into the E.R. lot. I followed her as she ran through the small parking lot and through the automatic doors. Inside, she flashed her badge to the security guard, keyed a code into a pad on the wall, and pushed through a door.

We passed a nurse. "Oh, hey Mel, what're you doing on this side?"

"MVA from this morning," Melanie replied without stopping. "Male, forties—"

"Upstairs," the nurse said with a grim shake of her head. "Trauma. Friend of yours?"

Melanie ignored her and continued to the elevator. The nurse nodded toward Melanie and said "Scoop and run" to someone else behind the counter.

We emerged on a new floor and I followed Melanie down a shiny white hallway. Ahead, I could see the small crowd outside a door: James, Mandy, Annette, Mom and Dad, and a doctor.

"What's happening?" Melanie said as she approached the group.

Everyone turned, and I noticed a look of surprised fury from both my mother and father.

"Who called *her*?" Dad said, and he guided Mom away.

Melanie was bewildered, but brushed it off and awaited an answer—as did I.

"They're operating right now," James said.

Operating?

"Are you the spouse?" the doctor said, glancing over her clipboard.

"Yeah ..." Melanie stumbled. "Well, girlfriend."

"Sure, sure, that's fine. I'll repeat what I just told the family—"

Melanie interrupted, "Just tell me if he's going to make it. How serious—"

"Much of his injuries are internal," the doctor said. "I don't ever like to say fifty-fifty, but this was a very serious accident."

"We can fill her in on the rest," James said, and pulled Melanie aside.

I slipped through one wall in search of my body, but it was a storage room. Beyond another wall, an empty operating room. I popped back into the hall, observed Melanie crying with the group, then passed into the opposite wall. This one was a break room with several hospital staff chatting over coffee and pastries.

I was nowhere to be found, and went back to the hallway and followed the path the doctor had taken. Around a corner and through a set of automatic doors, I found a busy area with staff bustling through the halls, and in and out of rooms. I finally found it. There were six people working on my body, tubes emerging from my mouth and nose, bloodied instruments buried deep inside my torso, suspended monitors with live views of the chaos inside.

Everyone spoke with calm, assured voices. I hopped onto one of the screens for a better view.

"Gauze," a maroon-clad doctor said. "Suture that, please, Joyce." He glanced back at the vital signs scrolling across the screen beneath me. "What the hell is this?" Others at the table glanced up.

"The static," a nurse said.

"Yeah," the doctor replied, rolling his aching neck, and began working in a new area. I jumped off the screen. "That's better. Phil, make sure I.T. checks that thing out later, okay?"

Phil grunted. The screen was fine, though. It was my presence that gave it the jitters.

"There we go!" the doctor cheered. "That should get our pressure up."

They should have let me die. All this just to have a warm body in a wheelchair, facing out a sunroom window.

"See this?" the doctor said. "That's from the seat belt."

"BMs?" a nurse said.

"He's got another eighteen feet of perfectly good tubing in there. Not worried about digestion. Pneumothorax and bleeding was biggest concern."

The doctor from the hallway poked her head in the room. "Status, Todd?"

"Looking good," he said.

"How good?" she replied, skeptical.

"You know my favorite idiom, CJ," he said with a wink, then returned to the apparently-ruptured intestines.

"Out of the woods," Doctor CJ said, smiled, and let the door close behind her.

* * *

Due to my mother and father blaming Melanie for my life falling apart, they made it clear to her that she wasn't welcome in my ICU room. It seemed to me that they weren't the best at handling the crisis at hand, allowing their fears to get the best of them and blaming the only available scapegoat. However, thanks to James insisting Mom and Dad leave the hospital for dinner, Melanie was allowed to sit with the unconscious Joseph. Annette left with my parents and James and Mandy walked off to give Melanie privacy.

She walked into the room slowly, carefully, as if to avoid awaking a baby. Her face was stricken as she came around the curtain—tense, with the same sort of apprehension it betrayed when she had walked around Uncle Dom. She did and didn't want to see me. Small steps inched her closer to the bedside, closer to the unrecognizable, human-shaped lump of purple and black. White tubes and wires. Fiberglass and polyurethane. Bandages soiled by still-weeping wounds. She brought one hand over her stomach and the other to her neck. She collapsed into the chair beside the bed, buried her face in the sheets, and tried to be quiet.

Melanie fought to compose herself. She cleaned her glasses, dried her eyes, and sat up straight, almost studiously.

"Hi Joey," she said. "The doctors say you're doing real well." She paused, seemed to contemplate before resuming. "I've heard about people … couples … They have problems, big issues and things. Stuff they can't get over between them. Mostly stupid stuff, but that's not the point." Another beat. "The point … *yeah* … I don't know the point—No, I *do*. I do know the point. What I'm trying to say is that you hear about these people … They're on the outs, pretty much wrapping up the business of calling it quits. Then one of them gets hurt—say, the man gets hurt—and all of a sudden the woman can't live without him. 'He was always so good to me. Sure, there were tough times, but blah blah blah.'" She made her circling hand "blah-blah-blah" gesture that I loved so much. "And then the guy either pulls through, or—well, let's just say for this that he pulls through, and everything is fine. He comes home, the wife takes care of him, he's appreciative, new lease on life, blah blah blah." She closed her eyes, shook her head with frustration. "But things just go back to the same old bullshit, you know? They maybe last another six months together. Maybe even things are *worse!* Anyway, the point. I'm trying to say that you and me aren't those people. We were never those people. We just got through what's gotta be the craziest fucking hump that a couple would ever get thrown at them. You know, like a test or something. Of course there's a ton more shit to go through 'cause you don't get off so easy when you do something like you did, but whatever. We'd get through it. We'd go through that *together*."

She got lost in thought, searched around the room, checked her watch.

"What I'm trying to say is that I'm not idealizing you because of this. I'm not seeing the world and our future and … *you* through any trauma-tainted glasses. I'm still pissed at you for Andrew! I'm pissed that all my co-workers are going to find out private things about me because there has to be hearings and a trial and all this bullshit because you went crazy. I don't understand how the hell this happened to you in the first place when you drive like a grandma in a parking lot! But I love that about you. It's *part* of you, along with a thousand other things that I could list off the top of my head. And now you know that it's not just because you're hurt and I'm scared or can't be alone. It's real."

Three light taps on the hospital room door. It was James with Mandy looking over his shoulder. He raised his eyebrows to verify everything was fine. Melanie nodded and put up an index finger to ask for another minute. She turned back to my body, put a tentative hand on my forearm—one of the exposed areas of actual skin.

"That's all I wanted you to know. That we passed that test. Everyone wants to think they're different from everyone else—making comparisons, pointing out unique things, but I feel like … I think we actually *are*. To someone else that would sound so dumb and condescending, I know—as in 'Oh, we're all the same, but somehow *you're* the exception!' I don't know, maybe it is."

I wanted so badly to tell her it wasn't dumb. We *were* different. And we had still been growing as partners. It was so early in our relationship. I'd looked forward to stages and more adventures and milestones. I wanted to tell her that I heard her, that her jumbled, beautiful, stream-of-consciousness message had been received. I don't know why that was so important to me. She'd been able to say what she wanted to say. That, in itself, was probably what she needed more than me hearing it.

"Mel, hon?" Mandy's gentle voice in the doorway.

"Yeah, I'm done. I'm coming."

She stood up beside my old, used up body, leaned over my tube-riddled face, and inhaled. I doubted she found much of any scent aside from alcohol and iodine. Her gaze held on the shiny, closed, blackened eyelids for a moment, then she turned and walked out.

17. Good

I t's perhaps a bit morose to stick around one's body and watch as friend after friend, uncle after cousin, co-workers and acquaintances come and visit. Morose because they know you are in a coma and may not ever wake up, and their sentiment therefore drifts somewhere between fragile hope and mourning. To know that their grief was for a friend of many years, family members sobbing over decades of moments shared with Old Joseph, the experience for me was not remotely narcissistic. Combine that with the fact that this was *my* doing, it was in many ways like I was a convicted murderer standing in a courtroom as the victims' families rebuke and share exactly what was taken from them as a result of my actions.

The nights at the hospital belonged to James. He stayed after everyone else had left and stared at the empty shell, perhaps waiting for his brother to miraculously awaken. He summoned nurses to check on Joseph at a greater frequency than their schedules required. He researched traumatic accidents on a tablet computer, and then asked doctors about the things he had read. Tests he knew they hadn't performed, experimental treatments from other countries. In the end, all he could get out of them was assurance that his brother needed time to heal, and could regain consciousness in weeks or months, but not days. One doctor stated that if Joseph was conscious, they would likely put him into a medically-induced coma for his own good. *Patience* was the message.

On my third night in the hospital room, just after James sent Mandy home with the kids, James began pacing. He peered out the window and waited to see his family appear in the parking lot. He was behaving suspiciously, and I didn't know what was up. I had been thinking about leaving that night so I would have enough time to travel, vet and study my next life. But I was glad I had stayed.

James glanced both ways down the hall and closed the door. He brushed past the curtain and looked all around the room, high and low.

"Frederick?" He finally said. "I know you're here."

I obviously couldn't answer, but I knew that the screen with the vitals streaming by would be sensitive to my energy. The lines and characters grew fuzzy when I was near it, just like the one in the operating room. I hopped on a counter, slid across the arm from the wall, and perched atop the monitor. It took a few seconds, but then James noticed it.

"Ah, is that you?" He said, and I slid back down the arm to let the screen sharpen, then returned. "Yes, it is you. Good, I'm glad you're still here. Listen, I know you have to leave soon to find a new body. Maybe … maybe you'll be more careful next time … entering, you know? So if you change your mind at any point, or for any reason things don't work out, you can let them go."

He slid a chair back and turned it to face me. He sat down and addressed the screen as me.

"You're going to do what you want to do, of course … I know this … And I know you have no reason to do what I say. But I hope you pick the *right* candidates in the future. You know what I mean by that. And don't seek out others like us. You're going to be curious, but … there are some powerful individuals out there that're … Well, they're not like me. Ours is a solitary existence but for the families that adopt us."

A nice euphemism, I thought. *More like we adopt them, not the other way around.* I wondered who these others were he had mentioned. He tells me not to be curious, but then gives me something to be curious about. Who knows if I would have thought to seek out others?

There're caves out there in the hills, Jimmy. Don't go in 'em!

James took a deep breath, scratched his cheek. "I'm not as self-congratulatory as you think, you know? About kicking you out? I have a lot of guilt about that. I justified it for years that you were bad, I was good, so everything was hunky-dory. I was going to show the whole family how perfect I was now, and every compliment about the 'new James' meant that I'd done the right thing. But I know I didn't. I'm just trying to make the best of it now. Live out this life to the very end, try to do good things, make people's lives better, and then move on.

"You weren't a bad person, you know. Annette exaggerates. That was kind of why I wanted her to talk to you. Your parents loved you. They thought you were hilarious. There were plenty of good times between the bad. I know because that was one of things they missed when I took your place. I was so focused on being good and helpful and smart that they would be sad when I didn't want to perform for them. You used to put on puppet shows and plays and things in the living room. They would say things to me like 'you know, you don't have to be like Jojo *all* the time.' They missed you. It hurt me to hear it, but I think it's important for you to know. Everyone missed you for the first couple years ... especially Joey. He loved the fact that I wasn't setting his baseball cards on fire anymore, or stealing his clothes and towel from the bathroom so he'd have to come out naked, but there was a ... I don't know ... *zest* you had for life that I apparently couldn't simulate. He got used to how the relationship changed after a while, but I knew I had made a bad choice that I couldn't take back."

He sighed, searched his thoughts for anything else he may have wanted to say to me.

"It might be meaningless at this point, but if there's anything positive you can draw from this experience, it's that you know where you came from. You have every blank space in your history filled in, if that's important to you. It was important to me and I'll never have it."

"Who you talking to?" A dry, weak voice.

We both turned to the bed, disbelieving. It was Joseph. He was trying to raise his hand. One eye appeared to be sealed shut, but the other rolled around wildly in an effort to take in all there was to see.

"Where ...?"

James leapt up, darted to the bed, held Joseph's hand down before he pulled out his IV.

"Jojo, oh my God, Joey, you're ..." He rambled on in this way for a moment before hitting the nurse call button dangling from the bed rail.

"Where's Mel?" Joseph croaked. "She was ... I think we were driving ... Is she ..."

"Mel's fine, Jojo," James said, holding his brother's hand—*my* brother's hand. "Nothing happened to her. I'll call her right now and tell her you're awake. She'll come."

"Is ... Is there something I'm supposed to be doing right now?"

James laughed maniacally. "No, no, nothing. Just relax. All you need to do is lay there and heal. You were in a car accident. By yourself."

"Don't 'member," Joseph said and tried to swallow. "Can I have water? Were you talking to me? I heard you talking."

This Q&A session went on for some time while James called or texted everyone he could think of. Soon, there would be hordes of people filling the room. And then James's face morphed into one of sudden distrust. He glanced at the vital sign monitor which he discovered to be crisp and clear (I had moved). He spun slowly around, scanning the room for some sign of me. Then he turned back to Joseph with a suspicious glare.

James said, "Whooshoo lie whar ermay sho srish inshuh?"

Joseph smiled weakly, blinked slowly, and replied, "Whar besher. Maysho srish laysha."

James sighed with relief, smiled wide, and stepped out of the room to track down a nurse. One was already coming, clearly in no hurry due to James's prior cryings of wolf.

"He's awake!" James called to her, and she stopped, stunned, then came running.

She unclipped a phone or radio from her belt and began calling people. In the room, she said hello and good morning to Joseph, checked his vitals, and began asking him questions. From the hall I heard people coming. They could have been hospital staff, or they could have been Melanie and members of the family. I didn't want to know. So I left.

* * *

Typically a story like this would wrap up with me sharing a brief, yet tantalizing summary of where I went next. My time with Melanie and the Clings had come to an end. That story was done, and I was the main character. Did I turn out to be a pro- or antagonist for you? It turns out that I *do* care. My concept of myself had been skewed from the beginning. I was never incapable of sympathy or empathy, I was just unsympathetic and selfish. I like to think that fact changed after my short stay in Frederick, but that is for you to decide for yourself.

I'm not going to say right now where I went next, because I find the story of Joseph, Melanie, and James to be more interesting at this point, and in this context. Because I did keep tabs. James and I are "friends" online, so I get all sorts of enlightening updates and photos from him.

Dr. Kalestian dropped all charges against Joseph. Some believe it was because he found out about the accident and Joseph's amnesia, which was verified to be genuine by a specialist. That may have touched his heart. Then again, the doctor's wife didn't want her husband's affairs (yes, with an oh-so-shocking plurality) to become public knowledge. How embarrassing that would have been for her. "You're going to drop this, Andy," I imagine her commanding as he nursed his plastic surgery wounds. The DA certainly wasn't concerned with such things, and he didn't buy Joseph's amnesia claims. He decided to still prosecute. Unfortunately for him, though, with an uncooperative victim, his case pretty much fell apart.

His legal troubles behind him, Joseph's job was waiting for him right where he left it, albeit limited to the office due to his bum legs. I wondered if Najafi thought his little search warrant trick with the judge was really gone from Joseph's memory. He had certainly been nicer to me after that. Scott Lieter knew about the illegal warrant, too, though, and as far as Najafi was concerned, Scott could have reminded Joseph of it his first day back at work.

My parents seemed to abandon whatever negative feelings they had toward Melanie. There is photo evidence of grand times had by all. For example, my mother planting a sloppy kiss on Melanie's squished cheek. Couples outings on the golf course (Joseph with his cane ... sorry). Clinked wine glasses over a Thanksgiving table. All of these photos show people enjoying the very happiest of lives.

Joseph and Melanie moved into the house together and were married a year later. Their wedding photos are amazing, and look like the sort of idyllic shots from wedding ring catalogs and resort websites. They honeymooned in Puerto Rico, of all places. Who the hell honeymoons in Puerto Rico besides Puerto Ricans? Melanie's idea. She had always wanted to go there. There are great self-taken photos of the two of them in front of the sorts of beaches I would expect to find in Tahiti or Acapulco. There are full shots of them taken by strangers as well. Joseph's arms around Mel's waist, her gorgeous poof of coils forever blowing in his face. Some might find this window into their oh-so-perfect life to be nauseating, but not I. And it gets better.

Melanie gave birth to a son this year. Yup. The newborn shots are anything but cute—the kid was more a tiny, gray pissed-off goblin than adorable baby. But he got better. Even at just one month old, the little one could be a model for Baby Gap. I can honestly say he looks more like me than Melanie. It's a little weird to say that, but it's true in every sense. Just a damned good-looking kid. *We* named him Frederick. You know, after the town.

*

Acknowledgements

Special thanks to talented author Marcy Dermansky for her keen editing of this novel. Gratitude goes as well to my faithful and forgiving beta readers: Alyssa, Angela, Bill H., Bill R., Eric, Jess, Karen, Stacey, and Vicky. And finally, my wife, Ana, to whom this book is dedicated, because without her, not only would there be no books, but I'd still be hunched over a keyboard all day, cursing my life (as opposed to being hunched over a keyboard all day, loving my life).

An excerpt from the prequel to A Warm Place to Call Home

The Many Lives of Samuel Beauchamp
(a demon's story)

My name—the one I currently use—is Geoffrey Cuion. I've lived in East Harlem, New York for nearly three years, moving here from Oklahoma City in 1956. I have a lengthy police record back in Oklahoma, Kansas, and Missouri. Assault and battery, mayhem, larceny, robbery, weapons possession, kidnapping, attempted murder, and manslaughter. Society would consider me an "ex-con," *if* society knew who I was. If they knew *what* I was, well ... that would be a wholly different matter.

My stocky body boasts countless scars—wounds obviously inflicted by knives and bullets—as well as a few minor burns around my legs. As the majority of ex-convicts claim, I had nothing to do with any of the aforementioned crimes, nor the incidents that led to my scars. I accept no responsibility for the ROAD DEVILS M C tattooed around a nude woman atop a flaming motorcycle on my right pectoral. Likewise, I did not select the vulgar tattoos on my right shoulder or left forearm. All are shameful vestiges of a life left behind, and I keep them safely hidden in public. The one thing I cannot hide is the thick, earthworm-like scar that runs the ridge of my jawline from right earlobe to chin. Though hair never grows there, I often knick it when shaving, adding scar upon scar.

I go by "Geoff." It sounds friendly, inviting. When people call me by name I light up. It must appear to the speaker that I am particularly elated to see them, when in reality it is simply an acknowledgement that I have them convinced. I am who they think I am. But beyond that, it means they do not know who I *was*. Well, who *he* was. Because they would have instead called me "Tinker," and being addressed by that name would mean that life, as I knew it then, was over.

Abilene, Kansas - 1956

I sat at the end of the bar and wiped the sweat from my pint of beer. Motorcycle engines roared outside Gracie's Canteen as the jukebox spun Hank Williams' "Your Cheatin' Heart." A wobbling fan overhead strove in vain to clear cigarette smoke from the air. A man in a crackled leather jacket and brown-tinted sunglasses sat at the middle of the bar, glancing back at the door every time it struck the hanging bell above. He had broad, square shoulders and little neck to speak of. His hair was greasy and long, slicked back and curling up at the neck. His big, bushy sideburns led to a handlebar moustache, and the right side of his jaw bore a large, raised scar stretching from chin to earlobe.

"You want sump'm, shitstick?" the man said, and I realized he was talking to me. I must have been staring, and with his sunglasses on, I couldn't see his eyes.

"No, sir," I said and looked down at my drink.

"Well, why you eyein' me like you know me? You know me?" Other conversations in the room quieted.

I shook my head and didn't look up. I reached in my shirt pocket, pulled out a dollar, and tossed it on the bar before heading to the men's room.

Wincing as the urine flowed into the steel trough, I waited for the pain to end. The burning down there had been growing worse by the day. A week earlier I'd had a bout of coughing, during which I'd spat bloody phlegm. Something was obviously wrong with Vernon's innards, and getting worse. When I returned his scrawny body to him, he'd find his health problems well advanced, and would have no recollection of traveling from Denver to Abilene, Kansas.

The restroom door creaked open behind me, the garbled sounds of conversation and laughter spilling in. The door closed and I felt someone lurk close to my back. I buttoned Vernon's slacks and spun round to see the scarred man from the bar, his jaw clenched, lips crinkled tight. His sunglasses sat on his head, angry cobalt eyes wandering over Vernon's gaunt face.

"Pardon me," I said as I tried to move around him.

"You telling me to move?"

"Ahh ... yes, actually. Asking. If you don't mind."

His nostrils flared. He raised his chin. His neck muscles tensed into a bulbous V, and then he snapped into motion, slamming big, gnarly hands into my chest. My legs smashed into the urinal edge as my back crashed into the wall, a knob or pipe jamming into my ribs. My rear dropped into the basin, soaking the seat of my pants. When I opened my eyes, he was arched over me. He grasped a clutch of hair on the side of my head and a switchblade clicked open an inch from my eye.

I knew he'd follow me into the room. I'd expected some choice words and threats—something to goad me outside for a fistfight. The man was clearly scum, as I'd assumed, but if this was the sort of thing he pulled when someone merely *looked* at him, I was certain he'd done far worse in his lifetime. And I had seen enough.

I eased out of Vernon and slid into "Tinker."

"Tinker, what the hell, man?" A fellow in a leather vest gawked from the doorway. "Gracie gonna ban you for life this time."

I stood upright and turned, washed my new hands in the sink, then looked over my new face in the mirror.

"You all right, Mister?" the man in the door asked Vernon. "Mister?"

I walked back into the bar in silence and strode across the room toward the exit, all eyes on me. Behind me, I heard Vernon's panicked voice shout, "Where am I?" as I raised Tinker's hand to pull the main entrance door, acting as nonchalant as possible. The overhead bell chimed.

I strove to curb my paranoid thoughts. *They know! Someone knows! Run!*

Outside, in the hazy sunlight, bikers lingered around motorcycles and a stock car on a trailer. I pulled Tinker's sunglasses down over his eyes and walked to my new motorcycle, the one on which I'd seen him arrive earlier. I was relaxed, cool, but also tough and scary, or at least that was the impression I was going for.

Someone nearby called, "You headin' out, Tinker?"

I glanced over and nodded, searching my pockets for keys. A tall man with spiked blonde hair and shiny sunglasses was moseying toward me. I found the keys in a breast pocket, mounted the motorcycle, and attempted to shoot a sinister look his way. He paused, peered behind him down the road, and then took another hesitant step toward me.

He tilted his head. "Bird said he was gonna come talk'atcha over here. You likely wanna wait a while for him to show."

I started the engine.

"Well, where's you headed?" he shouted over the roar.

I walked the bike back a few yards and throttled onto Highway 40, heading east, a trail of dust pluming in my wake. Buffeting wind beneath my shirt and jacket chilled the glaze of sweat on my chest. Tinker was a dirty, sticky man before I'd arrived, but my nerves and fear kept the perspiration flowing. Fear that a horde of tiny motorcycles would soon appear in my mirrors, speeding after me. Nerves about my stash—all my money and worldly possessions—stuffed into an abandoned well, covered with dead shrubs, all hidden beneath an old piece of plywood not twenty feet off an open road. And I fast learned that Tinker had actually needed to use the restroom—and not to urinate.

Exiting the highway onto the dirt side road, my rear wheel wobbled and slid. I'd had a bit of experience riding off pavement, so fortunately didn't fall. I glanced back down 40 in search of pursuers. None yet. The hazards and insecurity of body transitions had always been one of my primary reasons for delaying it as long as possible. And this biker I'd chosen—an unprecedented risk in character alone, a public transition, acquaintances on the way to a scheduled meet-up, numerous witnesses to my silent departure from the scene, not to mention my earlier decision to leave my belongings in so open an area. Taking Tinker at that moment had been a rash move, a fear-based choice. And now I had to retrieve my stash in the light of day.

I dismounted the motorcycle and realized I was shaking.

I'm such a coward, I thought. *Seemingly immortal, yet afraid of everything.*

My new stomach churned with stabbing pains, like an angry, violent criminal demanding release.

The wind shoved at me—quick, bursting gusts—like some invisible giant: intimidating, taunting, a thunderous voice in my ear. But the surrounding hills chose to embrace the wind, their blankets of wild grasses dancing and bowing upward, pleasant green waterfalls somehow flowing against gravity. I inhaled a deep breath and let the peaceful sight calm me.

Such a beautiful world.

My gut reminded me that despite the world's beauty, nothing mattered more than *immediate release*. I was mortified by what I needed to do out in the open—not a shrub in sight higher than two feet, and cars passing every minute. I dropped my trousers and squatted, facing away from the road to hide my face. Sweat gushed from every pore as I heard a big rig (of course a big rig) barrel down the highway. The brakes squealed momentarily, and then the ever-warping sound of a prolonged horn blast. *"Just lettin' you know I see ya, buddy,"* it said. *"Hang on a sec while I announce this over my CB."*

Defeated and ashamed, I cleaned myself as much as possible with bundles of barbed shrubbery and wide-bladed grasses, and kicked dirt over the scene. Relieved and re-buttoned, I stepped toward the plywood-covered well. And then my belly informed me that my relief had only been intermission.

A short time later, I observed my stash lying untouched where I'd left it. Relief after relief. It certainly wouldn't have worked after switching bodies to ask a perplexed Vernon if I could borrow his car keys for a moment. "Just need to unload a few things, stranger." Especially looking like this Tinker character. In this body, I might as well have had a sign on my back that read: "MURDER." No, when I passed Gracie's in Vernon's car earlier, I knew at once I needed to do a drop. There were sure to be body choices aplenty beyond those well-worn doors.

I lay down in the dirt and reached into the pit with both arms, grabbing my canvas clothes bag, money bag, then the crate. This was going to be difficult. I knew the instant I'd mounted the bike that I was making a decision to leave some things behind. I'd been accumulating treasured non-monetary keepsakes for twenty-three years. After stowing the cash I'd amassed (about $280,000 at that point, primarily from an inheritance I'd arranged), the bike's tasseled leather saddlebags wouldn't hold much more.

I sat up and folded my legs together, squinting again down the highway. Still clear.

The crate first. I reached in and grabbed my Buck knife. *That* I would *not* be giving up. A gift from one of my fathers, a railroad bull named Dabney Fuller.

Early on, I'd lived as a young hobo named Rip whose life had simply been too difficult for me to endure. In his body I'd been beaten and robbed countless times—forever walking a thread between hunger and true starvation. There was something about Rip's slight body, or perhaps some aspect of my personality, that drew abuse to me. It was as though I exuded weakness.

In Cheyenne, Wyoming, I (Rip) had joined a band of younger 'bos (short for hobos) who, like me, had no families. We'd been waiting in the trees to board a freight, watching as a bull (railroad guard) walked atop the boxcars with a pistol in his hand, searching for folks between the cars. When they were gone, we rushed the tracks and climbed aboard, but only a minute later the bulls came back.

"C'mon down now, you little shits!" one said, banging his club against the side of a car.

It had probably been a trap, but either way, we were yanked off at gunpoint and walked to the edge of the rail clearing. We sat for a moment while the other bulls hurried to come have a look at us. We could tell right away which one was the leader, because right after he stepped up to us, the other bulls' postures improved and they started chuckling to themselves.

"You search 'em yet?" he asked, floating a lantern across each of our faces.

"Not yet, boss."

"Well, strip 'em then," he said, and walked off.

"You heard my Pa, you tramper shits! Strip!" This bull was a fairly young kid. He couldn't have been much older than me, three whiskers scattered across his ruddy face, and a uniform that hung wide off his shoulders.

The four of us stripped down to nothing, terrified of what might come next. "Fortunately," all they did was go through each pocket and hem, extracting coins and bills from every hiding place. I'd thought for some reason they'd forget about our shoes—the toe of one of mine held twenty-eight hard-earned dollars. They didn't forget about our shoes.

When the bulls were done searching our clothes, they stuffed all of our money into a coffee can and threw our clothes back at us. The two grown ones walked off cackling, leaving the young mean one to "send a message."

While he beat us with his club, he called out, "Tell m'Pa to wait up fer me, all right! I's almost done!"

His name was Aaron Fuller, age nineteen, and he didn't beat or rob any more hobos after that day. Not after I jumped in there. That's the optimistic outlook on leaving Rip, but I'll share more about him later.

Despite occupying a taller, thicker body, I hadn't quite escaped the torment of others. Aaron's father was an extraordinary contradiction: loving and proud, yet rageful and volatile. One day he would embrace me and kiss my head and tears would well up in his eyes as he choked out doting, often poetic words, like "Yer better'n me, boy. Yer gonna be sump'em. Yer love is like a mountain on m'chest, boy." Other days it was as though a feeble dam held a black lake of wrath. He never balled a fist to me, but the rapid-fire slaps from his meaty hands nevertheless painted bruises and rattled my skull. He would scream, "Yer just gonna leave me! After everything I've done fer you! You never cared a lick about me!"

Unlike prior transitions, when I left I was somehow able to slip from Aaron's brain without tearing his consciousness out with me. It might've had something to do with never quite feeling at home in him. I'd always been aware of his presence there with me; he was a sleeping predator in the darkest corner of its den. I used this technique from then on when borrowing bodies, ever mindful of the other one with me. Aaron awoke in his home, frightened and confused, but then rapidly accepting, as if awakening from a too-real dream wherein he was beating a group of young 'bos. I was just relieved to see him awaken, and I didn't stick around to witness any revelations of missing time.

Another big rig roared past me on the side of the highway. I tossed Tinker's dull, greasy switchblade, and stuffed the Buck knife into my pocket.

Rubber-banded stacks of notes and letters, my Kodak 35 Rangefinder camera, the Mason jar full of coins and keys and trinkets. Everything had some level of sentimental value, but I needed to select a few choice irreplaceables that would fit, and then move on.

My books.

I was Jerome Johns for the early half of the 1950s, and it was as him that I lost my virginity, began my education, and enjoyed a few years of relative serenity in Colorado before events took a turn, and an accident forced me to leave. My friend and mentor at that time, Quincy Holbrook, had given me many books: Graves' Goodbye to All That, Lawrence's Seven Pillars of Wisdom, Descartes' Meditations, Sartre's Being and Nothingness, among others.

I generally prefer not to think of Colorado. While I can attribute some of my highest highs to that period, the converse is also true. I would gladly give up many of the good memories of that place if the bad ones went with them. But this is not how memory works, is it? And so I do my best to bury the bad, highlight the good.

Over the years, fortunately, I had managed to disconnect my books from their associated memories. No longer did they trigger a series of recollections, but for the longest time I couldn't even look at them without succumbing to the weight of the past. They would just reopen wounds. I flipped to a dog-eared page and found a scrawled note: "Strip everything else away ... What do we know for sure?" Quincy loved Descartes.

I don't want to talk about Quincy right now.

I closed Meditations and spread all of the books out side by side in the dirt next to Tinker's motorcycle. My fingers had flipped each of these pages multiple times, wishing I had a hundred more. I couldn't bring all of my books, nine total, so I selected four, wincing at the other five while consoling myself that many other copies existed in the world, and one day I'd have them again.

I opened my canvas bag and picked through the articles of clothing I'd collected over the years. A hand-painted tie, an austere work shirt from the early 40s, coveralls. During World War II, I lived in a commune in New Mexico where we made clothes and repaired vehicles for the nearby town's residents. There I learned to ride and refurbish motorcycles. It was a peaceful pocket of land in a chaotic world, where no one exactly admitted they were avoiding the draft, but observing men forgetting their assumed names had become a regular occurrence.

"Hey, Bill, you on kitchen duty tonight?"

(No response, "Bill" keeps walking.)

"Uhhh ... Bill?"

("Bill" stops, looks around, remembers these people call him "Bill.") "Oh, hey! What was that you were saying?"

"Kitchen duty."

("Bill" acknowledges he's on kitchen duty tonight.)

I can't tell you how many times I witnessed this exact exchange, with only a simple change of name and subject matter. It was actually rather humorous.

At the commune, I was a recent German immigrant named Anton Wiltzcheck. Ironic, no, that I was surrounded by others with assumed identities? It felt good to not feel like the only liar in town.

Apparently, Anton had not ranked high on the U.S. list for service, as they never called for him. We had no radio on the commune and were therefore successful in ignoring the imploding outside world. While it was peaceful, though, I do not look back on it fondly. The people there I considered friends were, in fact, just friendly. I was always an outsider, kept at arm's length and never truly trusted. Perhaps I shouldn't have worked so hard perfecting my German accent.

Despite the heartache, delicious foods were prepared in abundance there, and I had grown fat as Anton. Bread was my biggest weakness. I could eat it all day, and still do. And so began a pattern of my host bodies slowly swelling.

I had kept a pair of wide-waisted trousers I'd sewn there, and decided I'd still keep them. At least one item from each life, I determined, and rolled the trousers, gathering a few more knick-knacks before returning everything else to the well. Perhaps one day I'd return here. Maybe my valuables would lay safe long enough. The good weather would certainly continue for a couple months.

But I never returned, and rarely looked back.

With the motorcycle loaded, I gazed once more down the highway, started the engine, and rode south. I continued on until I reached Oklahoma, then turned toward my true heading: east to New York City.

The warm wind at my cheeks and hair, the smells of hot soil and big bluestem grass basking in the afternoon sun, I felt alive and ... *almost* free. There was only one problem—one sour nut in the bowl.

Tinker...

Like young Aaron Fuller, Tinker was a furious, powerful presence in the back of my head. I'd hated him within a minute. I didn't like what I was thinking about doing to him, but the more I considered it, the more reasonable and appropriate the idea felt. In my early days, "wiping" a person's consciousness had been an inevitable, unintended result of leaving their bodies. It was only after Aaron that I learned to exit bodies "gracefully," keeping the original consciousness intact so they could resume their lives (albeit with some memory loss).

I pulled off the highway and found a quiet spot to park for a moment.

I'm sorry, Tinker.

Continued in

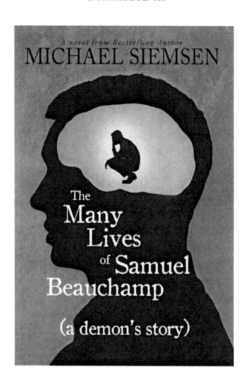

About the Author

Michael Siemsen lives in Northern California with his wife, three kids, dog Brody, cat Atom, several fish, and two chupacabrii. He is currently at work on several new novels, including the follow-up to A Warm Place to Call Home.

Connect with the author:
facebook.com/mcsiemsen
michaelsiemsen.com
twitter: @michaelsiemsen
mail@michaelsiemsen.com

Also by Michael Siemsen:
The Many Lives of Samuel Beauchamp (a demon's story)
The Dig (Matt Turner Series Book 1)
The Opal (Matt Turner Series Book 2)
Return (Matt Turner Series Book 3)
Exigency

CPSIA information can be obtained at www.ICGtesting.com
Printed in the USA
LVOW06s1644150915

454264LV00006B/1077/P